EPIC AND LOVELY

Epic and Lovely

A Novel

Mo Daviau

WEST VIRGINIA UNIVERSITY PRESS · MORGANTOWN

This is a work of fiction. All of the characters, organizations, and events portrayed in this novel are either products of the author's imagination or are used fictitiously.

First edition published 2025 by West Virginia University Press
Printed in the United States of America
ISBN 978-1-959000-62-4 (paperback) / ISBN 978-1-959000-63-1 (ebook)

Library of Congress Cataloging-in-Publication Data

Names: Daviau, Mo author
Title: Epic and lovely : a novel / Mo Daviau.
Description: Morgantown : West Virginia University Press, 2025.
Identifiers: LCCN 2025008710 | ISBN 9781959000624 paperback |
    ISBN 9781959000631 ebook
Subjects: LCSH: Genetic disorders—Fiction | Self-realization in women—Fiction |
    LCGFT: Novels
Classification: LCC PS3604.A9446 E65 2025 | DDC 813/.6—dc23/eng/20250506
LC record available at https://lccn.loc.gov/2025008710

Cover design by Kimberly Glyder
Book design by Than Saffel

For EU safety/GPSR concerns, please direct inquiries to WVUPress@mail.wvu.edu or our physical mailing address at West Virginia University Press / PO Box 6295 / West Virginia University / Morgantown, WV, 26508, USA.

In memory of
Susan DeFreitas (1977–2025)
The scorpion was her idea.

From a spiritual/attachment perspective,
if you continue to believe, do, or engage with people
who have hurt you, either consciously or subconsciously,
you've made an agreement. You've said yes.
—Chrissy Tolley

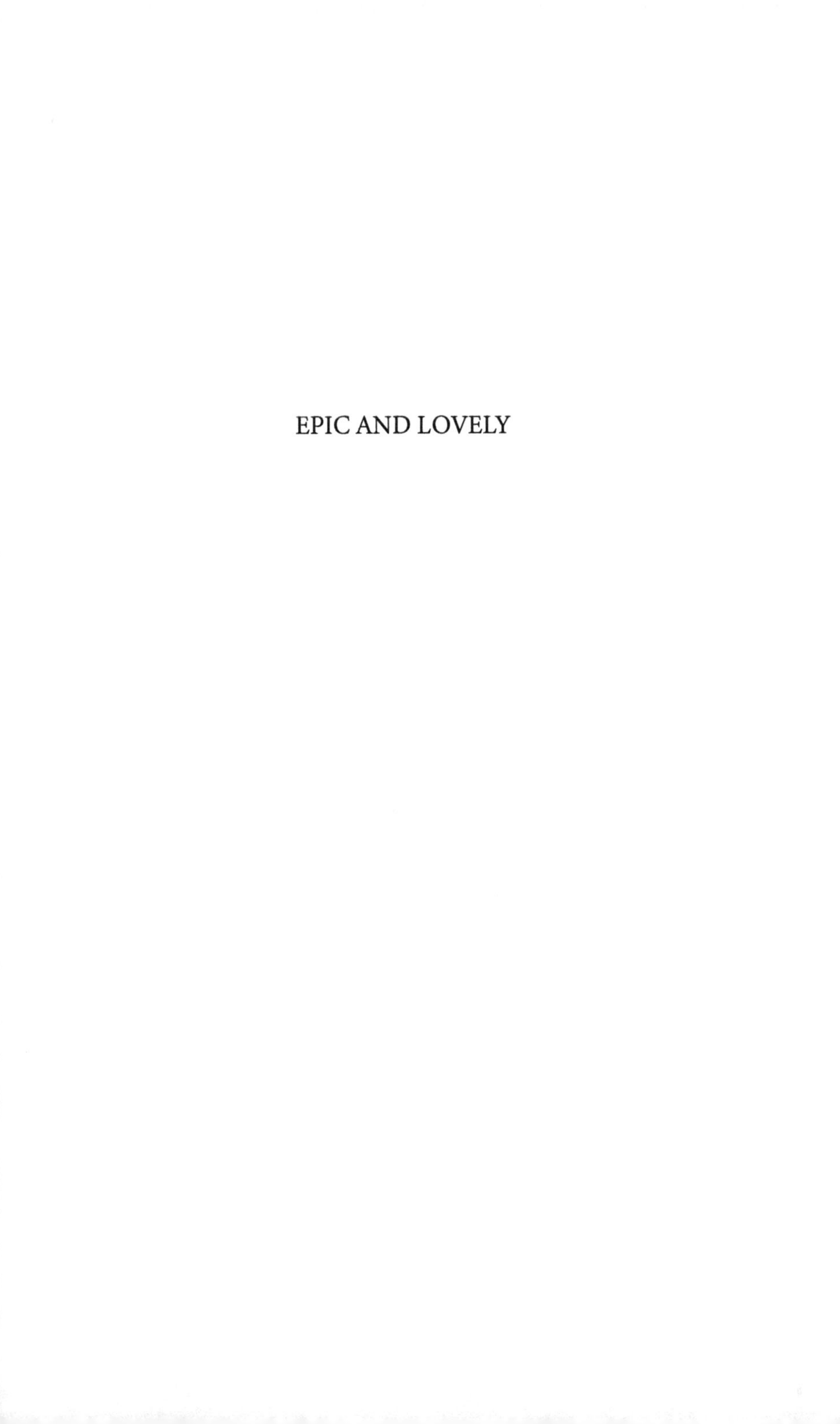

EPIC AND LOVELY

1

Dr. Tabitha Chen, MD, PhD, Clinical Director of UCLA Medical Center's Rare Disorders Clinic:

I was eleven when you told me to my little lopsided face that I wouldn't live past the age of forty. My mother, standing beside me in a too-tight miniskirt and platform sandals that made her wobble like a stack of plates, screamed at you, and tried to get you fired for saying such a horrible thing to a little girl. In twenty-nine years, though, I've never told you how happy you made me that day. How relieved. How special, even. The news that my life would be short set me free.

I was eighteen, on a routine visit to your office, when you sighed heavily and took my hand—*that* hand—and advised me to never have a child. That a full-term pregnancy would break my already-broken body. You told me, with love, that I should do pretty much anything else with the two decades I had in front of me. So I did. I listened to you. I've always listened to you, Dr. Chen.

You were like a mother to me. And now, you are the mother of the five-pound, four-ounce baby you cut from my uterus hours ago, leaving me to bleed, to grieve, to wonder how it could have been different. These last hours of my life, all joy and warmth and wonder from holding the beautiful rump roast who I claimed as my daughter for mere minutes before I handed her over to you for a lifetime. As you have sequestered me into this plush room in the Steven K. Elwood Wing at Stanford Hospital, with the pink blankets and the pale blue walls and view of the campus and the family of stuffed elephants you had sent over—because you remembered me saying once that I loved elephants—I have approximately seven hours left to finish writing you this letter, to tell you what I need you to know about the last few months of my life so you understand me, or at least try. I thought I had found the one person who could understand, but I was wrong.

You should know that there's more to my choice of you as adoptive mother of my little sweet potato than the inevitability of my passing. And please don't ever say that my passing wasn't inevitable. After three decades of being told I would be dead by now, to live beyond this day would be insulting. I planned for this. Honored it. Made choices around it. Even if I came to you desperate for a few borrowed days or weeks of motherhood, drunk on all these spicy hormones, I would want you to tell me no.

Like I said to you in your office, and on that night in my house in Los Feliz when you found me crying and hyperventilating on the floor: I never want her to know me. I never want her to miss me the way I missed my dad, with that deep ache that never lessened with time. This is the greatest gift I can give the little pumpkin you are hiding somewhere in this hospital. My full, loving, wholehearted absence.

Did you know these last few hours of living are so sweet, Doctor? This is the first time I have ever felt real peace.

I, the once and former Nina Simone Blaine, the only ever documented female patient born with A12 Fibrillin Deficiency Syndrome to give birth to a live, wriggling, A12-free sweet potato six weeks past her fortieth birthday, finally got to taste that elusive thing called happiness. Whomp, there she was, all in a single mad rush of oxytocin and dopamine. Sorry, I don't sound like the Nina you've known and taken care of all these years. Rump roast. Sweet potato. Oxytocin. Dopamine. Whomp? I was never cutesy, was I, Dr. Chen? Things have changed.

Sigrid. My sweet potato. My sugar nugget. The love of my life. Sigrid Alma.

Thank you for all you did for me over the years, Dr. Chen. Not only for focusing your career on a rare genetic disorder that mainly affects the children of much older men. Or for violating HIPAA like the madwoman you are and bringing together all your A12 patients so we could feel like family. You knew I'd never have a real family because we talked about that between blood draws and reviews of my MRIs. But you admitted to missing out on something, too. After I had grown up and left Los Angeles, I came to see you and noted one afternoon, while staring up at all the diplomas on the wall of your office, that you had lived a very accomplished life, and you told me you felt otherwise. You had missed out on being a mother, not entirely your choice or fault, but parenthood had passed you by like the last bus out of town. Too much time at work, you lamented. Few potential fathers worthy of your gifts and brilliance. You laughed a little, tried to wipe those tears before I saw them, and mumbled something about trying IVF at forty-four and nothing happened, but maybe that was for the best, because you had student loans, you had a tiny, messy condo, and you didn't have the means to pay for IVF until you were forty-four. You'd acted as the responsible oldest daughter you'd always been, never risking a mistake. Then you cried and I passed you a napkin I found on your desk. I reminded you that you had us, misshapen children of the elderly semen demons of greater Los Angeles and the young, beautiful women who loved them and their money.

Thank you for your medical and research service, which came at the expense of having children. You took care of us, the A12ers who passed through your practice. You gave me Sylvia, my dear friend of thirty years, you gave me the praise and support I didn't get at home, and you even gave me Siggy. All those times I asked about getting a tubal ligation you told me I couldn't have an elective surgery because anesthesia might kill me, so we had to save it for emergencies. Why wasn't frequent sex with Cole considered an emergency?

Allow me to be the one to repay you for your kindness and sacrifice.

I always hated it when certain woo-woo LA people say, "My child chose me as their parent," because no way in hell did I choose the two mismatched weirdos with which the cosmos saddled me. When I told you that Tracy and Eddie were a bad act to follow, I meant it. I meant it when I said there were reasons beyond my A12 decrepitude why I could never be a mother. There was no way, emotionally, for me to take good care of my sweet potato, at the standards to which I would hold myself. And, as I knew my time on earth would be short, I did not cultivate those standards. That baby didn't choose me, Dr. Chen. Never, ever say that to her. Don't even mention old, forgotten Nina Blaine. Tell her she had a sacred vessel who loved her so much that she trusted you and only you to keep her safe.

The scaffolding of my life was wobbly on a good day and unlike my own mother, I would never allow myself a misstep.

I would have chosen you, though, Dr. Chen. To be my mother, if choosing your parents were a real thing. I get to choose you now for Sigrid, with absolute confidence that you are fit for the job.

One of the things we agreed to four months ago, when I told you I was going to barf up my lunch because I was pregnant, was that we'd leave my mother out of this. And Cole, too, whose return I await here in my hospital room as I finish writing this letter. You insisted we leave him out of this transaction as well, even though his single testicle had everything to do with this, biologically and legally. Like me, he was not long for this world.

When I came home to Los Angeles last March, I was thirty-nine years, three months, and twenty-two days old. My life already felt long. My hands were gnarled, my back stooped, and I couldn't work at my soon-to-be-ex-husband's restaurant anymore.

According to your research, the oldest known A12er died at forty-seven. Our A12 bodies relent to gravity. Our bones snap. Our lungs collapse. Our aortas tear open. Our muscles atrophy. Our skin melts, our brains drip out of our nostrils, our feet grow talons, and we sprout wings and fly, but only to the ocean to plunge to our deaths.

Whatever you think of us, we politely request that you resist pity. We always knew our time would be short. We were never anything less than messy Hollywood offspring, tragedies too grotesque to be made into gossip. We had as good a time as we could on this effed-up ball of dirt. But truly, Sigrid Alma, a name I chose because it means Warrior of the Soul, does not share our affliction. Ten fingers and ten little toesies. Believe me, the last thing I did before you took her out of my arms was to count them. And as I touched each one and said the numbers out loud, I said a prayer for my baby girl who will be raised by you, who would love my child even if she did look like me: May her future be so epic and lovely as if to be divine.

<h1 style="text-align:center">2</h1>

A year ago, I called Sylvia crying, as my long, dull marriage had finally ended. "Come home, Blainey," Sylvia said in her nurturing voice. "We have a death cult here. A bunch of A12s living and dying together. The food is amazing. Don't be alone in Connecticut. Come be with us."

I got on a plane. For Cole, mostly, but for Sylvia, too.

Our geriatric Twelver support group was called the Friends of the Good Thumb. You knew all of us, of course. Aunties and uncle-ies who would have loved the snot out of Sigrid. They would have showered her with kisses, expensive gifts, and every beautiful dream we never made come true.

Jorie Kruse, our six-foot-two-inch goth with smeary tattoos up and down her skinny arms, gave our group its name. Every Sunday we gathered in the garden at Sylvia's cottage in Echo Park. Her house was a luscious pink space that Syl had built to feel like a womb. We'd sit around her backyard wicker table, eat expensive food, drink wine, tell stories, and maybe sing karaoke if we were feeling it. One afternoon, Jorie told us that when she was a little girl getting dragged by her actress mother to the very same office at UCLA Rare Disorders, she caught a glimpse of your mentor's description of her body in his notes. Dr. Ghosh had written:

Patient Jordan Elodie Kruse (DOB 09/21/1981) is the daughter of father Abraham Kruse (age 75 at time of birth) and mother Annemarie Batten (age 26 at time of birth). Jordan is 176 cm tall and weighs 43 kg. Congenital hand deformity on the left, ring and pinky finger no longer than one cm, index and middle finger normal length, thumbs good. Profound pectus excavatum (Haller index 10.25) with heart displaced to left thorax.

It was true: The five of us who gathered every Sunday had good thumbs. Normal, well-shaped, operational thumbs with strong, healthy nails. We held them up as we sang our official club song, which began with Syl blowing a hearty C into her pitch pipe:

> *Rise and shine, O children of old men*
> *As we gather with our sad song again*
> *Our lives are foreshortened because theirs were so long*
> *No one tells a man what to do with his Hollywood*
>   *schlong*
> *What we gave up in fingers we inherited with pluck*
> *A12 Fibrillin Deficiency, of which no one gives a fuck*
> *We are the Friends of the Good Thumb*
> *Strong of heart and then some*
> *Bereaved as children, aggrieved right now*
> *Our thumbs are perfect, and how!*
> *We have good thumbs and we are friends*
> *You need Good Thumbs to hold you at the end.*

Old men fathering children? That's a rich man's folly. For every Rod Stewart, Mick Jagger, hell, every Eddie Blaine, Harris Notley, and Abe Kruse who tempts genetics, there is a kid like me, fatherless, fingerless, but born into privilege the same.

A12 mainly affects the babies born to men over age sixty. Which is such an LA thing. Old man, young woman, money, power, the gossip, the lust, the mentions in *People* magazine, being unable to read a clock.

Trust us when we say we can't complain. Anyone who doesn't walk through life with a body like a Hefty stretch sack will shut us down if we suggest that our birth was anything short of a miracle, that we were conceived in love and light, and that our fathers were supposed to live to be one hundred and ten and, don't you know, this is LA, baby!

A12 isn't the worst. It doesn't affect one's intellectual ability. We Good Thumbs were alumni of prestigious American institutions, though I did not graduate from Yale, and Cole didn't graduate from anywhere. While it kept us all out of varsity sports, we enjoy light exercise and occasional physical exertion with no negative effects. Most of us walk until the very end. And what is abnormal about a so-called physical abnormality? Sylvia, a beautiful Black woman with a sweet demeanor, looked normal. Whatever A12 does to our eyes didn't happen to her. If you didn't look at her hand, you wouldn't know she had a genetic disorder, and she didn't let her hand stop her from playing the piano like her daddy. Jorie was hauntingly pretty, with her too-big eyes and lengthy fingers and bony shoulders that jutted fashionably from her slinky tank tops. I loved her from the moment she described me as looking like Margaret Hamilton as the Wicked Witch of the West. Jorie was a gifted visual artist and bitingly hilarious and wore her eye patch grudgingly—she loved her milky, bulging eye, decorating it with black eyeliner and a spendy palette of eyeshadow she bought on Rodeo Drive.

Sylvia owned a small, successful winery in the Santa Ynez Valley. She was also the face of her late father, jazz pianist Harris Notley, and gave talks about his legacy at universities and in every jazz documentary on PBS. Jorie worked as a tattoo artist, even though her A12 skin couldn't hold ink very well, so her own tattoos were bluish spider webs. We often talked about her career at our Good Thumbs gatherings, between karaoke songs, because that's what we did: ate rich food, shot the shit, and sang like our lives depended on it.

I had forgotten how bright the sun was in Sylvia's garden. I'd gone days, weeks, even, without spending time outside in Connecticut. I lived my life by the oven light for almost twenty years, standing for hours in Dansko clogs pulling bread and cakes out of an industrial oven and sculpting fondant into roses, daisies, dinosaurs, and little graduation caps for the finest cakes in all of Connecticut. You'd think all the sun over Los Angeles would disinfect the people a bit—dry out the lies, shine the light on the truth, but fictions continued to thrive here. I thought about this while riding shotgun in Cole's dirty minivan after he picked me up at LAX, Cole doing a slow 45 mph in the right lane down the 10 with the view over the mountains in the yonder and the houses that didn't match: This was the city that let my parents get away with their false identities and their age gap. Part of me wanted Cole to turn the van around and take me back to the airport to go back to Teagarden, Connecticut, where things were dull but seemingly under my control.

That first afternoon back with the Good Thumbs, Sylvia gave us her spot-on impression of Whitney Houston singing "Didn't We Almost Have It All," and, exhausted, reclined on her pink furry chair with her shoes off.

"Do you ever get tired when another idiot shows up and asks you for another Vampyrica sitting on top of the cat tattoo?" we asked Jorie.

Jorie shrugged. She was a shrugger. "Vampyrica is money. When those hipster fucks got super into my dad's films, that was money. An upper arm Vampyrica done by me is five hundred, minimum. What sucks is when customers come in and comment that I look like an Abraham Kruse movie monster. What the actual fuck? You say that and then you trust me to tattoo you? Syl, do you get mad when another jazz historian wants to talk to you about your dad, or God forbid, asks to sit at his piano?"

Syl reached across the table for a king crab leg. "I want them dead."

"Chris?" Jorie asked, to be polite. We knew Chris's biography.

Christopher Kyriakis, the most indolent and recalcitrant of the Good Thumbs, rolled his eyes and said, "No one ever writes to me about anything. I'm nobody. Just a deformed ball of money." Christopher's father was Antonakos Kyriakis, a Greek banker and robber baron, unfamous in the US unless you were in the know about high-dollar arts patrons. There's a hotel in Thessaloniki bearing his name. Chris was the last of Kyriakis's eleven children. His mother was a '70s American television star whose name I'm not allowed to mention. His inheritance had been astronomical, and he had done nothing of note with it.

"And you, Nina?" Jorie asked. "Don't you hate it when someone comes at you singing an Eddie Blaine song with the voice and the trill? Like some Vegas cheeseball wearing gold chains in his chest hair? Like Eddie Blaine cosplay is something you're going to be turned on by?"

Without missing a beat, the fifth member of our gathering of the walking dead came out of Sylvia's house and down the brick walkway. He was trailed by his German shepherd, who was clad in a hot pink collar, matching his master's loping gait, as it was aided by a cane. He arrived where the four of us were sitting, wine glasses in hand, as the breeze wafted through the bougainvillea and Chris warmed up his voice to sing, yet again, "White Wedding" by Billy Idol.

This man was handsome in a way only someone with A12 could be handsome, like a melting bronze statue in a faded green T-shirt, brown cargo shorts, and rainbow-striped knee socks marching up his stick-thin legs. His longish dark-brown hair was held back in a yellow bandanna that matched his yellow eye patch. He was handsome in a way that was beyond any object of beauty that had been presented to me in my life up until four days before this very moment, when this man found me half weeping on the curb at the LAX Terminal 3 pickup area, put me in the back of his white 2004 Toyota Sienna, and drove me to a far corner of the parking garage to make good on the months' worth of filthy text messages he had sent me as I transitioned from dutiful wife to divorced middle-aged slut with a clock ticking over her head.

As the German shepherd whined in the direction of the crab legs, this man began to sing:

> *Beautiful girl*
> *Moving in the moonlight*
> *Come closer*
> *Come closer to me*
> *The moon is bright and shining*

And my heart, my heart was pining
For your tender touch
Your tender kiss
Beautiful giiiiiiiirl
Standing beside meeeeeeee.

He kneeled on the patio in front of me, no mean feat for a man as poorly balanced, asymmetrical, and extremely A12 as he was. He let his cane drop to the ground with a loud clack, took my three-fingered hand into his own, and sang the last few lines of my father's biggest hit, "Somber Mountain," first in a baritone before switching to a full falsetto.

"Nina Blaine, from the bottom of my very soul!" he exclaimed, smiling like he'd won the biggest teddy bear at the carnival, showing off his missing front tooth. "There you are," he said, pretending that he hadn't spent the last four days in my bed, licking my bellybutton and making me scream. "You're a blur in my one remaining eye, but a beautiful blur, just the same." His German shepherd, Bruno, licked the crab juice from my hands and collapsed at my feet.

Cole. Finally. Truly. There he was. My confederate. My love. My everything. My heart did a flip-flop, and I felt stupid and alive.

***

In 1990 Eddie Blaine, a Jew famous for his Christmas albums, passed away as loudly as Cedars-Sinai ever saw. He was an old man, a has-been, and no one made much of his death, save the Jewish media and *Entertainment Tonight*. It was only a footnote that he had left behind a daughter, Nina Simone Blaine, age seven.

Dr. Chen, promise me you'll watch the episode of the game show *Big Money!* that aired on April 2, 1980. It's a louche twenty-two minutes, but Siggy's origin story and mine are in the glitzy folds of its quick money and gaudy repartee. The overexcited blonde with the watermelon tits stuffed into that pink minidress? That's my mom, Tracy. It would take decades for her to admit that, yes, the day she appeared as Contestant #3 on *Big Money!*—put up to no good by her University of Texas Tri-Delt sisters—she was high as a kite and hadn't had more than a cup of coffee and a bite of Danish. Such was 1980. Such was the life of a button of a girl from a Dallas oil family who always got what she wanted, and this time, what she wanted was the tobacco-stained, grouchy old man who asked her on national television if her brassieres were made by NASA.

For three months in 1980, while the regular host of *Big Money!* was drying out at Betty Ford, the semi-legendary crooner Eddie Blaine donned a brown suit by Botany 500, wielded the silver telescoping microphone, and cracked wise, handing booze-soaked housewives and college kids handfuls of cash, wood-paneled floor-model television sets, or the keys to a brand-new Mercury Zephyr. *Big Money!* was tacky, short-lived, and had a hideous cardboard-looking set with a backdrop consisting of the world's currency symbols drawn in gold paint.

Whenever I watch that episode, and I do, because how fortunate am I that the meeting of my parents aired on CBS right before the *Evening News with Walter Cronkite*, I can't believe in what a terrible-looking world those two found each other. Eddie Blaine, an odd troll of a man by 1980, aggressively flirting with any and every woman in his path, stuffing cash down my mother's dress on daytime TV. And Tracy? A giant pink cloud filled with uppers, misogyny, and hope carried her onto that set and into Eddie's arms. That she stayed there still surprises me.

Eddie Blaine was worse for wear by the time Tracy showed up. Long abandoned to the entertainment purgatory that was Las Vegas, he earned his late life keep at the mercy of producer Mike Watson, who, as my mother would tell anyone, was a crazy old womanizer who happened to like Eddie Blaine's albums and didn't want to see the old man starve. My father, once the velvet-voiced vocalist who honed his craft not in the recording studios of Hollywood or on stage at the Flamingo, but in the Grand Ballroom at Klinger's Hotel in the Catskills, was tired and wanted to go home. The thing was, he didn't have one; he knew it, and he hated himself for it.

Home for the man once known as Sandy Blattner was an elusive memory, not in California, but back in New York and New Jersey, the land of Jews and honey that he hadn't seen in decades. Sandy had gotten his start during the Great Depression, and while the Blattner family avoided destitution during this time, they were not exactly keen on Sandy leaving for the Catskills to sing love songs to housewives. Eli Sanford Blattner, born on Halloween night 1916, was their oldest child and precious only son. They wanted him to run the shoe store, but such pedestrian expectations tired young Sandy. He was different. A cad. A flirt. A weirdo in a bowtie. The thought of smelling socks all day made him ill, but he couldn't tell his parents that he'd rather choke on a bottle of shoe polish than work at the store while they were paying his tuition at Rutgers. He spent a single year in New Brunswick chasing girls and failing math, but Sandy Blattner was meant to sing. He had been cantor of his own bar mitzvah. He idolized Bing Crosby. And, of course, that voice.

In the summer of 1936, Sandy applied to work as a waiter at Klinger's Hotel, which not only featured a certified kosher kitchen, shuffleboard, and watercolors class but also had live entertainment five nights a week. When he arrived, suitcase in hand, he knew he was made for better things than carrying roast beef platters to picky old men and their wives. Whatever Sandy Blattner had in mind the first day he put down his tray and, with the blessing of Mrs. Klinger, commandeered the microphone in the Grand Ballroom and sang, with his trademark lilt, "Blue Moon," it was not, "when I'm sixty-three years old, I'm going to be the fill-in guy on a game show on goddamn *television* and I'm going to make a move on a shiny piece of Texas ass who has an orgasm every time I stuff a Benjamin down her dress."

For seven years, Sandy Blattner was the shining star of Klinger's Hotel. There was no smoother, more inviting voice on the Borscht Belt circuit. Sandy's handsome face was printed in black and white in Klinger's advertisements in the *Forward* and every Hadassah newsletter on the East Coast. In 1940 he married his biggest fan, Ruth Levy, a chubby, hilarious Cornell coed who had suffered the indignity of four weeks at the hotel with her grandparents, who complained about the rye bread and the pillows and the smell of the grass. That summer, Ruth pretended to go to bed at eight but was down in the Grand Ballroom at 9:30, mai tai in hand, listening to the dulcet sounds of Sandy Blattner's voice hitting the high notes, and then the low notes, before turning his back on the crowd to take a deep breath and wipe his forehead with a clean, white handkerchief. On Ruth's third night sitting on the edge of a red velvet chair right smack in front of the stage, Sandy got down on one knee in front of her and sang "I Can't Believe That You're in Love with Me," while gazing into her eyes. Ruth cried the entire time. The next day, Sandy borrowed a coworker's Buick and took Ruth to dinner one hotel over, to Leininger's, whose tummler had been trying to poach Sandy for the previous two seasons. He knew that schmuck would give him and his girl free steaks and as many Manhattans as they could drink and would keep the fans away when he took Ruthie on the floor to dance.

When Sandy's father was hit by a streetcar in 1942, his mother and sisters expected Sandy and Ruth to come home and run the shoe store. But Sandy was going to Hollywood. He had big dreams and a big voice and a big recording contract at Capitol Records. And a big wife, which he soon found out was something the Capitol boys all found laughable. Milky, plump Ruth, with her loud voice and stinky sweat, became pregnant with their son two months into their move to Los Angeles. Ruth grew as big as a whale, and even after Evan Howard Blattner came into the world in the summer of 1943, Sandy knew there was a price to be paid for loving Ruth. "Could you at least shave your armpits and spray some perfume?" he would beg Ruthie when she stuffed her body into an old dress that no longer fit. He couldn't even remember what he'd seen in the girl. When one of the producers at Capitol laughed and asked if the fat-assed broad who brought Sandy his lunch was his sister, he said yes.

Ruthie was served with divorce papers sent over by Sandy's agent. No conversation, no explanation: only a plane ticket to LaGuardia and a check for a thousand bucks. Sandy, renamed Eddie Blaine, had gone into the USO in 1944 and came home married to a dancer he'd met on base in Germany. They were divorced by 1946. She was nothing, he'd assure anyone who stopped to listen to his life story, and that included me. Adult me, who had been gifted by my father's manager and best friend, Addie Chambers, a series of videos she'd made of her interviewing my father at the end of his life, so I could hear his stories from his mouth.

My mother was also a "nothing," though he never said as much on those videos. Tracy was his third and final wife, forty-one years his junior. Eddie Blaine chose women who were beautiful in the way Hollywood had taught him to believe. Blonde, tiny waist, demure, beckoning, smiling, teetering on too-high heels. Women who you looked at and maybe slapped around a bit—Addie had stopped him on one of the videos from elaborating on what he meant by that. But to my father, there were women you slapped around and women you didn't, and Tracy was the former.

It's important to note that, as one of the two people who were present at the hospital the day my father died, a gray-skinned Eddie Blaine, staring down God with tubes in his nose, looked into my seven-year-old face with sincere confusion. Moments earlier, he had kissed my forehead and said, "I love you, Nina, so much! My beautiful girl! I'm so lucky I got to be your daddy and I'm sorry it couldn't have been for longer. You're wonderful and I'm so proud of you!"

But as the end came, something in him darkened.

"Ruthie?" he said, scared.

He tried to sit up. The nurse pushed him back down. "Ruthie, where is she?"

What I learned that day, the day Eddie Blaine exited stage left forever, was that Ruthie wasn't nothing. Ruth, who my father divorced for being an embarrassing reminder of who he truly was. Ruthie, who moved back to New York and married a man who appreciated her. Ruthie, who I met by accident when I was sixteen at a restaurant in the town where I attended boarding school, who remained the only person (until Cole) who ever looked me in the eye and told me it was terrible that an old man like Sandy Blattner thought he had any business making a baby at age sixty-six.

Tracy, who was at home waiting for a phone call from the lawyers the moment Eddie passed, was nothing. Ruthie had been something to him. I knew this. I held onto that sentiment my entire life. To a girl with bulging eyeballs and eight fingers, that was money in the bank. It meant I might not be looked at, but I could be loved.

3

The Friends of the Good Thumb was a death cult. You'd set us up for this constant awareness of the calendar, each passing day another one closer to The End. We couldn't fight it, so instead, we reveled in it. Our gatherings were bacchanals: With his gazillions, Chris ordered and paid for our food and booze, which we consumed in Sylvia's backyard as the hot Santa Ana winds caressed our faces.

We lounged about in Syl's garden, drank wine, laughed, and laughed some more. Syl had a karaoke player in her backyard, with a monitor that attached to the wall on her patio, speakers so loud and crisp that they irritated her neighbors, and a sick selection of tunes that she had curated over the years, which didn't matter because we all tended to do the same songs over and over. I wanted to melt into the floor and scream when Cole got up to sing his songs, which were either "Midnight Confession" by the Grass Roots or "The Stroke" by Billy Squier.

I always sang Pat Benatar's "We Belong." Sometimes "White Rabbit."

You, Dr. Chen, brought us Good Thumbs together: We were your first patients, now all around forty and facing down our expiration dates with bravery and aplomb! That you violated patient privacy laws to bring us together was a lovely gesture that we'll repay by leaving the bulk of our fortunes to UCLA Rare Disorders.

"You, the enchanting Sylvia Notley," Cole said last April when we celebrated Christopher's fortieth birthday, holding court over the Good Thumbs after a bit of pinot gris and Chinese barbecued duck. "You are a gifted jazz singer in your own right, and, like Jesus, you turn water into wine, and yet here you are, choosing to exist merely to extend the living memory of your father, the greatest of all our fathers. Your life has been an endless jazz funeral. Harris Notley's little time traveler. The irony, then, that the man with hands that spanned two octaves gave you that little tripod chicken claw. Your life, littered, like the streets of New Orleans after Mardi Gras, could have been a lively celebration of you, your manifold talents, and your sexy long legs, but no. Because your old man's name is spoken in the same breath as Duke Ellington's."

Sylvia flipped Cole the bird. "Father Harris would tell me to slap his name out of your stupid mouth."

Cole winked at Sylvia. "Are we doing this, Sylvia? That's so hot."

Cole crossed and uncrossed his legs before pointing at Chris with his wine glass in his hand. Chris was looking at his phone and chewing on an egg roll when Cole started in. "Kyriakis, you're spending what is probably your last birthday on this stupid planet with this pack of ingrates? You, who have made it to the A12 Methuselah age of forty thanks to Daddy's drachmas, could have flown us all to Amsterdam for poppers and whores, but instead, we're in Notley's backyard again eating takeout while you know damn well none of these uptight birds are going to give you the shag you so desperately need. What gives, good sir?"

Chris swallowed his egg roll and shouted, "Hey, how about for my birthday, you shut the fuck up?"

Cole gestured toward Chris's birthday cake, sitting in the middle of our roasted duck bacchanal: a three-tiered round cake with peaks of white buttercream frosting, topped with pink and purple fondant roses. Structurally, it was a wedding cake. My professional expertise told me that cake took a full day to bake and assemble and probably cost Chris around $500. My cakes, and I do say this to brag, were delicious. There was something about this cake that told me it was more for show than for flavor. That cake had a bad attitude. Baker's intuition.

"You bought yourself a wedding cake, Buddy. You know Nina could have made you a cake for five bucks, right?"

"I'm excited to taste it. Does it have fruit?" I asked Chris, immediately regretting my question, watching his face fall.

"It has cake," Christopher said.

Cole hopped up on his chair, almost falling on top of Bruno the Dog, to lavish us with a grand announcement. "Friends of the Good Thumb, before I do what the birthday boy asked and shut my mouth, I want to thank you for having a wretch like me at your fancy garden parties. I love knowing there are other eight-fingered freaks out there who like to have a good time, and I especially love you for bringing the exquisite Nina Simone Blaine into my life, my arms, and my sex van. As we inch ever closer to our deaths, I am glad to flame out completely in love with Sylvia's hot-as-hell boarding school roommate. Have you all seen Nina's book of poetry? Published by some press I've never heard of."

I had never told Cole about my poetry collection that came out twelve years earlier, but he pulled my magnum opus from the back of his pants and held it up for all to see. "*World War You.* Killer title, Sweetie. Nina, you're the prize at the bottom of the box of junky cereal that has been my life. I love you." Cole took my left hand and pressed a kiss into each gnarled finger and one good thumb.

Silence, the deafening sort, filled the space. Cole dropped my hand and said, "Community support? Hello? You freaks saw me make a grand romantic gesture and you can't even clap?"

Sylvia clapped. Chris and Jorie did not.

"What do you losers know about love?" Cole continued.

"More than you!" Jorie yelled.

"How many times have you been divorced?" Chris yelled.

"Cute, Chris. You're cute. Happy birthday. I'm in love with Nina. Thanks for listening. I will shut up now. I'd like a beer, though. Wine is for rich kids." Cole sat down on his chair and made a zipper gesture over his mouth.

Jorie turned to me and whispered. "For what it's worth, Nina, Cole trailed me to a horror convention in San Diego years ago and told me he wanted to have sex with someone who looked like him and assumed that I, too, wanted to have sex with someone who looked like me, or my father."

"I totally look like your daddy," Cole turned to us and said loudly. "Abraham Kruse was a colossus of fibrillin deficiency."

Jorie lit a cigarette—end of life and all, why not? "When I told Cole that I'm gay as hell and he's a fucking dildo, he told me I could make an exception for a fellow Twelver. Gross."

Cole laughed at that. "I am a dildo. A dildo in love with Nina Blaine!"

Sylvia would later compare Cole on this day to Tom Cruise jumping on Oprah's couch, losing his mind over Katie Holmes.

"Fake and rubbery and larger than life, and in love with the heart, soul, and pectus excavatum of Nina Blaine! Whatever, Jordan, you love me. Not like Nina, of course, but just as well since you're so open about your vulva-devouring predilections and your ugly shoes."

Jorie squished her working eye shut. "I've heard about your A12 cock and ball situation," she said, drawing a circle in the air over her crotch. "Be glad that I only want pussy."

"Do you have the A12 cock and ball situation, Kyriakis?" Cole yelled at Chris. "Do your balls hang low? Do they wobble to and fro?"

Chris pounded his fists on the table. "Could you please stop ruining my birthday? For fuck's sake!"

"I'm not ruining anything. Cut your wedding cake, you lucky son of a bitch. Look at you, making it to forty as a Twelver and you didn't hire the LA Gay Men's Chorus to sing us Barry Manilow songs while we ingest that painted-whore monstrosity of sugar and flour. Did you at least get ice cream? Why are you so friggin' cheap?" Cole, at forty-five, was the eldest of the Good Thumbs, a detail he emphasized when it suited him.

"Kyriakis, seriously. Just because you know you're not going to bang Nina or Sylvia, and definitely not Gertrude Stein over here, doesn't mean that you should be a little bitch and not cut your five-hundred-dollar cake."

Chris picked up the cake knife, held the point an inch from Cole's throat. "I asked you to shut the fuck up! Let me remind you I'm rich, dying, and have nothing to lose."

Cole's plate of rice and dumplings and duck bones flipped upside down as he quickly shot up from the table. He pulled his pocketknife out of his shorts and held it to Chris's nose.

"Are we doing this? Because I'm down if you are." Cole moved his knife slowly toward Chris's neck. "Because if you really want me to leave your extremely fun party, I can take Nina home, sing her Eddie Blaine's 'Mistletoe Mambo' like I mean it, and make her come until she sees Jesus while you sit here and cry like a baby when you damn well know there ain't gonna be another wedding cake with a birthday candle in it for you."

Cole pressed the point of his knife to Chris's nose. "My parents never gave me a penny, Chris, and I still turned out to be a loser. What's your excuse?"

I pulled the knife from Cole's hand. He gave it to me without a struggle. Should I have anticipated a struggle?

Chris, his forehead beaded with sweat, threw the cake knife down on the grass and stomped off into Syl's house.

Cole laughed and spun around on the grass like a ballerina. "If you change your mind and want me to cut you later, let me know, Sweetie!"

***

A few years before this meeting of Los Angeles's A12 senior citizens, I got an email out of the blue from a guy named Nick Sullivan, a name I had known for years. He had become an acquaintance of Sylvia's thanks to you, Dr. Chen. This was before Nick Sullivan saw God or got subpoenaed—the story changed often—and renamed himself Cole Courchaine: Cole, a nickname of Nicholas that wasn't Nick, and Courchaine, after a furniture store he remembered seeing as a child on a trip to a funeral in Buffalo. And, as Nick Sullivan, he said what I had been thinking about love, death, everything, and he made me laugh harder than anything or anyone. We began writing to each other every day.

When that first message landed, I hadn't had sex in eleven years.

For most of my adult life, I was not an interesting person. I chose a small life. I married the first man who looked at me without pity or disgust, and I worked in his restaurant six days a week, went home, and occasionally watched a movie. That's what I told Cole in those years before he met me in the flesh at the curb at LAX. Less than an hour after meeting, I cried into a handful of In-N-Out Burger napkins after he railed me in the back of his ancient white minivan, which he had outfitted with a sheepskin rug and silky red pillows.

You? Not interesting? Nick/Cole responded in that first online exchange. *Liar. You're trying to hide something, and I am absolutely going to find out what.*

Dude, I wrote back. *I make cakes for a living. And that's it!*

Nah, I googled you and found something you wrote for that fancy boarding school of yours. DANG. Someone interesting is in that A12 meat suit. Right?

Nicholas Joseph Sullivan was born in August 1976, the ninth and distantly last child of an Irish-Polish Catholic couple whose extreme fertility became legendary when his mother, Rosie, pushed out her final babe six months shy of her fiftieth birthday. Joe Sullivan, Cole's father, was an even sixty, in accordance with your A12 hypothesis on older fathers. The eldest Sullivan sibling was twenty-six when the youngest was born— little Nicky had two nephews who were older than him.

Cole's childhood was fighting over the television, over-cooked chicken dinners, pierogies on Christmas, yelling, more yelling, having snowballs (and worse) thrown at him by bullies on the walk home from school, wearing thick glasses, keeping his Star Wars figurines in immaculate condition, and being dragged to Latin Mass by his mother. He had five older brothers, and had to wear their outgrown sneakers until he was a teenager and could buy his own with the money he earned working at his twin older brothers' used car dealership. "Spoiled ingrate!" he would yell and point at me and my $300 orthopedic shoes, and I'd remind him that my mother sent me to that fancy boarding school so her husband didn't have to look at me.

We could suck it.

He loved this speech.

When Cole first saw film footage of me as a child sitting on Eddie Blaine's lap, footage that Addie Chambers allowed UCLA Rare Disorders to use for fundraising, Eddie in a powder blue tuxedo holding up my A12 hand and saying to the camera, "She's perfect except for this three-fingered business!" he asked Sylvia for my email address so he could contact me. She warned me ahead of time: *Remember the guy from the Wired magazine ad with A12? He wants to meet you. He's funny and tells good stories.* Syl didn't know I'd followed him online ever since I'd found that letter.

Hey, three-fingered business, he wrote to me. *Me too. Lefty or righty?*

After a lifetime of having to explain to everyone I've ever met, minus you and Syl, what A12 Fibrillin Deficiency Syndrome is, to have that moment of sweet recognition, to have my body preternaturally understood by a man who looked twice as A12 busted as me? *Lefty or righty*, Dr. Chen. *Lefty or righty*. A clarion call from the angels to my crooked ears. Of course I wrote back.

I was still married the day he asked me that question. Paul and I lived in a white house down the hill from the wrought-iron gates of the Ethel H. Bondurant School for Girls, where Sylvia and I were members of the class of 2000. Our marriage had flatlined. I had flatlined. Though my life there was dull and circumscribed, the thought of ever leaving Teagarden, Connecticut, made me want to die.

Nick Sullivan was nominally a resident of San Francisco, though his emails came from an IP address in Bangkok, and then Vancouver, BC, and finally, Los Angeles, from where he sent the one that announced his name change and said, *Hey, I'm divorced now! What about you? Divorced? (wink)*

I insisted to Cole that I was not interesting. I was smart but did not live up to my potential. Except for that slender book of poetry, which was a lark. But the dull life I'd chosen was beginning to fade away, or at least my husband was. Paul Luciani, sixteen years my senior, was a stout, rugged, no-nonsense man. He spent his waking life in his restaurant, Stella di Capra, an upscale Italian place across the street from my boarding school's front gate. I washed up in Paul's industrial kitchen as a nineteen-year-old college dropout. Paul offered me a job even though I didn't ask for one, after I told him that I had left Yale for mental health reasons and was living in a room at the bed and breakfast next door because Bondurant was the only real home I'd ever known and didn't know where else to go. Paul grew up in New Haven and reserved a special hatred for Yale. "You're not one of them," he said repeatedly as he trained me to make his signature garlic rolls, or how to properly sanitize the countertops. I insisted that I really was one of them.

Paul called himself a family guy, but he didn't have a family. He said it was because no woman wanted a three-hundred-pound workaholic, but I argued that at least a few did, and he took that to mean me. At nineteen, I had never been kissed, on a date, or had sex, and assumed those rites of passage were only for girls with ten fingers, though Sylvia enjoyed her fair share of male attention at Bondurant and then at Stanford, but Sylvia was Sylvia—a force of nature, loved, protected by her family. I was me and not those things.

In our online courtship days, I told Cole that I married Paul because he was the first guy who ever showed interest in me, and I couldn't take the risk of him being the last. He wrote, "Girl, I'm a slumped-over, monocular, monorchid weirdo with eight fingers and a nasty growth in my left armpit, and the acquisition of pussy on the free market, such as it is, has never been a challenge for me. Women entirely unafflicted by our shared condition can't get enough of my A12 asymmetries and anomalies, and yet you seem to have banked your future on the idea that no man would have you because of your magnificent *Twelvitude*? Darling Nina, how wrong you were!"

Dr. Chen: Let's be reductive. Paul was a good man, based on behavior and choices, and Cole was a bad one. But you'll forgive me, please, for being so drawn to Cole's grandiosity. While my marriage to Paul—who trawled the bottom of the self-esteem sea along with me, which was largely why we were together—had changed for the worse, I would have never said that out loud to you, to a therapist, or to anyone except for this A12 sex bomb colossus on the other end of my computer. I married Paul not because I was in love with him (And I loved

Paul! Don't ever think I didn't!) but because of who I was or wasn't. I watched Sylvia attract men, break their hearts, and try again like it was no big thing because her mother told her that she was beautiful. Sylvia grew up with choirs of Notley relatives singing the same song. Tracy and her Barbie doll–producing family couldn't hide how horrified they were by my body. If Tracy noticed me so much as looking at a boy that way, she'd yank me aside and remind me I wasn't like the other girls and to act accordingly.

Nothing was ever asked of Tracy Westervelt besides her beauty, and though I had been avoiding my mother since she aged into AARP and a short, tight pixie cut, I couldn't imagine her going quietly into the good night of her senior years. Tracy was the youngest of three sisters, each of them shimmeringly blonde with a turned-up nose and a svelte figure. They were glorious examples of American beauty: real prizes on the marriage market of Dallas's upper echelons. They modeled in the Juniors' section at Dillard's, waved from the homecoming court throne, and were labeled Biggest Heartbreaker in their high school yearbooks. Tracy was, in minor ways, the black sheep of the Westervelt girls—unlike her sisters, she stood five foot two and had a pair of bazooms that no triple-D department store bra could tame into social propriety. Everything she got in life, she got by being a looker, and she had no idea what to do with a daughter who was, per the prevailing standards that Tracy understood, ugly.

My mother did not care for my wavy brown hair, my bumpy nose that pulled from Eddie Blaine's Ashkenazi ancestry, or the hairs that sprouted from my upper lip when puberty came. As she whined to you in your office some thirty years ago, it was all of my little A12 anomalies that needed to be fixed: my sloped shoulders, the dip in the center of my chest where my sternum bowed inward, my bony feet with toes that looked like type-writer hammers, and of course, my left hand, bearing the A12 Fibrillin Deficiency Syndrome calling card: the nonexistent pinky and ring finger, represented by two pearly nubs where the bones failed to grow. Little Nina was proof that life was unfair, and that Tracy had been dealt a terrible hand, which was the song she sung as she attempted to bully me into plastic surgery as a teenager, and, failing that, hiding me away as best as she could. When I was thirteen, Tracy took me to Venice Beach to see a psychic, a tiny Armenian woman with whiskers on her chin who wielded a gold medallion on a chain while she stared at my left hand. "Will Nina ever find a man to marry her?" my mother asked the woman in front of me. The psychic closed her eyes. "No. Will be impossible."

Paul, whom you heard about but never met, was many things, but he was not fun. He did not tell jokes, he did not watch television, he occasionally read paperback thrillers but was mostly asleep by ten. At the height of the pandemic, he ended his years of sobriety and rejoined the Catholic church. In the last few years of our marriage, he stopped speaking to me for the most part, other than to criticize me, bark orders in the kitchen, or point out that I should "be over" certain things by now. And then, the thing happened: His younger sister's car skidded under-neath a semi on an icy stretch of the Jersey Turnpike, killing her and her oldest child instantly. Left behind were her two younger children. Those kids' father had been a deadbeat for years and didn't answer when the courts came a-calling. That left Paul and, by extension, me, to be their caregivers.

I didn't have it in me to devote what little time was left to Paul's niece and nephew, who were bereaved and had needs and requirements. One of them was a violin prodigy, and overseeing artistic greatness in a child was not what I had on tap for the end of my life. My body was failing. Dragging the fifty-pound flour bags to the bins hurt my hands and I couldn't lift them anymore. Many times, I became lightheaded in the kitchen and needed frequent breaks on the wooden bench in the lobby to catch my breath. My life as Paul's blushing, baking bride was over, all but for the official retirement, which he frowned upon. I could work for about an hour before I had to lie down and nap. Lifting the bowl out of my industrial mixer became an impossible task. My cakes were starting to look shabby and uneven. Paul looked at me like I was shabby and uneven and suggested I was playing up my disabilities to get out of taking in his sister's kids or having to do anything I didn't want to do, because suddenly doing things you didn't want to do became virtuous at our house.

Wasn't it better for me to leave than to be another caregiver who died on those kids in a year or two? I took a cue from my own life. Staying and making those kids watch me die would only hurt them in the long run.

Paul, Catholic again and seeming more like a sanctimonious stranger than my long-time partner, told me that no good woman got out of being a mother, whether that was by the usual way or by divine intervention. I was a good woman; God was testing me. When I told him that he was implying I was a bad woman for not being a mother, he smirked and said, "God makes the rules, Nina, not me."

It was true: Paul's niece and nephew didn't have anywhere to go. Those kids appeared in my tiny house after work one day, wearing their filthy sneakers on my hand-braided rug. I had never felt one way or another about these children, or anyone else's children. On those Sundays in late May that I hobbled out to the stone front steps of Stella di Capra to watch the Bondurant graduation procession go by, I didn't feel how those fundraising letters told me I should about the next generation of Bonnie excellence. I only felt loss, watching all those young women in their navy blue caps and gowns smiling and waving and carrying that long chain of laurel on their shoulders.

And what started out as a guilty crush that was destined to go nowhere became a guiltless crush that I intended to pursue. What did it matter if I left my marriage for some guy in California, abandoned those kids, and quit a job I couldn't do anymore? I was going to die. You said so yourself, repeatedly. Your voice was the shrieking ghost in my head that told me to choose myself.

Paul expected me to go to Los Angeles to sell Eddie Blaine's house in Los Feliz, which became my house when Addie died of the virus a year earlier. We didn't need the money before, but we needed it now for a bigger house now that we were, in Paul's words, "a real family." Hearing *a real family* come out of his mouth made my skin crawl. Paul would tap his computer screen as he showed me the estimated value of my father's house. Like Christopher, I felt like I was little more than a deformed ball of money.

But I needed that house: Eddie Blaine's 1970s monument to himself was all that was left of the old man. Nine hundred square feet of blood red wall-to-wall carpet, mirrored walls and ceilings, garish chandeliers dangling over velvet sofas in what had once been a quaint Spanish-style cottage belonging to a silent movie starlet who sold it to Eddie for a song because he sat with her in her dotage and made her laugh at SAG screenings. It was glorious, it was hideous, and it was what I needed. Addie Chambers lived in it for thirty years and never updated the decor, except for the refrigerator, replaced only because the one Eddie bought in 1975 finally died.

"I'm not coming back," I whispered to Paul, who I asked to drive me to La Quinta at Bradley Airport the day before my flight to LA. "You can divorce me so you can marry someone else. I'll sign whatever you want." He hunched over the steering wheel of our rusted Subaru, not looking at me. Looking tired. Defeated. It would be the last time we ever saw each other. I had one foot hanging out of the car door touching the curb in front of La Quinta. I ran my finger along the dusty dashboard, knowing this would be my last ride in the car we bought together a decade earlier, back when we still had sex.

Paul stared forward, drumming his thick fingers on the dash. Where once there was warmth, there was now a freezer blast of hostility. Behind him was the full weight of society's messages about childless women, women who didn't sacrifice for others, women who put themselves first. I was no saint, and I didn't want to be a saint, and he could saint without me as far as all of this went.

My phone buzzed.

I looked down at it. So did Paul.

"Who's Cole?" He gestured at my phone.

He saw the text: *I can't wait to find out what A12 pussy tastes like! 24 hours to go before I fuck that sweet deformed ass of yours into the next dimension!*

Paul continued to stare at my phone. He could paint me as the whore and liar I was. Fuck it, I thought. Another man wanted me. If that hurt him, so much the better. I wanted him to know that when I left this car for the last time, there was someone on the other side of the country waiting to do to me all the things he couldn't or wouldn't. If I was a bad woman because I didn't want to spend my last two years of life looking after someone else's kids, great. I'd take that. Fuck you and your nonfunctional dick and your shitty politics, Paul Luciani.

Paul never knew the deep, dark, dirty reasons why I couldn't be anyone's mother. Or if he did, it was an inconvenience he shoved away. Why, when he told me he'd gotten a vasectomy in his twenties after a girlfriend had an abortion and he never wanted to go through that ever again, I kissed him on the cheek and told him that made me even more attracted to him. Maybe there was some motherliness in me, but A12 took it first, Tracy stomped on it with her little feet second, and I needed to keep the rest for myself.

On the curb that day at La Quinta, I felt seasick. Everything was a blur. Paul couldn't see me. He never could, and that was what hurt most in this moment. He didn't know that asking me to mother was asking me to disappear. "I know you think you're about to die. That's been a thing with you for as long as I've known you," Paul said coolly. "You act like you want that, though. Like it means you can have your way without any consequences."

"Yeah, it does," I said and slid out of the car, cold and nauseous. "I'm not selling Eddie's house. I'm going to live in it and I'm going to die in it. That's all I have left of him, and you can't take it away from me."

He was quiet for a bit. That was better than another lecture from Paul on how I should feel about my dead father. "Goodbye, Nina."

I sobbed like a wounded animal on the flight back to Los Angeles. Cole took receipt of the scared, broken Nina and fucked her back to life in an airport parking garage. That enormous, life-giving man, Dr. Chen. That deity of life itself. Cole raptured me to a better place. Cole was the medicine I needed to heal the wound and carry me to the end.

So you'll forgive me if I am confused about who the hero of this story is.

***

Cole was, for a hot minute in the late 1990s, somewhat, minorly internet famous. Famous-ish for being a Silicon Valley bigmouth, a lesser Capote for the Web 1.0 crowd. In his heyday, he worked as a bartender at a pub frequented by gossip-worthy tech bros in San Jose and repeated everything he overheard, and a few things he made up, on his blog. He loved talking trash about the various early internet players: who was rude to a waiter, who got caught doing blow with a prostitute, who farted on a hot mic at a tech conference. Cole was most famous, at least to Nina Blaine, for placing an advertisement in *Wired* magazine, looking for the mother of his child. I had read that ad many times. You could even say I was a fan of that ad.

Cole told the baby advertisement story to the Good Thumbs over oysters that Chris had flown in from Maine. I thought about that ad and reread it so many times over the years that it felt like my story, too.

Cole stood over us as we ate around Syl's backyard table. He straightened his back with the help of his cane and, with Bruno standing at attention to defend his wizened master, began his lengthy tale.

"Ah yes, the baby ad. It ran right before Christmas in 1999. Sixty-three women wrote to me. Some sent nude photos! I deleted those straight away. There was one woman I was wildly attracted to, a copper-haired goddess with a cool science job, but she lived in Pittsburgh and wanted me to move back to raise our child near our families. My mother had seventeen grandchildren, for Pete's sake. *Do you think that we'd be getting free babysitting?* I asked her. I didn't want to leave California. I narrowed it down to three Bay Area locals and chose a woman named Hannah Maes, because she was the nicest and the prettiest.

"Hannah was nine years older than me and a widow. She taught French at a private school in San Francisco—I didn't want anyone with a Silicon Valley job. Her father was a big-name luthier from Belgium who made these zillion-dollar violins and cellos. Three years before she wrote me her very kind letter, her husband had died climbing Mount Everest. She thought she'd never be a mother, until a friend tipped her off to my impassioned treatise printed in *Wired*."

I could recite from memory Cole's full-page ad from 1999. It was the first time I saw any mention of A12 in the mainstream media. If I had found the essay when it was published and not years later, I would have thrown in my lot to make a baby with Nick Sullivan, despite your prognostication that a full-term pregnancy would kill me.

"I have that letter memorized," I admitted.

Syl nodded and said, "Nina's wanted to marry that ad for years."

Cole loved that I indulged him, and that was all that mattered. "Go ahead, my turtledove," he said, pulling me by the hand next to him as he orated from his imaginary stage.

I took a long sip from my gin and tonic and stood up to tell Cole's story. "Friends, if I have them, I beg for your attention: Today I, Nicholas Sullivan, an accident of biology and Catholicism, will wear my heart firmly upon my sleeve," I began.

Cole made smoochy lips at me. "Yeah, baby. Give it to me."

I recited from memory: "Roe v. Wade was passed three years before I was a bun in my mother's too-old oven. Forty-nine years old, with eight children, one of whom had two kids of her own by the time I came along. Rose Krupa, that sturdy oak from the mean streets of Erie, Pennsylvania, planned to marry her high school beau, to whom she was engaged since the age of fifteen, but the boyfriend ate shit in Okinawa, changing up Rosie's plans. After high school, she took a bus to Pittsburgh to look for work. Rosie found a room at a boarding house, and, after attending mass at St. Stanislaus for nine months, she met the still-single-at-thirty Joseph Sullivan. He was cold and rough, but he came back from the war in one piece. Family legend had it that he told young Rosie that he didn't think she was pretty, but a year later he mercifully slipped a ring on her finger in front of God and a hundred cousins.

"One thing my old parents left me with is a little-known and little-understood affliction called A12 Fibrillin Deficiency Syndrome. When I came out with only three fingers on my left hand, an off-duty sternum, and an eyeball that bulged so far out of the socket that a doctor mercifully removed it, my parents shrugged it off. It was only when I read about the daughter of the great jazz pianist Harris Notley, also of advanced age when he brought her into the world, having the same number of fingers and this thing called A12, did I get myself to the doctor for a diagnosis.

"A12 isn't the worst thing in the world. I can do odd things with the skin on my belly, like pretend to be a plastic grocery bag. The deep dent in the center of my chest explained that I am not merely a human bowl for dips and sauces, but a mutant who shouldn't be able to breathe but can.

"But A12 does have the pesky side effect of taking us out around the age of forty. Forty-five if we're lucky. I'm twenty-three. Still young, yes, but even that doesn't give me much time to guarantee my presence at Baby Sullivan's high school graduation.

"Which means that if I want in on this parenthood thing, which I do, I need to get on it quick if I am going to be around to see this kiddo grow up.

"Consider this to be the lengthiest, whiniest personal ad in the history of the genre.

"Me: Constitutionally unattractive, mouthy, banned from at least three tech offices in Santa Clara County, carrier of a genetic disorder that there is a chance our child will inherit, seeks bright, witty, educated saint to mother my child. I ask that you be my age or older, want to have a child more than anything in this life but don't have one yet, and employed because I don't make much being a provocateur/bartender. Trust funders welcome. No one with the last name Sullivan, please. Email inquiries to letsprocreate408@yahoo.com."

To indicate that I had finished, I took a bow. Cole hobbled up on his cane to give me the standing ovation I deserved.

Two months after Cole chose Hannah Maes as the winner of his sweepstakes, they went to San Francisco City Hall to lock it down. Sadie Bryn Sullivan was born in June of 2001, and Nick considered his mission successful. A photo of him holding up his drooly baby like a trophy graced the pages of *Wired* two years after his treatise. I had that photo saved on my computer for years. It felt like my victory, too.

"And what is Bryn up to these days?" Sylvia asked.

Cole fiddled with his wine glass. "Berkeley. Pre-med," he said. "I think she skis, too."

"You think?"

"She didn't get the 12 and has good balance, how about that?" Cole mumbled.

"Genetics is a funny thing," I said.

"You *think* she skis?" Syl asked.

"Did you even go to her high school graduation?" Chris asked.

Cole turned his back to Sylvia and said to no one and everyone, "Nina thought my *Wired* ad was genius. She printed it out and had it taped on her wall for twenty years." This wasn't true, but he liked to claim it was. "She should've been Bryn's mama."

I should have been Bryn's mama, Cole said.

Me too, I thought. I could barely contain the joy I felt. Remember opening a fresh pack of Starburst and finding that the first one in the stack was your favorite flavor, cherry? It was like that only a million times better.

But there was something else about that statement, something that a thoughtful person might notice, in that someone really was Bryn's mama. Someone I was told by a reliable source was a great person. I didn't know this the day Cole declared me the preferred uterus holder for his genetic line. I did think it, though.

The group turned quiet for a bit. Even I didn't have anything to add to the conversation. Cole's face softened. He looked like he could maybe cry. "A12 or no, I really wish I found you sooner, Nina. That you would have seen that ad in time and wanted to make a double A12 baby with me instead of shacking up with your meatball man in Connecticut, crying in private and having to be on top all the time."

The Good Thumbs turned to look at me. The combination of wonderful and terrible things in that statement messed up the wiring in my brain. "Paul never made meatballs," I said, to be fair, because I was always fair, and Cole didn't need to be insulting a man he'd never met. "He was more of a Bolognese guy."

Cole's face darkened. A lightning bolt of fear shot through me. How wrong I was to correct Cole.

4

Before Cole came into my life and ordered a case of paperback copies of *World War You: Poems by Nina S. Blaine* directly from its independent publisher, I would forget, for months at a time, that I wrote and published a book of poems. In its earliest incarnation, my poetry collection was a project commissioned by a Bondurant student who had heard me read a poem I wrote for my class's ten-year reunion banquet and who had gone on to form her own independent press. The poem was six pages long, and the f-word appeared thirteen times. A real rager, my classmates said. Pissy, rude, aggressive, completely out of character for me and out of place at such an august event as a Bondurant reunion banquet, which had been held in the same airy, flower-filled ballroom as Daisy Day and our graduation. The director of alumnae sent me an angry email after I read it in front of sixty Bonnies and their assorted plus-ones. She threatened to rescind my alumnae association membership until I threatened to ban her from Stella di Capra. The only other restaurant in Teagarden was the Subway inside the Sunoco station, so she backed off. Sylvia helped me edit it. When I watched the video of my reading at the Bondurant reunion, I loved the version of Nina Blaine who stood up in front of the Class of 2000 and called her own pussy an engine of destruction.

Some of my classmates seemed to like that poem a lot, though. So did the Bonnies who were working the event as servers and dishwashers that night. *World War You* didn't make me a star, but it did, for a year and a half, make me a bit of a guru among the Bonnies. A legend in the minds of a few misfit daughters of privilege who felt the same rage I felt about how goddamn hard it was to be alive.

They were prose poems about loving yourself. Not an original premise, but that's what I was feeling back in my twenties, as an accidental pastry chef who had given up her dream of law school, of writing a book, of doing whatever I was thinking of doing before leaving college—not that I've ever been ambitious. I was supposed to want a career that left my mark on the world, but the execution of that goal seemed out of reach, and besides, I was going to die at forty, and I liked baking. Then I married a man who did not want those things for me. Chef Paul told me that there was nothing wrong with being a college dropout. He paid for me to get my culinary certificate at the local community college, making me persona non grata among certain segments of Bondurant's alumnae but a beloved member of the Stella di Capra back-of-house family.

I wrote that as a woman, you must love yourself because the odds are high that no one else will. You will not stagger out of the gates of the Bondurant School without someone, sometime, for some bullshit reason, absolutely fucking with you. Women must love themselves.

You know that there is life after mommy and/or daddy and this pretty dream school, that you will get older, you will be judged by the size of your tits and the weight on your ass and not the degrees on your wall or the lines on your resume. Your education will stop mattering, but what will hurt the most is that your heart, your love, your goodness, will also stop mattering. This is life under patriarchy, and everything you learned at school will sit like an undigested biscuit in the pit of your stomach.

That I wrote anything incendiary or influential is laughable to me. I am, as Sylvia says, forever up my own butt in sorrow and pity. She thought maybe my stepfather would try to sue me for including references in the book to his sexual assault court case, but he didn't, probably because he, literally, couldn't read. The book is dedicated to Sylvia.

Should I have thought it strange that Cole ordered twenty copies of my book? For five people, one of whom was the author?

I was at another Good Thumbs gathering, this time on a rainy Sunday in Sylvia's living room, sitting on her pale pink sofa with four different charcuterie boards and six bottles of wine laid out on the coffee table, and our shoes parked by the front door, all of us digging our misshapen feet into her soft sheepskin rug. It was only me, Syl, Jorie, and Cole—Chris was elsewhere that day. Harris Notley's famed piano had been pushed up against the wall and was covered in orange sheets tamped down by framed family photos. The biggest photo, right in the middle, was of an aged Harris Notley with white hair and a red bowtie and a wide grin, seated at that very piano, with two-year-old Sylvia on his lap.

Cole dinged his wine glass with a spoon to get our attention. "Attention, siblings in disorderly disorders! Today, the Good Thumbs are reading Nina's book for our book club. We did not have a book club prior to today and we'll never have a book club again." Cole placed a copy of my book into his dog's mouth to deliver to each Good Thumb. "Good boy, Bruno! It's important that we understand this book and are prepared to speak of it intelligently so that we will all be on the same page when it comes time to go into battle with Kailey Elwood."

"Battle?" Sylvia asked.

"You know, Cole, you get really obsessed with stupid, unimportant people," Jorie said as she walked around the living room pouring a very nice cabernet from Syl's winery. "You wasted your youth beefing with Silicon Valley douche villains and conning baby-hungry widows into marrying you. Maybe recognize that although the Good Thumbs aren't exactly the world's mentally healthiest people, we're not into vengeance, either."

Cole arched a brow at Jorie and reached across me to grab a handful of Marcona almonds. "You know, dear Jordan, you shouldn't know what a Kailey Elwood is, unless you have some sort of Instagram addiction you've been hiding from the rest of us. Do you dream of twee meadows and organic baby food in glass jars?"

"She's the twenty-something consort of your boy Steve Elwood, who is some also-ran tech billionaire you used to swap blowies with when you lived in San Jose," Jorie blasted back. "Like, less famous than Bill Gates but mentioned in the same breath as Bill Gates."

Cole laughed. "So basically, he's the Eddie Blaine of Silicon Valley. Less talented than his peers, but still capable of bagging a sweet young blonde."

I had a sick feeling in my stomach. This was going nowhere good.

"Cole, can you chill out? No need for all this," Syl said, but of course, he ignored her.

Cole put his hand on my knee. "Like Eddie Blaine opening for Peter Lawford at the Flamingo during the spring of 1965, Steve Elwood's contributions to the world of software are minimal and slightly embarrassing. I will warn you, I have prepared a PowerPoint presentation that may shock and offend our Nina, as it pertains to her fine book of verse."

Slide one appeared on Cole's laptop: a photo of a nude man shaking a cocktail shaker.

The group groaned. "Cole!" Sylvia yelled. "Get rid of that!" She jumped to her feet and slammed Cole's laptop shut. "Not in my house!"

Cole smirked, proud of himself. "I thought you ladies were mature adults." He opened his laptop again and covered the offending part of the photo with his hand. "In spite of your puritanism, I beg of you: Sear into your minds the sexual malfeasance of Steven K. Elwood, founder and CEO of Exegesis, the immoral and frankly banal leader in furtive government contracts for overpriced bank encryption software."

Cole clicked to his next slide, a black-and-white photo of what appeared to be Steve Elwood's 1970s-looking high school graduation photo. "This cheeseball who lies, still, about graduating from Stanford, and resembles a defecating panda when going shirtless in public, married his oldest kid's college roommate, this human puff pastry named Kailey Evers, now Kailey Elwood. She owns an organic baby food company and here we have on slide three, what she wrote about our Nina on Instagram."

Slide three: A photo of Kailey, pale and freckled, her cornsilk hair in long braids like the Wendy's corporate logo, wearing a gray cashmere sweater, holding an infant in a white cap to her chest, staring gravely into the camera.

Our beautiful daughter, Zinnia Grace, was diagnosed with a rare condition called A12 Fibrillin Deficiency Syndrome. We learned that Steve's age might have had something to do with her having this, but that advanced paternal age as a factor is anecdotal. Apparently, the majority of people who have this are the children of famous people? Why have I never heard of this?

Steve and I are donating $5 million to the UCLA Rare Genetic Disorders Clinic for increased research to put an end to this crippling illness. Our Zinnia will struggle to have a normal life.

Cole laughed. "Look at this room full of strugglers we've got here. Struggling to have more wine and sing another karaoke song!"

"I thought you said she mentioned me?" I asked.

Cole cleared his throat. "Baby, I didn't forget about you! I would never forget about you." He clicked to the next slide, where he had enlarged and highlighted the following text: *It has been brought to my attention that the author of a little book called* World War You, *Nina Blaine, suffers from A12, and that part of her book is about growing up with a different body. A friend of mine sent this book over, and . . . wow, this was supposed to make me feel better? A book with a poem called "Ugly Girl Manifesto"? My daughter is NOT ugly. Maybe Nina Blaine is ugly—I don't know her, and I don't want to. But her way of speaking of herself makes me sick.*

The gang looked at me.

Jorie said, "I'm taking you for fro-yo after this, Nina. You don't deserve this."

"Wow," was all I had to say. I didn't know this Kailey Elwood from a hole in the wall, but the idea that she would rather have a "normal" daughter (whatever that means, and never mind that Steve Elwood already had two other daughters with the right number of fingers) than a daughter who would write a book like *World War You*, where she admits to liking herself in spite of being told she was either a freak or a pity case was pretty awful, although I would have preferred to not know anything about Kailey and her A12 baby at all.

Cole began, "I know we all have feelings right now. I think we're all on the same page in that we hate this stank bitch and want to put hot sauce in her douche bottle?"

"Fuck her!" I yelled.

"Hate's a strong word," added Jorie, and Sylvia threw in a totally expected, "I don't hate anyone. Hate is for losers."

Cole walked behind me and put his hands on my shoulders. "Maybe Nina Blaine *is* ugly! Look at this beautiful woman! She got her father's nose and her mother's boobs, and she wrote a groundbreaking book of poetry about self-love that they sell at Erewhon. This gold-digger Kailey has some cojones speaking about our girl like that."

I sprung up from the chair to get Cole's hands off me. They didn't sell my book at Erewhon, and I didn't know why Cole said that they did. "Syl knows this story, but did you know that my mother didn't know who Nina Simone was when my father put it on my birth certificate? If she had named me, I would have had a name like Kailey. But the 1982 version, which was

Amanda Joy. Can you all hear my dad responding to that with, *more like Amanda Goy, am I right?*"

The other Good Thumbs looked away as Cole put his arm around me and sang, "No man will ever hurt you now that you're miiiiine. No man will ever look at you like you're a swine!"

"It's *In my arms forever, you are divine*," I corrected.

"No one wrote a love song like Eddie Blaine."

"My Aunt Addie wrote his songs. But sure."

"No Kailey Elwood will hurt you now that you're miiiiine," he said loudly to the group, and then in a whisper in my ear, "I mean that."

"They don't sell my book at Erewhon," I said.

Cole still needed to hold everyone's attention. "Good Thumbs! Good Thumbs minus Christopher because he's off getting his scrotum waxed or talking to his lawyers! Do we agree that we are siblings-in-arms against this slanderous c-word attacking our beloved Nina? I have so much dirt on Elwood. It would bring me no greater happiness than to let Elwood's child bride know that she has declared war on the wrong social club of connective tissue-disordered orphans."

Cole came up behind me and planted a long, wet kiss on the base of my neck. "In vino veritas: I am here to protect Eddie's little girl."

The magic of Cole was that he could return to me the long-gone feeling of my father's love. How did he do that, I often wondered, tangled up with his gangly limbs in my torn-up bed sheets, staring at the ceiling, feeling as loved as I did once upon a time as a little girl. Such magic.

"In vino veritas," Cole said again, his hands rubbing my shoulders, his mouth grazing the side of my head. A spray of his saliva landed on my ear, as if directing the ghost of my father from his lips straight into my heart, "Anyone who hurts you will have to answer to me, Nina."

***

Dr. Chen, Sylvia and I often reminisced about meeting you for the first time when we were kids and you were fresh out of medical school; the young, cool doctor with a streak of pink in her hair. That you chose us—the forgotten and forgettable children of rich old men—to focus your career on has meant a lot to us, and not even from a research perspective. Thank you for taking our blood, mapping our DNA, and speaking to the media every time another aged one-percenter dropped his sperm into a young model, actress, or UT Tri-Delt sister.

Once, during a lunch outing in which I sobbed all over your white coat after eating two bites of a Cobb salad, you held me in your arms in that booth at Du-Par's and asked me what would change in my life if you successfully stopped an age gap couple like my parents from having a baby. I was in my twenties and had flown back to Los Angeles behind my mother's back to attend Sylvia's wedding and to give you six vials of my precious blood. You and I talked about whether I'd be able to have a baby of my own without dying of lung collapse or turning into an overstretched Hefty trash bag, as Paul and I were sort of discussing adoption at the time and I asked you if you advised the elderly men who come in all sad and mad over their eight-fingered darlings to knock it off with the elder reproduction. You told me you had, just once in your career, because the man in question seemed to have several young women—not only a single wife but a harem, as it were, and was expecting to be a new father three times over in the span of a single year. You refused to tell me his name because that was a HIPAA violation, but you told me this monster was crop-dusting his semen on the eggs of Los Angeles's fertile maidens and creating a future generation of the Friends of the Good Thumb.

What I didn't say was that setting a child up to miss their parent from the jump was a particular form of cruelty. It's one thing to lose a parent young to a car accident or cancer. That wasn't the plan. Eddie's dying when I was a little kid was always the plan, as much as Tracy denied it.

If we were talking face-to-face right now, if I wasn't sitting here waiting for my suicide mission pregnancy to be over, you would tell me that the feud that Cole started with Kailey was meant to mirror the ongoing feud I had with my mother. That in talking to me, he somehow grokked the Nina-Tracy vibe and was replicating it with his mortal enemy's third wife. He was bonding with me through a shared enemy.

You, Dr. Chen, are well-known among the Good Thumbs as a violator of patient privacy. I would never do anything to cause you trouble or get in the way of your important research. I suspect there is job security in being the only doctor interested in a rare genetic disorder that mainly affects the rich. But when my mother left a message at your office to ask if you had seen me recently, your job was to tell her that you could not disclose that information! Patient-doctor privilege mattered here, and it was wrong of you to share with Tracy that that we had been meeting for lunch at Lemonade every Wednesday.

I would convey to the Human Resources department of UCLA Medical Center my disappointment in your actions if I didn't need you to raise Sigrid.

Know this, Dr. Chen, since you think it's okay to overshare: I flamed out on this life thing after months of having tons of intense, imaginative sex. Cole, old for having A12, equipped with but a single testicle that hung two inches above his knees like a golf ball in a strawberry taffy sack, was an insatiable sexual warrior who bent me over, threw me down, ravished me, and did everything Trent Reznor sang about and then some. I almost came to you about a urinary tract infection and maybe herpes. I went to Planned Parenthood instead because you would have known who had given me cooties and disapproved. You would have told me to stop. I wouldn't have. Not a police officer, SWAT team, moving train, or team of wild horses could have dragged me away from that man.

Which is to say, as the days left of my life dwindled into the single digits, there was a brief window of time when I thought maybe I wouldn't die at forty. That maybe you were wrong. That what would prolong my life was not whatever you were cooking up at work, but Cole and his sexy magic. He made me see colors. He made me leap over mountains. For six whole weeks, I was the shiniest star.

***

The Eddie-Tracy marriage was on its way out at the time that Eddie himself was on his way out. A pack a day smoker for sixty years, Eddie was known around our basic Burbank tract house by his seal bark death cough. A few times a day, I would look up from my crayons or my Beverly Cleary book from the library and watch my father hit the center of his chest with his fist, clutching the kitchen table to steady himself as he horked his lungs out, each hack and gurgle a reminder to young me that my father was old, that old people die, and that my father was soon to be an old person who died. He would then go to the sink for a glass of water which he would take a long drink from and resume his coughing, leaving his blood-spattered paper towels on our yellow kitchen countertops.

By this time in their marriage, Tracy had been marched back to work, and not as an actress, as she had long hoped. Mike Watson himself had told her to her face that she was a lousy actress and the only side of the camera she'd ever be on was the one she didn't like. Watson got her work as a makeup artist for the soap operas as a favor to my dad, who had finally accepted the end of his life as an entertainer and intended to spend the rest of his days with his albums, his spiced rum, and his favorite little girl.

"Nina bella, if anyone at that goddamn school gives you guff about your hand, you punch 'em right in the nose," he'd tell me when I'd come home from first grade crying that some kid had been mean to me about my hand. "Your mother's gonna tell me I can't raise you like it's 1925 Jersey City, but you know what? She can take a walk. No one ever called Tracy an ugly Jew."

I did punch that girl in the nose the next time she called me an ugly cripple. Jew, cripple, all the same to Eddie Blaine. The school called home and Eddie picked up the phone. The school told him he had to come pick me up for punching Jennifer McFuckface or whoever. Dad told them to go pound sand, refusing to pick me up or to punish me for my actions. In his grimmest bad guy character voice, I heard him bark over the phone between phlegmy coughs, "I told her to do it, you bunch of pansy cowards! I am not coming to get her. She did what I told her because you let that spoiled brat talk to my Nina like that. No, you listen to *me*. You punish my kid and I'll punish you with the business end of my Colt 38, you stupid fuck."

I went to private school after that.

The thing I knew, and that I assume Eddie knew—which would explain why he acted like the crazy perp in a '70s cop show at the end of his life, especially where I and my three-fingered business were concerned—was that my mother was on the side of the school. Tracy always sided with the school and the bully. She never outright said it, but I knew.

Tracy and Eddie had a blow-up fight about his teaching me to punch bullies and threatening the school principal with a gun he didn't really own. Tracy wrote him off as a crazy old man, proving once again that anyone you deem beneath you, be they a woman, a Jew, old, or merely inconvenient, can be written off as crazy. Women do it as much as men. Tracy has done it with me for decades. If I disagree with her, I'm crazy. Sylvia, who sides with me in all matters concerning Tracy, is also crazy, as is her mother, Dr. Cassandra Hill-Notley, professor emeritus of Musicology at USC and the recipient of a Guggenheim, who once got in Tracy's face for canceling my birthday plans as punishment for calling Greg Hodges an asshole.

The only man to call me beautiful growing up was Eddie, and he was, according to my mother, crazy.

He was crazy.

She still says he was crazy.

But he loved me, I'd tell her, and she wouldn't hear me over the din of her own father's voice in her head, telling her she wasn't as beautiful as her sisters. Big Jesse owned Tracy's head the way he owned Grandma Arlette, Westervelt Oil and Gas, a new Cadillac every two years, and that garish white house with the columns in Dallas. I know she'd look at her fluffy blonde nieces, each angelic facsimiles of the original three Westervelt daughters, and wonder, why not her? The universe had been unkind to Tracy, and anyone who said otherwise was, of course, crazy.

***

As the days dragged on, Cole became obsessed with L'Affaire Kailey. He had a bone to pick with Steve Elwood, but why? Cole never worked in tech. He never coded, never had a job at a start-up. In his twenties, he'd been a bartender in San Jose, after following a girlfriend out to California when she got a gig at Apple. While she worked a hundred hours a week, he refashioned himself as Nick Sullivan, blogger, gossip monger, and gum in the hair of the architects of Internet 1.0.

"Do we really need to jump in the shit pit with her?" I asked him one night after three hours of porny sex followed by the consumption of a large pepperoni pizza and a liter of Dr Pepper. "Another mother who can't even deal with her misshapen baby. . . . Well, at least she's super rich, right? What about the A12 babies of poor people?"

"There aren't any, because only rich people pull this shit."

"Your family wasn't rich."

Cole shrugged. "They were Catholic, and I wasn't dead or bleeding all over the floor, so they never took me to a doctor about my chest or my eyeball or the fingers Jesus kept for himself."

I gazed at his A12 hand, a big manly, three-fingered specimen of a sexiness that I never thought I'd know. Cole's left hand, with the three remaining fingers bent sideways with arthritis, was, to me, at least, the most magnificent manifestation of pure animal bliss. I wanted to lick it, love it, honor it, worship it. Those gnarled fingers had made me come harder and faster and with a power I had never imagined, and it felt so holy that I would leave this planet confident that I had been fucked good and proper by a man who knew my body in a way no one else could.

He stared at me with intent with his one eye. Cole's eye was brown like my eyes. In a way, I felt exposed by this look. Cut open, even.

"I love the shit out of you, Nina. You're brave and crazy, just like me."

I smiled. I flushed. I was boring and more than a little scared, but if Cole wanted to say otherwise, I'd take the compliment. Feeling in love with someone who looked like me was an exercise in transcendence, and I thought Cole felt the same. If he had been a normie, Cole wouldn't be part of my story to the extent that he was the thesis and the villain and the punchline. My meatsuit fueled my shame, doubt, and the disgust of others. Cole was, objectively speaking, worse off than me. I could put on a high-necked dress and gloves, and no one would wonder out loud if there had been lead in my mother's drinking water. Cole had an eye patch and a cane, and those magical tree-root fingers and he was *insane*.

"My love? Would you like to see a photograph of Steve Elwood wearing frilly red panties, circa 2000?" he asked me so sweetly, nuzzling his face into my breasts. I said yes.

Dear Kailey Elwood,

In response to your Instagram post citing my book, *World War You*, which, truthfully, was not written with the twenty-eight-year-old trophy wife of a sixty-something tech billionaire in mind. You have it all, right? And all figured out. Congratulations!

I suppose you believe that I wrote my loser book for losers because of my disability. A12 doesn't affect one's intellectual abilities. It does make me look like a stretched-out trash bag, and there's the finger thing, of course, which I am a little tired of talking about. It shot my piano playing career, oh well. And the joke always went, I don't need a ring finger because who's going to marry me anyway? Right?

No one batted an eye at me as an adult living in the tiny town in Connecticut where I went to boarding school and never left. My mother, a Texas beauty queen turned West Side of Los Angeles mom, whined and wailed about my disorder and when I got older and mouthier, responded by disappearing me from view. If you look at the announcement of her marriage to former Rams lineman Greg Hodges that ran in *People* magazine, you'll see that she allowed them to doctor the photo to cut me out and allowed my conventionally attractive, able-bodied cousin to take my place. She replaced her daughter to please her new husband. Did it never occur to her that this would hurt and humiliate me?

The truth is you did this. As the majority of A12 children were born to fathers over the age of sixty. Your husband is over the age of sixty. There are risks to fathering a child at such an advanced age. There's very little research, because no one is going to tell Steve Elwood that he can't sow his seed past his expiration date. So maybe believe the anecdotes?

If you want to be a supportive mother to your child, do not say things like "Zinnia will struggle to have a normal life" in public where she will one day see them and know how you feel about her. And quit having babies with your husband. Your first husband, that is. I imagine there will be more for you.

Sincerely yours,
Nina Blaine

5

Tracy was thirty-one when Eddie died. After the funeral, with our house in Burbank quiet and strange, all of Eddie's stuff in boxes that Tracy stacked in the garage, we drove across the desert to Dallas to visit her family. When we arrived, the first thing her father, Jesse Westervelt, a menacing man with a thick Texas drawl, said as he looked down at her still-golden head was that she needed to get her hair done, lie about her age, go shake her moneymaker at a new husband, and not ask him for a dime.

Jesse Westervelt had a way of making everyone feel small. He stood six feet eight and was built like an angry door. He wore a bolo tie and smoked his fat cigars in his house, a seven-bedroom mansion with white marble floors where I got lost as a child trying to find a bathroom.

When Grandpa Jesse was young, an army recruiter came to his high school in Henrietta, Texas, to get the boys to sign up for the war. The recruiter took one look at Jesse and told him he was too tall to join up. His older brother went, though, and when he didn't come home, Jesse became the sole owner of his family's business, Westervelt Oil and Gas, where he terrorized his employees for nearly forty years before dying of a heart attack on the links at the Dallas Country Club.

"Did the old man at least leave you enough money to get that girl some finger surgery?" I remember Big Jesse, a cigar between his teeth, asking my mother as we sat in their gold and green living room in Highland Park sipping hot Lipton tea, my mother watching me like a hawk in case I spilled a drop on the couch. Big Jesse liked Cuban cigars. He leaned back in his leather chair, his long legs spread wide as he puffed and swirled a whiskey neat around the glass. For all his money, Jesse Westervelt's pants never reached his ankles. He only ever bought pants off the rack at Dillard's. His shins were a yard of brown sock.

Eddie Blaine didn't leave Tracy penniless, but Big Jesse didn't give a damn about that. A woman living without a man was simply not done in Tracy's family, and Eddie Blaine, in the eyes of my grandfather, did not count as a man. Tracy's abrupt move to Los Angeles after her college graduation and her elopement—which she managed to keep a secret from her family for an entire year until her sister Wendy turned up on the steps of the house in Burbank, having hired a private investigator to track her down—were all her father needed to prove that she was not only the least beautiful of his daughters but was the dumbest one as well. He compared her often to the puppy he shot as a child because it kept wandering away from its mother and crying when it realized it was lost.

Jesse Westervelt thought of himself as a behemoth—his massive size, his wealth, his command over my grandma Arlette, who made it her life's work to be as invisible as possible. She hid in the kitchen while her husband roared at my mother. "You married a man older than me, baby girl, and you're surprised that he died? You didn't have your head on straight. You married the first man in Hollywood who wanted to jump in your jeans. Nina, baby, watch that cup. Set it down on the coaster there, please. Tracy Jane, you come back around here asking me for money like I'm a fool? Like I didn't raise you up right? I didn't raise no ugly girls. Go find yourself another husband before you embarrass yourself even more."

When Tracy became a widow, Jesse stopped trying to hide that he loved her the least. He called her a disappointment, and worse. Tracy's sisters, Julie and Wendy, went from the Westervelt mansion in Dallas to a perfunctory year or two at Southern Methodist to locate a proper husband and were considered finished on the day that Big Jesse walked each of them down the aisle at Highland Park Presbyterian Church, aglow in their gauzy white veils. Tracy, a bit of a rebel, spent all four of her years at UT majoring in art and dating a string of tortured poets and sweaty musicians rather than getting a diamond ring from a scion of industry like she was supposed to.

On that visit after Eddie died, Grandpa Jesse's living room filled with smoke from his Cuban as he glared at his youngest, waiting for her to answer for herself. Grandma Arlette, who rarely spoke, cowered next to the door to the kitchen, one hand stuffed in her apron pocket, the other around a glass of vodka and orange juice. "You can move back to Dallas, sure, baby girl," my grandfather said coldly, taking a long drag on his stubby cigar, "but it's embarrassing, to me and your mother and your sisters especially, to have you crawling back here after you done gone out to California and made a damn fool of yourself on the TV with that dirty old man."

Tracy cried on that green velvet couch with the quiet dignity that she had been raised to perform. Her mother dutifully ignored her and made me a plate of cookies. Grandpa Jesse rose to all his height, reached down and handed Tracy the telephone, a white landline on a very long cord. "Call up your sisters and tell them you're sorry for humiliating them with your old man husband and your mutilated Jew baby."

Tracy took her marching orders. Five years later, Grandpa Jesse walked her down the aisle at Highland Park Presbyterian to marry Greg Hodges, an NFL quarterback with an expressionless face, a womanizer who held open contempt for her daughter. Someone at CBS had set them up on a blind date and Tracy, who had turned down a couple of very nice men in the meantime, said yes when he slid four karats worth of Westervelt family approval on her finger ten months later. Tracy barely looked at me on her wedding day, except to say that I had smeared my mascara, and she didn't care for my attitude. She was finally getting her big day, doing the one thing that would make her daddy love her. I'll never forget the way she smiled, weeping for the camera while walking beside her father on his arm. It was the only day I ever saw Tracy happy. Like, truly happy. The same day the man she married joked to his football friends that he wanted to put a bag over my head for the ceremony. The friend offered to lock me in the trunk of his car. When I told her what her new husband had said, she told me I was lying and if I continued to try to ruin her life, I could move in with the Notleys.

Grandma Arlette held my A12 hand in hers that day to hide it. Maybe she did that out of love, so that no one could see it and I could be a gauzy white bride like her girls someday. What I really wanted was for her to say she knew I'd never be like her girls and that she loved me anyway.

***

Cole dangled my ringing phone over my head. It was seven in the morning. I did not want to open my eyes. The bed was old, and it sagged in the middle—it had been Addie's bed before she moved into the retirement home where she caught the virus—and now it was a sweaty mess. I'd bought cheap pink cotton sheets at Target when I arrived at the Eddie Blaine Manse in Los Feliz, not realizing they'd be stained and threadbare within a month thanks to Cole.

Cole crouched over my face in bed, dangling his nut sack onto my forehead while Bruno tucked his head into my armpit.

"La Tracy would like to speak with you."

I looked at the phone. I didn't want to talk to Tracy. Mentally tabulating the number of months since I had last spoken to her took the place of speaking with her, and the number had grown large.

I took the phone from Cole. "Mother? Why are you calling me so early?" I demanded, sounding raspy and tired on purpose.

"It's not early in Connecticut. Where are you?"

"Does it matter?"

Bruno let out a few loud, sharp barks.

"Do you have a dog, Nina?"

"No."

"Are you in Los Angeles? You're in the Los Feliz house, aren't you? Or you're with Sylvia?"

I didn't respond.

"I tried to call Paul," Tracy said. "Did he change his number?"

He had, but that information was given on a need-to-know basis, and Tracy did not need to know. "Nope."

Tracy continued, "Justice said he saw you with a guy wearing a bandanna and an eye patch eating lunch at Grand Central Market."

Truth be told, I wouldn't recognize either of her twin sons, the Royal Princes Hodges, if they hit me with a football. I hadn't seen them since they were five. They were with their nanny when I came to LA for Tracy's husband's awful court hearing, and I hadn't seen my mother in Los Angeles since. Tracy had sent photos of her sons over the years. They looked like their marble slab of a father, all angles and muscles and vacant eyes. And who the hell picked out those aggressive names? Justice went to law school, obviously. Hunter, named for the practice of killing animals, played football for the University of Utah and was coaching some Canadian team with a goofy name that would never fly here in the US of A.

"How would Justice even know what I look like? Los Angeles has other A12ers besides me and Syl."

"He knows what his sister looks like. He knows Sylvia, too. He said you were with that eye patch fellow. Nick Sullivan?"

Cole, still naked and dunking his junk in my face, dropped my laptop on the pillow next to my head. It was open to Instagram.

Tracy pressed on. "You left your nice husband for an eye patch-wearing terrorist?"

"I have no idea what you're talking about."

I looked at Cole's screen. He blew up the text of a recent comment on Kailey E.'s account. I had forgotten about L'Affaire Elwood. Sparring with some idiot rich bitch on the internet didn't hold the same wonder to me as it evidently did to Cole.

Cole slapped the screen of my laptop to bring to my attention this comment:

@tracyblainehodges: First of all, congratulations on the birth of your beautiful daughter, Kailey. I know my daughter Nina believes that she got A12 because her father was older, and that her friend, @sylviamnotley, also shares her situation and her beliefs. Their pity party has been going on for years, and they aren't going to change their minds. But the thing that Nina never understood and refuses to acknowledge is how much her father and I wanted her. That she has only ever been loved and cherished, especially by Eddie when he was still alive! He adored his little girl so much. Was I a perfect mother? Of course not! But Nina will tell you I favored her younger brothers and allowed *People* magazine to replace her in my wedding photo with a model. What Nina leaves out of that story is that she had already left the wedding by the time we got around to taking family photos and the photographer assumed that her cousin from Dallas was her, and even magazines make mistakes. Kailey, feel free to be in touch with me, and thanks to you and Steve for your generous donation to the UCLA Rare Disorders Clinic.

Tracy asked, "Who is this Nicky Six Six Six? On Instagram? That's Nick Sullivan, right? I remember you laughing over something he wrote years ago. Is he the one with the baby? He was the other person you knew with A12 besides Sylvia."

Cole cackled. "She tagged Sylvia!"
And Sylvia clapped back:

@sylviamnotley @tracyblainehodges Mrs. Hodges, living with a visible disability, especially as a woman of color, has not been easy. Even with, as you point out, the privileges that come with wealth. Speaking honestly about our struggles is not a "pity party." And the least you can admit is how badly the *People* magazine incident hurt Nina, as well as the incident with your ex that derailed her college education. Both events devastated her. I was there for your wedding, there with her for the immediate aftermath of the *People* incident and know that she has always seen that as you rejecting her. You never apologized; you never pursued a retraction with the editors at *People*. We had a teacher at Bondurant who knew someone at *People* who confirmed you vouched for that photo. You certainly didn't take her side when your ex humiliated her to dodge his sexual assault allegations. Kailey and other women of extreme privilege (money is great, but it isn't a white hand with five fingers!) are going to do whatever they want, and that includes having babies with rich old men and seeking attention on the internet about it when the baby isn't perfect. A12 is not the worst genetic disorder you could have but tell that to someone with 2.2M Instagram followers. Please don't respond, Mrs. Hodges, as I'm going to block you. You have willfully mistreated your daughter for far too long.

"Make me a cup of coffee," I said to Cole.
"Whatever mistress wants," he said, slipping on his boxer briefs and disappearing into my messy kitchen.

Twenty minutes passed. Longer than it takes to make a cup of coffee. And then I hit refresh.

He had taken his laptop with him to the kitchen.

@nickysix66 A message to the third Mrs. Steven K. Elwood: a lot of people love Nina Blaine, even though, per your estimation, she is worthless and pitiable for writing truthfully about her life, for not getting plastic surgeries, and for pointing out that some of us have harder lives because of the attitudes of people such as yourself. I knew your husband back when he was on marriage #2 (your college BFF Ava's mother) and only worth about three mil. Back then, he was a sniveling, spoiled rich kid who built up a fortune to avoid the truth about himself—that he was a no-talent user whose only happiness came from firing his underlings and getting cornholed by whatever rough trade he could find. You're nothing special. You're just young and dumb enough to be part of the expensive infrastructure Steve needs to not face the fact that he's a fraud, a liar, and has never had an original idea. Nobody thinks you love him or are with him for any reason but the cash money, honey. If little A12 Zinnia isn't good enough for you, I'd be more than happy to adopt her and give her the loving and accepting home she deserves. Sounds like you see her as little more than a defective Amazon order and you'd be satisfied with a return. Maybe someday you'll come to your senses and learn to value others for their humanity instead of their appearances, but I won't count on it. Take care, sweetie, and have a nice day. P.S. Nice to meet you, @tracyblainehodges. I'm a big fan of Eddie's.

My mother had hung up. Two minutes later she called back.

"What? What?" she said, pulling her innocent little girl act on me.

"What the hell is wrong with you?" I hissed. "Get a job and stay away from Instagram, *Tracy*."

"You and your friend Nick should leave Kailey Elwood alone. You don't know what you're talking about."

I stood up from the bed, ready to let my mother have it. One of the advantages of staring down my A12 expiration date was that I had no reason to be nice anymore—honesty was the policy, and I felt no qualms about letting Tracy know exactly what I thought of her. "You don't know what you're talking about. If I were you, I'd humble myself around Sylvia Notley and shut up about me and my body and my friends."

"You don't understand what *Kailey* is going through, as a mom of a baby with A12. You never worried about a child. She's trying to be a good mother—"

"Unlike you! You were a shitty mother the entire time! Selfish and ridiculous."

"Oh wow. A woman without children calling *me* selfish. That's rich."

"You—who married an old man because you thought he'd make you famous and spent thirty-five years whining that he didn't have enough money to make it worthwhile—are why I didn't have kids! I can't have them! I have A12 because Eddie was old! Also, people with A12 don't live very long!"

"You think you're going to die soon because you're almost forty? I don't think that's right, nor is that an excuse to be rude online. As your mother, I was embarrassed—"

"You don't get to speak for me, Tracy! You don't! The day you stood up in court and said, 'Your honor, my daughter Nina is disfigured and therefore too ugly for a man like my husband to sexually assault,' was the day you quit getting to call yourself my mother. Now go beg your he-man sons for attention and leave me alone."

"That's not what I said!" she yelled. "You can't seem to let that court thing go."

I winced and hung up the phone without saying goodbye.

Cole appeared with my coffee.

"She told me that me and my 'friend,' meaning you, should leave Kailey alone because we don't know what we're talking about."

Cole and I looked at each other, mouths agape. He laughed.

"We don't know what we're talking about?" He pointed to each of his dazzling A12 physical anomalies. "Like she doesn't know what this town thinks of washed-up old hags who keep running their mouths after no one wants to bang them anymore?"

I swallowed a sip of coffee, tamping down my anger. My phone beeped. A text from Syl: "She's still a piece of work!"

"Syl," I said, holding up the text on my phone.

"Oh, Sylvia. Righteous anger. Good on you. Bruno? Go in the living room." The dog obeyed, and Cole shut the door behind him.

He straddled me as he pressed the power button on my phone and threw it across the room. It slammed against the wall before landing on a pile of my dirty clothes on the floor.

"Repeat after me, Nina Simone Blaine: I am beautiful."

I must have rolled my eyes, but I did say it. He shot me a disapproving look.

"I am beautiful," I said.

Cole flipped me the bird. "Fuck you. You don't actually believe that."

"Well, no."

"Rule number one of Cole: You don't lie to Cole."

"You lie all the time."

Cole arched a brow at me. For a second, I thought he was going to slap me across the face. He would have, I figured, thinking it made him sexy and commanding instead of terrifying. He didn't, though.

"Nina?" he said, lifting my chin with his finger. "You're beautiful. Say it."

I couldn't say it. Why would I say it?

Cole's hand moved down to my throat. Lightly at first. His eye narrowed. His face gnarled into something sinister.

His grip on my neck grew tighter. "Say it. Say it. Nina, say it. Don't be a whiny little bitch like Chris Kyriakis. If I have to fuck self-love into you, I'll do it."

I tried to dislodge his grip on my neck. The tiny bones in there began to bend and I wondered if he would go far enough to break them.

With my left foot, I pushed Cole and his hand off me, coughing, launching myself off the bed in a haze of adrenaline and cortisol. My eyes could only see bits of white light.

"I didn't say you could get up," Cole yelled as I stumbled into the bathroom coughing, uncharacteristically locking the door behind me. Instinct told me to hold the door closed as Cole beat on it, but my arms were noodles, worthless against someone only slightly stronger than me. It only took him a few seconds to rip off the doorknob. "A bathroom door is a privilege, not a right," he boomed as he lunged at me. I hit the back of my head on the rim of the toilet as he dragged me out by my ankle.

6

At the end of his life, Eddie Blaine sat in the living room of the house I had inherited and told his life stories to a future version of me via a Panasonic video camera on a big tripod. Addie's idea. Since I wouldn't get to know my father as an adult, I should hear his stories directly from his mouth as told to her, recorded for posterity. The year I turned twenty-five, Addie had the five VHS tapes transferred to DVDs. Later, the DVD transfer guy modernized his business, and for an additional fee, he uploaded the videos to a password-protected cloud site so that Eddie, slightly drunk and in a bad mood, would be with me forever.

On a Monday that I had nothing to do and no one to see, save for maybe opening the thick envelope addressed to me from a law office in Hartford (spoiler: I never opened the envelope), I typed in the password (S0mb3rM0unt@1n) to watch the Eddie-Addie videos and listened to two people from another era with Jersey accents talk to each other.

There was Eddie, one of his Pall Malls dangling from his lips, parked on his gold couch, which had been Addie's couch all the years she lived in the house. It was still in the living room when I arrived, covered in dust and cat pee. Addie had sprayed it with Febreze, but the smell was so awful I had the whole thing removed, feeling a small pang of sorrow over getting rid of a piece of furniture that my dad had once sat on. Some of his cigarette smoke still lingered in the house, after all those years.

In the video, Eddie wore a yellow Polo shirt, the bottom of his hairy belly poking out over his polyester pants. He occasionally took sips from a Snoopy mug.

***

ADDIE: Ed, put out the cigarette, Babe. Do you really want Nina to see you like that?

EDDIE: (takes a long, hard drag) See me like what? An old man down on his luck? That's the truth, right, Addie?

ADDIE: Jesus Christ, Ed. Okay, what do you want Nina to know about you?

EDDIE: (belly laugh) I could take Dino *and* Vic Damone in a fight.

ADDIE: Come on, Ed.

EDDIE: No, okay. Kids today, they don't like Damone. Fair. Okay. I don't like Damone. I want adult Nina to know that one of the best moments of my life, and I mean this, was when she had chicken pox. She was three years old. I stayed up with her all night because she couldn't sleep. I had taped mittens to her hands so she wouldn't scratch, and she and I cuddled on the couch and tried to watch TV but there was nothing good on at two in the morning, so we went outside. This was at the house on Magnolia, of course, and I carried her down the street under the moonlight and she was crying, getting snot all over my jacket, and it starts to rain. And you know what was open at two a.m.? Remember The Remington, that old bar down from Mike's office? I took my little Nina and she sat on my lap at the bar, and I had a gin and tonic and she had a ginger ale. I told her that if this had been the last time I ever had a drink at a bar with a girl,

I was glad it was with her. She was the best company, even
though she was sick.

ADDIE: (pause, surprised) You took a sick toddler to that
filthy bar?

EDDIE: Yeah, I did. (Addie snorts) Oh, look at you, Miss Perfect. You make it sound bad! It wasn't bad. We had a good
time. She wasn't sleeping anyway. She drank two cups of
ginger ale.

ADDIE: She had the chicken pox and you took her to The
Remington to breathe on other people? With all the cigarette smoke? That dump always stunk real bad.

EDDIE: Why do you even talk to me when all you can do is
accuse me of being the worst father in the history of America? I love my little girl and she wasn't sleeping and—

ADDIE: What did her mother say about taking her to the
bar, Ed?

EDDIE: Tracy, eh! (he waves his hand around like Tracy was a
bad smell) My princess can go to a bar if she's with her old
man. That's my rules. What is it with you, trying to make it
sound like a bad thing?

ADDIE: (sighs) Okay, next question. Why did you name her
after Nina Simone?

EDDIE: Excellent question. At a party in 1974. I was sitting
next to a woman who looked like my former wife, Ruthie:
Jewish nose, eyebrows, a face I'd seen all over the Catskills.
She was on drugs. This girl was expressing admiration
for Leonard Cohen. I hated Cohen, probably because he
was a Jew who looked like me and wrote better songs than
me. That schlemiel rubbed me the wrong direction, you
know? He was some young hippie poet, and I was this

old slob singing about mountains and being a loser. I was embarrassed.

ADDIE: I thought you named her that because you liked Nina Simone.

EDDIE: Nina Simone is (pause for emphasis) the actual voice of God. I'm not a religious man, but I believe that. Anyway, this cute Jewish girl who was high as a kite had a Nina Simone album on and she told me that Nina Simone was singing a song written by Leonard Cohen. That song, "Suzanne," you know? A boring song. Like I said, he rubbed me the wrong direction.

ADDIE: He rubbed you the wrong way, not the wrong direction.

EDDIE: Nobody likes it when you try to correct me, Addie. Back to my story: When Nina Simone, who was a better singer than me and every drunk son of a bitch I ever shared a stage with, sang "Suzanne," it was like she took that turd of a song and turned it into a diamond. And I knew when you were born, Nina, with your hand and me being old and all, that life for you was going to be hard, or at least harder than it was for your mom, which was not hard at all. And I wanted you to be like Nina Simone. Taking garbage and making it the most beautiful thing. So, sweetie, before your mother put some dingbat *shiksa* name on your birth certificate, I beat her to the punch and named you Nina Simone.

ADDIE: I did not know that, Ed. Okay, next question. Describe your childhood.

EDDIE: (smiling) It was perfect. Horace and Esther Blattner were excellent parents. They owned a shoe store.

Montgomery Street Shoes, in Jersey City. As a boy, I put the aglets on the laces. Do you know what aglets are, Miss Smarty Pants?

ADDIE: You kill the mood at parties with your damn aglet story.

EDDIE: Important shoe fact! Aglets are the taped-up ends of the shoelace, so you can thread the laces in the shoes. If your laces didn't have aglets, you wouldn't be able to get the laces in the shoes. Back in those days, we wore boots with laces. My sisters Miriam and Ann ran the store when my father died. I was up in Tannersville with Ruthie and our dog, living at the hotel. It broke my father's heart that we did not want to run the shoe store. Ruthie's folks died when she was a young girl and she was raised by her grandparents in Forest Hills, Queens. Ruthie was a smart girl. She went to Cornell, and I made her quit school and live with me in the boonies so I could sing "Bei Mir Bist Du Schön" at a room full of old Jews eating soup. You were asking me about my childhood?

ADDIE: Yeah. Tell Nina about your sisters.

EDDIE: (raises his eyebrows) Two short ladies who smelled like armpits all the time. BO! I don't know how anyone could be around them, but they were popular. (laughs) They were sisters! Miriam was two years younger than me. She took over the shoe store. She married a Catholic with a head like a tomato. In 1966 I had gone out to New York to see my son Evan graduate from college, and I went to Jersey City to see Miriam and her family. And her husband, I swear to God, he called me to my face a no-talent phony crooner and asked me why I abandoned my family. I said I didn't abandon my family; I followed my dream. And he said that Ruthie had come by the store with her other son to buy him shoes and I held my fists real tight by my side, I wanted to punch him. But I didn't want to make trouble with Miriam, so I didn't. My other sister Annie . . . Annie died two years ago. She was four years younger than me. She caught the flu. She and her husband left Jersey City and moved down to Pompano Beach when their kids were little. They have a daughter named Karen who's very pretty. A lovely girl. I remember seeing pictures and wondered how a couple who looked like them made such a pretty thing. Annie's husband was a lawyer, kind of a dull, slobby fellow. Always had a schmear of food on his shirt. I wouldn't say nothing bad about him other than he told boring stories all the time and no one ever pulled him aside to tell him he was putting everyone to sleep.

ADDIE: Do you realize that you talk about Ruth in every question I ask you?

EDDIE: No, I don't.

ADDIE: You do. Do you keep in touch?

EDDIE: (pauses for a long time) You know, since Evan died, it seems kind of . . . awful to call her out of the blue and say what? Ask her how she is? Her son died. She don't want to hear from me. She married that nice doctor and had another son. She still has the other son. She don't need to hear from that jackass Sandy Blattner that got rid of her on top of losing her son.

ADDIE: What about your other wives?

EDDIE: What other wives? She doesn't need to know about you-know-who.

ADDIE: Okay, fine.

EDDIE: What—oh, Tracy? What do you want me to say about Tracy? That's her mother. She knows Tracy.

ADDIE: Never mind then. Why don't you tell the story of meeting her mother?

EDDIE: (thinks about it, long cigarette drag) Nah . . . it's not a good story. It makes me look like a dirty old man. Maybe I was a dirty old man. I wouldn't put nothing past me. A twenty-two-year-old wants to get in bed with a funny-looking *alte kaker* like me? On what planet does that happen? Oh right: Hollywood. I'll tell Nina the truth (leans forward to the camera so his face fills the screen, waves at me with his cigarette) Your mother was on drugs the day I met her. She liked the (points at his nose, sniffs), you know? Stay away from the nose candy, baby girl. You may end up with a guy like your old man, making messes and farting up the whole place, and I won't be around to help you pick up the pieces.

ADDIE: (pause) Ed, is that necessary? Why do you do that?

EDDIE: Because her mother has her head in the wrong place. Up her *tuches*, that's where.

ADDIE: Okay, but really, Ed, what made you fall in love with her? With Tracy?

I positioned my finger over the pause button. Did I really want to hear this? My father's weird body language, amped up from ratting out Young Tracy, Snorter of Cocaine, wasn't going to tell me anything I wanted to know. At least he lit up when he talked about me.

EDDIE: (another long pause) You know, Addie . . . when I left behind Sandy Blattner and became Eddie Blaine, that was . . . that was . . . he was a whole other man. And Eddie Blaine wanted girls like Tracy. Nothing wrong with Tracy, she's a good girl, she's fun. She'll make another man very happy when I'm dead and gone. Good for her. She's beautiful. But that's Eddie's wife, not Sandy's wife. Sandy and Eddie are two different guys and maybe you understand that? You gotta understand, Addie. No one else would understand. Sandy wouldn't be married to a girl like that. Tracy . . . Tracy would be the shiksa with the knockers that's friends with Sandy's daughter. Not the man . . . not the man who married a real woman and stayed with her through all the bad stuff. Ruthie and I would have had a lot of bad stuff, but we would have made it if I hadn't been so stupid. Eddie made Sandy a lonely man. Tracy Westervelt. I don't know, let her go home to Texas where her family is if that's what she wants. I feel bad about that.

ADDIE: You feel bad about what?

I hit stop. I didn't want to know what my father felt bad about. Because if he said he felt bad about me, about bringing me into the world, then that wasn't information, it was ammunition. I didn't need that message from the grave.

Did he feel bad about dying, leaving behind a seven-year-old?

I hit play.

EDDIE: That she thought she was marrying a big Hollywood guy. Not some has-been schmuck. (laughs) No one but her ever thought of me that way. And that's . . . that's sad. But that's why the old guys like to get with the young girls. They don't see how moldy and rotten we've gotten, do they? (Eddie laughs, but it's a sad laugh)

***

When I went to boarding school, I refused, on principle, to go back to California for holidays. That was a waste of time, money, jet fuel, and effort, and besides: Why would I fly six hours and take a taxi from LAX to that ice-cold house in Malibu to be ignored at the Thanksgiving table or have what I put on my plate policed by Tracy? That was the whole point of boarding school—to not be in that house. People think Tracy made me go to Bondurant. Nope! That was my idea.

Greg Hodges, my former stepfather, maybe said five sentences to me the entire time he was with my mother. One of them, at their engagement party at an Italian restaurant in Dallas, was delivered maybe six inches away from me, as I sat at the head table licking Italian cream cake off my fingers. With a look of disgust, he pointed at me and said, "Do you have to be here?"

The answer was no. One of Greg's staff members—his equivalent of Addie Chambers—appeared moments later to take me back to Grandpa Jesse and Grandma Arlette's house. I was thirteen, maybe too old to be licking whipped cream off my fingers. The slightly melted, tilting-to-the-left child in a floral dress was ruining his view. And he knew that my mother would side with him—God had given him a magnificent body: masculine, powerful, and strong. He was a man above all others, a man other men wanted to be. My mother's body complemented his in meeting its classically gendered expectations, and that's why he chose her. Personality, compassion, intellect, kindness?

Not really a thing with those two. Tracy was three years older than Greg, but she starved herself and had work done so she could fit the bill. Feminine bodies are diminished, after all: small, weak birds with clipped wings who need manly strength to protect them, to maintain their survival. And Grandpa Jesse ate that pairing up. Bragged all over the country club about his new son-in-law. There was no way she was going to protect me from any of this.

It was okay to be a broken doll at the Bondurant School, though, and I had friends who lived in New York or Connecticut who would invite me home for Thanksgiving dinner. Sophomore year, I stayed on campus, alone in Teagarden all weekend with a reservation at Stella di Capra for their thirty-five-dollar Thanksgiving meal.

At four o'clock that day, I bundled myself in my red woolen coat to walk down the hill and out those iron gates to have my supper, which was prepared by my future husband, though I didn't know that at the time. I sat at a two-top table in the corner of that rustic, wood-paneled dining room and ate my salad, my roasted turkey, my sage and sourdough stuffing studded with mushrooms, my mashed potatoes, and my French green beans dripping in butter. I liked eating alone. For one day, I didn't have to talk to other Bonnies about classes or gossip or college applications over a meal.

As I was about to put my fork into my slice of bourbon pumpkin cheesecake, a dark-haired man in glasses with a short, clipped beard approached my table. "Hello, this is awkward, but I have a question for you. Are you Nina Blaine? Or Nina Blattner?"

That he would know Blattner threw me a bit. "I am."

"Nina!" he said with a warmth that felt like he knew me. "I'm Jeremy Cohen. My mother, who is sitting over there, is Ruth, your father's first wife. She's been looking at you and saying that girl over there is the spitting image of Sandy Blattner and wanted me to find out if it was you."

I looked across the room at the plump woman with curly white hair, looking my way while sipping from her water glass, clad in a red sweater with eyeglasses suspended on a chain resting on her breasts. Jeremy, the "other son" that Eddie Blaine groused about, smiled down at me.

"Oh wow," I said, shocked. "Hi."

Jeremy reminded me of a cool counselor at summer camp. "My mother would love to meet you. In fact, she would love it if you would join us."

I stuffed down my immediate response to this scenario, which was to cry, and with sweaty hands, picked up my purse from the floor and carried my slice of pumpkin cheesecake over to the famous Ruth.

Ruth gave me a big, warm smile. "Nina, you look so much like him! Your father, of course. I'm sure you've heard that from people who knew him."

I sat down in the seat next to a woman holding a baby. "You met Jeremy, my younger son. This is his wife, Lisa, and my grandson, Noah, who is turning six years old next week," she said. "And the baby is my granddaughter, Frances, named for Frank, my husband. My other son, Evan, your half-brother, passed away twenty years ago, as you know. Died in that plane crash. Frank passed away last June, and I'm still feeling that, so that's why we're eating Thanksgiving dinner in a restaurant."

"I'm very sorry about your husband," I said to Ruth. "Why are you at Stella di Capra in Teagarden, Connecticut, of all places?"

"Jeremy and Lisa live in Stamford. They like coming here. It's cute."

"I go to the Bondurant School."

"Oh, that school looks very cushy. But kind of sad, right? Your mama sent you away to school? Gosh," Ruth rolled her eyes in disapproval. "I never understood that. You have eighteen years with your child when they're your child, and one day, that's over forever, and they're adults. I could barely get out of bed when this one left for NYU, and that's only a train ride from our house."

"She likes having me gone because of this," I said, holding up my hand.

Ruth nodded. "I see. I see your hand, Nina. Look, I'll say it. He was too old. Too old to have you. But you couldn't tell Sandy Blattner nothing."

"He was too old to have you" was not a sentiment that I had ever heard come out of another person's mouth. People, no matter their relationship to me, would try to talk me out of thinking that. It was a truth that the world conspired not to let me have. It pissed off Tracy something wicked when I said it myself, arriving at that proclamation as a kid and, to this day, never changing my mind on that. Tracy got to be young and stupid, and I had to pay the bill for it with my body.

"That's a lot to put on a little kid," she said. "Watching your old man get old and sick and die when you're still a child."

"Ma, it's Thanksgiving. Don't make her cry," Jeremy started.

Ruth covered my hand with hers. She had chunky gold rings on every finger. "It upsets me that this girl is alone on

Thanksgiving three thousand miles from her home and that Sandy, who had his manager put me and our baby on a plane back to Queens because my behind was too big for Hollywood, is responsible. It hurts me that this girl is hurting, and that Sandy is causing people pain from the grave. And what was your mother thinking? She was only a kid and she married an old drunk who wasn't good enough to sing with Sinatra in Vegas?"

I wanted to say, "Keep going, Mrs. Cohen!" but Jeremy shushed her. She shushed him right back. "Jeremy, I gotta let the girl know, her father was only a legend in his mind."

This version of family truth was the flame to which teen Nina-as-moth couldn't pull herself away from.

"He named you Nina Simone, like Nina Simone, huh?" she asked. When I got older, I understood it was a fitting move on my father's part, giving me a name that would always belong to someone else.

"Yep," I said. "As a big middle finger to Leonard Cohen, which made no sense to anyone but him."

"He wanted to name Evan Bing, after Bing Crosby. Bing Blattner. I put my foot down. There are no Jews named Bing."

Jeremy's wife, sensing I was about to lose my composure, asked if I'd like to hold her baby.

Ruth smiled as I took baby Frances into my arms. "Nina, what do you want in life?"

A real family, I thought. *Like yours, Mrs. Cohen.*

"I don't know," I said, slightly embarrassed that I couldn't spit out something that would impress her.

"I'm going to say something to you, Miss Nina, and Jeremy, you can know this about your mama: Nina, I loved your father so much. He was the sun and the moon and the stars. When he stood on that stage at Klinger's and sang like an angel, I wanted to die. That man was death. If I could have died in that ballroom when I was nineteen years old with Sandy singing 'Blue Orchids' right into my face, then I would have been satisfied with that short amount of life, because Sandy set me on fire and God's truth is that I never had that fire again. And sometimes, I have missed that fire. But Sandy Blattner didn't love me. That wasn't love. That was him looking into my eyes and seeing a doting young girl and liking what I reflected back at him. He was also a controlling son of a bitch and couldn't stop pretending to be someone he wasn't. But at the time, I was young, and it was okay because we had fun. Sandy Blattner hated Sandy Blattner and changed his whole entire self to this phony-baloney Eddie Blaine, a name that meant nothing, was from nowhere, and was made up to please people who wouldn't have given them the sweat off their backsides if they knew he was a Jew whose family sold shoes in Jersey.

"Moving to Los Angeles changed Sandy, and I'll never forget the hatred in his eyes when he told me I embarrassed him and to get lost. I'd done nothing but love him and help him with his singing career, but in the end, that hatred had nothing to do with me. Two years after a couple of goons in suits dumped me and baby Evan at the airport, I married a very nice man named Frank Cohen, who made eyeglasses for a living and bought me a house in Rye, New York, who never complained and came home every night and kissed my forehead. Who raised the so-called Eddie Blaine's son as his own, sent him to Cornell, and cried until he passed out cold on the floor when Evan died in that plane crash. Frank Cohen loved me. That was real love. He was there for me and my sons every day. Came home from work, praised my cooking, did homework with the boys, and fell asleep next to me every damn night. Frank never made me feel like I wanted to die. He never grew to hate me because I dared to remind him of who he really was. Now, Nina, listen to an old lady: Choose a consistent man. Stay away from a man who makes you want to die. Be a little bored. That's what love is. Don't do whatever the hell you grew up seeing. People in Los Angeles only love themselves. Choose a man who can love someone other than the person he sees in the mirror. Don't choose the guy on stage with the spotlight on his face waiting for his applause."

Jeremy looked me in the eyes, calibrating his words to something appropriate for a lonely teenage girl. "Ma's a little dramatic sometimes, but she means well. She cares about you."

Baby Frances started to get fussy, so I passed her back to her mother.

"Jeremy, you're boring as hell," Ruth said, smiling at her boy. "Look at you. A psychotherapist, this one. Married to the daughter of his father's colleague at the optometry office, who's a counselor at the Jewish school. I did a good job," she smiled even bigger. "I did a good job with Evan, too. He graduated from medical school a month before he died. He was going to be a cardiologist. Your father felt guilty about Evan, which is probably why he wanted another shot at fatherhood."

I couldn't hold back the tears.

"If you need anything, Nina, you let us know. Jeremy and Lisa are right down the road in Stamford. I'm in Rye until I break a hip or something. You shouldn't be alone like this. I'm sorry, but it upsets me that your mother lets you live like this. Come here and give me a hug."

I never told my mother about meeting my father's beloved Ruthie. She didn't need to know how hard I cried into that old woman's red sweater that day. When Ruth passed, I drove to Rye for her funeral and sobbed in the back of the temple until Jeremy sent over a friend of his to walk me to my car. Maybe I was crying for my father. Maybe I was crying for the mother and grandmother I wished I'd had. But I knew she was the one Eddie loved the most, so I loved her, too. I loved her because she knew my father, and she knew the truth. She was the truth. You couldn't spell truth without Ruth.

7

Dr. Chen, I met Cole's daughter, Bryn, hours before Siggy was conceived. Just as Nick Sullivan changed his name to Cole Courchaine when he moved to Los Angeles, Bryn had changed her last name to Maes, her mother's last name.

Challenging Cole as to why it upset him that his daughter renamed herself went nowhere. Her identity rebrand made him angry. He didn't change his name to mess with his parents, he insisted. They were long dead by the time he became Cole, and he never changed his name legally like Bryn. He insisted his was for social convenience and Bryn's was a big ol' middle finger to him and him alone.

But why would she give you a big middle finger? I wanted to know. Cole's *Wired* magazine ad baby?

I already loved her.

***

"Real actual question," Cole asked me as I drove his minivan with squeaky brakes up Interstate 5 toward the Bay Area, taking loud slurps of iced tea from his In-N-Out Burger cup. We were driving to Berkeley so he could introduce me to his amazing daughter. "Would you adopt the A12 Elwood baby if you were given the chance?"

"No," I said. "What part of 'we're going to die soon' do you not understand?"

"Let's say that Dr. Chen was wrong. Is wrong. That we're not about to die."

"What about Christopher?" Syl had texted both of us that he was in the hospital with some sort of heart thing.

"That bro is suicidal. You watch, if he makes it out of the hospital, he's going to hang himself off the side of his yacht. You are not going to kill yourself. Your epic and lovely death is going to be just that. As epic and as lovely as you. Not like Chris because he's a coward who has nothing to offer anyone besides foie gras and a bad attitude."

I'd never thought of Christopher as a coward. A sad sack, sure, but not a coward. That Cole was so casually mean about him felt wrong.

I ignored the sickness in my stomach. "Do you want to adopt the Elwood baby or something? This keeps coming up."

"I would do it, sure. Those shallow idiots don't deserve an A12 baby."

"I don't think 'deserve' is really the issue here." Cole's minivan kept trying to veer to the right.

"They're going to mess her up in the head, like you're messed up in the head. Telling her she's deformed and ugly and not as good as the other girls in her extremely wealthy orbit. You turned out okay. A little under-ambitious but someone had to bake pretty cakes in small Connecticut towns, I guess."

"My cakes were amazing."

"Yes," Cole said, lowering the car window to toss his empty cup into some scrubby Central California farmland. "Eight-fingered cakes. So good you can't even taste the two missing fingers."

Cole had *littered.* My mind went blank as I considered what, if anything, I might say about it. Where was Woodsy the Owl when I needed him? Was a single paper cup blowing down a row of almond trees worth detonating Cole over? Cole, after all, saw all that was wrong with me, and let me know what he saw. No one else would tell the truth about me, he said, because they were being too nice. Sure, I didn't toss cups out of car windows, but I was shy, I made strange noises, and cried too much. My ex-husband looked like Fatty Arbuckle, my mother's hubris was unbecoming on such a haggard, unimpressive old woman, and Eddie Blaine was corny.

Why risk it for some almonds?

The cup wandered into the orchard carried by the wind and my tongue went numb. Cole cranked a Led Zeppelin song on the stereo. I felt a chill. He grabbed my thigh, hard, and inched his hand up toward my crotch. I pushed his hand away, muttering "driving" so quietly that I'm sure he didn't hear. He found the zipper on my jeans and began tugging at it. I stared ahead at the road. My own iced tea sat half-full in the cupholder, and I wondered if he was planning to hurl it out the window as well when he gave up on trying to unzip my pants while I was driving.

It took me four hours, two bathroom stops, and a lengthy visit to a St. Louis–style frozen custard place in San Jose that Cole had loved as a young Silicon Valley know-it-all, to work up the guts to confront him on tossing his cup out the window. I ordered a medium vanilla custard with hot fudge and marshmallow sauce and ate it quietly in the car while Cole made phone calls by the dumpsters and only ate three bites of his large vanilla with hot fudge and sprinkles before hurling the whole thing, spoon and all, into the hood of a parked Tesla.

"Do you know the owner of that Tesla?"

"Saint Francis of Assisi," Cole barked as he climbed back in the car. "I had to call animal control on him, and he was pissed. Hey, baby doll, do me a favor and go back in and get me another sundae, please?"

I stared straight ahead. My face began to burn.

"Please?"

"You threw yours at a car," I said. "You made a choice and you've got to live with it. And what the fuck was up with you throwing your iced tea cup out the window?"

Cole didn't crack a smile. "Well. You sure told me. I made a choice! You learned to be a scold like that from your little friend Sylvia Notley, didn't you?"

I stared straight ahead, spooning the last melted bits of my sundae into my mouth.

"Sylvia is always telling everyone what to do. Including me, which she should know is a huge no-no and how you end up in the trunk of a car on Lerdo Highway with nothing but a broken lighter and one shoe. How have you been friends with that overbearing schoolmarm for thirty years? It really explains a lot about your meek personality because that stuffy little hussy has been controlling you since you were a kid."

"All this over an ice cream?" I asked.

"I didn't think asking you to get me a fucking ice cream was going to end up some sort of teaching moment, Miss Blattner, but here we are."

I slouched down in my chair.

Souza's St. Louis Frozen Custard has been in business since 1937, Nina. That's a long time to serve the good citizens of San Jose with their quality family custard recipe. Such a dependable and revered local business. Ma Souza died in 1998, back when I first moved here, and you know what the family did? On the day before her funeral, they handed out free cups of custard to the public. Tell me, Nina, when have you in your whole stupid life ever done anything as benevolent as that?"

"Wow," was all I could say.

"Your father was singing in the Jewish Alps in 1937, of course, so he would not have been among Souza's original customer base, but I bet he would have. Eddie B. knew what was good in this life, yes?"

Did you really need to drag my father into this? Again? I didn't say this. I only thought it. It had become a habit, and a strange one at that, that an hour couldn't pass without Cole bringing up my father. I knew my father's house had ugly furniture, but did it need to be commented upon daily? What my father sang in that annoying shower with the too-low shower head (Eddie was five feet five, okay?), which D-list starlet he may or may not have banged in the house and in what position, or why Addie didn't bother to buy a new couch all those years (because, according to Cole, she was in love with my father, even though she lived in the house with a woman I knew to be her girlfriend for fifteen years?).

"The Jewish Alps?" I asked.

"The Adirondacks or whatever they're called."

"The Catskills."

"Maybe you want to quit with the Jew-ography lesson and get me another ice cream, Nina Simone?"

I stared at him, and he stared right back. I mentally assessed the situation. I could go inside and get him another sundae, which cost five dollars, but it seemed to be, I guess, Parenting 101 that when your child throws their ice cream at a stranger's

Tesla, they don't get rewarded with a new one, and I did not want to parent Cole.

Cole held my gaze as he began to sing very softly, "*Angel in the moonlight.*"

"Stop it."

He smirked. "*A smile as bright as Manhattan. A look as sweet as Boston Cream Pie.*"

"Shut the fuck up."

"*It's no mystery that history has given us this one most passion-ate kiss-tery.*"

I flung open the door to the car and, clutching my purse, went back inside Souza's and ordered the damn ice cream sundae. When I got back to the car, he had taken the drivers' seat. I thrust the cup of frozen custard at his face, but he refused to take it.

"I'm driving us into Berkeley," he announced. "Don't force that shit on me."

"Take your ice cream."

"You eat it," he said in a whiny voice. "We're going to be eating dinner with Bryn in, like, two hours. You can get fat like your husband if you want, but I have meetings and stuff."

***

Over the years, I saw pictures of little Bryn Sullivan on the internet. Like the star of a long-running sitcom, I had watched Bryn grow up from following, nay, studying, Nick Sullivan's blog. Over the years, he posted photos of his cute little kiddo in a frilly pink dress, or in a Ramones T-shirt shoveling cookie dough into her mouth, or winning an award at school, or going through a merciless puberty with braces and bright red acne and a defeated look on her face.

Now, Bryn was a senior at Berkeley, pre-med, and a serious student. "She's a big nerd," Cole told me, and a few days later he'd change his story, that she was very pretty and very cool. Maybe even a little basic.

Dr. Chen, you've known Bryn her whole life. She was a special interest to you as one of very few babies born to an A12er. I've read your journal articles about Baby B, who was born with all her fingers and toesies, whose fibrillin wasn't deficient in any way. Who, despite her father being a Twelver, couldn't inherit it because her father was only twenty-four years old when she was born.

So what is it that you have learned about A12 being a spontaneous mutation rather than a heritable disorder via the future Dr. Maes? I wondered if it was Cole or Bryn's mother who put her in the car, drove her to Los Angeles, and let her be tested, examined, poked, and prodded for hours by you for the sake of science? I never asked you, even though you would have told me in spite of whatever privacy laws you loved to violate. I knew you disapproved of my relationship with Cole, but I didn't understand why.

You didn't like him, and that was fair. To most, he came in as sweet cream and soured quickly. Sylvia once noted that she missed the guy she had met at the UCLA Rare Disorders fundraiser ten years earlier. The strange, flirty man who sat with her and listened to her talk about the boring details of the fundraiser, which she had planned and hosted, and then took her to Denny's after, where they shot the shit over mozzarella sticks and coffee until three in the morning. For a few years, Sylvia had been the public face of your A12 research—she did all of your PR and was pretty and smiling and pleasant enough to further the cause, until someone at that fundraiser asked her some version of the question "Do you think it's harmful to the child for men as old as your father to parent so late in life" and she, unexpectedly, burst into tears. You knew that crying in front of an audience was not her style. Syl's sobs filled that room like a bad fart and your boss made you get rid of her.

Let me posit this, Dr. Chen: You failed. Majorly. You studied our DNA and pinpointed what and where and how it all went wrong, but you didn't check on our emotional states. We didn't miss our fingers. We missed our dads.

True, if Sylvia Notley, who was attractive enough to be your public face of A12, stands up in front of a bunch of folks who paid top dollar for dinner and a show to support your work and she can't answer the question because she's crying, she gets booted and told she won't be hosting fundraisers ever again. Sylvia has never said much about how she felt about her father's absence from her life. That was private, she would say and change the subject.

Which was just as well. Our truths and your bottom line didn't match up.

***

Bryn Maes lived on the second floor of an old apartment building not far from the Berkeley campus, Spanish style with arches, a shabby red tile roof, and outside corridors, clearly occupied by students. A dull gray paint covered what was once a beautiful stucco. Beer bottles littered the grass. Bikes, dying plants, and empty canvas grocery bags sat in front of each apartment. A row of shoes—mostly men's shoes, with one pair of hot pink Asics sneakers that I assumed belonged to Bryn—sat beside the front door to apartment 203. Cole stomped up the stairs ahead of me and pounded on the front door. Bruno sniffed the shoes. He must have recognized the smell of Bryn's feet, as he yowled when his snoot landed those hot pink sneakers.

A young man in a blue Cal T-shirt and gray athletic shorts opened the door and poked his head out. "Hey, do you have— oh, sorry, I thought you were the delivery person."

"Depends on what you ordered," Cole said.

The young man looked us over, paying special care to identify Cole. "Fuck!" He quickly shut the door, clicking the lock.

Cole pulled up on Bruno's leash. "I know that kid. That's Peter Tan. Kiddo's friend from school in San Francisco. His mom worked for Elwood, if I recall correctly."

The door swung open. Peter Tan had in his hand a tire iron. He let it dangle casually by his side.

"Is that you, Peter Tan?" Cole asked, the tone of his voice indicating that Peter should be embarrassed by answering yes.

"Mr. Sullivan? Bryn's not here. She and I both have exams next week and she is basically living at school these days."

Cole stared at him. Not to be menacing, per se, but a look that said, no words needed, that he thought this kid was stupid.

Peter Tan smacked the tire iron against his palm and said, "We have to get a 3.8 GPA this semester or else our med school acceptances get rescinded."

"Med school, that's great! Congratulations," I said.

Cole shook his head. "Peter Tan! From Presidio Knolls! The kid who put Oreos inside my laser printer?"

Cole was making Peter nervous. "You still got to bring that up, man?"

Cole took a step closer to Peter Tan. "You live with Bryn?"

"I live here, yes."

"You banging her?"

The boy winced. "Wow. You're really something, Mr. Sullivan."

"You can call me Cole. You're not banging her? Why not?"

Peter Tan looked my way and then at the floor. "You really have shit boundaries, man. Bryn and I are strictly friends. Sorry to disappoint you."

"Your generation, man. Kids today don't fuck, and Old King Cole here doesn't get that. Hey, can I use your bathroom? We've been on the road all day."

Peter pulled on the doorknob, crushing himself into the door jamb. "Nope! Sorry, it's really dirty. You know, college kids. And we can't have dogs here."

"I'm going to aim my piss into the toilet. Not gonna touch anything. Bruno can stay out here."

Cole reached past Peter Tan and tried to push the door open, and Peter countered by sliding back in, pushing it shut, and flipping the lock.

"What's going on here?" I asked.

Cole kept pounding on the door. "I have no idea. This is not customary behavior for a nerd like Peter Tan."

Cole yelled through the door, "Could you tell my daughter her old man is here and wants to see her? I am loathe to admit this, but the number I have for her doesn't work."

Cole looked back at me and smirked. I didn't like that smirk. He handed me Bruno's leash and walked to the end of the hallway, where a neighbor had left a hammer leaning against the wall, returned with it, and took a hard whack at the window beside the door. It cracked into a spider web.

The door flung open and out came a young woman in black yoga pants and a Bikini Kill T-shirt. Her dark brown hair was tied in a ponytail. She had a heavy textbook in her hands and used it to shove Cole in the chest as he approached her with his arms out for a hug.

She then threw the textbook at Cole, who ducked out of the way enough that it only nicked him on the shoulder. Pointing at the cracked window, Bryn yelled, "What the fuck is wrong with you? You broke my window! Stay the fuck away from me and my friends and my apartment!" Bryn cast her eyes over at me. "Oh, of course you brought a *woman* with you."

"My beloved daughter, this is my girlfriend, Nina Blaine. She and I both have A12 and we're at that age where we start dying, so I want to take you to dinner. And look, it's Bruno! Bruno is a dog who loves you! If you want to invite Peter Tan to come along, or whomever else you've got in there—"

"You broke my window!" Bryn yelled, pointing at the spiderweb crack. Peter Tan slipped out the door behind Bryn, reached down for one of the pairs of Birkenstocks, and ran down the steps and down the street with them. A neighbor poked his head out of their door. "I'm going have to pay for that to get fixed because you're a drama queen terrorist! A broke asshole who lives in a van and seduces rich women so he can eat." She looked over at me, making sure I'd heard what she'd said.

"Speaking of rich women, how's your mom? Hold up your hand, Nina," he ordered, and I did as I was told, not sure what the A12 salute was meant to mean here.

She looked at me like I had crapped at her feet. She turned to me and said, "You know you're a stupid cunt, right? To be dating this guy? You must be dick-drunk beyond all measure.

He broke my window in front of your dumb face and you're standing there like 'yes, I will absolutely fuck this psychopath later today knowing that his own daughter wants nothing to do with him.' Do better, lady."

Cole shouted, "Language! I raised you better than that."

Bryn trained her eyes on me. "Get your loser boyfriend and his dog out of here, now. If you consider yourself half a decent person and not some simp who's getting played so hard . . ." She took a step closer to me, pointing at me with her index finger.

I didn't respond, as I was struck full-force by the real, in-the-flesh Bryn from the internet, being the opposite of every idea I had about her. She was beautiful, with the sides of her dark brown hair shaved like the punk-ass bitch she undoubtedly was. I noticed a swirly tattoo on her wrist as she was pointing at me. I had hoped that my relationship with Cole would have brought me, not a daughter, per se, but a friendship with a representative of the younger generation. She didn't have to love or even like me. But Bryn, the girl who I watched grow up in dribs and drabs in images that always made Cole look like an awesome dad, was a real human, it turned out. One who had called me a stupid cunt to my face.

I barely heard Bryn when she said something along the lines of, "I want to tell you something. You're dating a man whose kid doesn't want anything to do with him. He's going to make up some garbage story and blame it on my mother, tell you that she turned me against him, even though that's not true. And you'll believe him because to not would get you put out on the street like yesterday's trash. You'll never hear Nick Sullivan apologize. He can change his name, wear an eye patch to cover the rotten black hole that leads directly to his nonexistent soul, and tell the world that every Silicon Valley billionaire thinks he's a worthless shit smear, but they're right. He is a worthless shit smear."

The fiery light in Cole's eye seemed blown out.

Bryn crossed her arms over her chest and looked straight at her father's face. "Seriously, Cole, when was the last time you made someone happy?"

"This morning," he said, staring into the middle distance. He gestured in my direction. "You can ask Nina how good it was."

Bryn reached down and started stuffing her feet into those worn pink Asics. When she finished tying her shoes, she looked straight into her old man's eyes with an icy glare and said, "Nicky boy, the waste of space. I got six sons and two of 'em ain't worth a damn. One's on drugs, the other thinks he's John F. Kennedy."

Cole yanked at Bruno's leash, and in response, he began to bark at Bryn. "You're going to make one hell of a doctor. Saving people's lives like you're smart or something."

Bryn stepped back from the dog. "I should say it in a Pittsburgh accent, so it lands correctly: Nicky, get over yahself, ya ain't nothin' special."

Cole's eyes went blank.

Bruno stopped barking and gazed up at Bryn, licking her shins, wanting something. She looked down at him with a look of pain. I could sense she wanted to get down on the ground and pet him, but she wouldn't let herself. She took another step back. Bruno was Cole's ally, and Bryn didn't like Cole's allies.

"Y'ain't nothin' special, Nicky boy. Y'act like ya beddah dan everyone, ya make yahself look like a jagoff," Bryn yelled, imitating her grandfather, as if she had been rehearsing for this moment her entire life. "Get a job and quit living undah my roof if you think your mum and I are so goddamn beneath ya, Nicky."

A battered red Honda Fit appeared on the street below, screeching to a stop. The driver laid on the horn. Bryn gave me another filthy look and turned to lock her door. She ran down the cement staircase to the car, the driver pounding the gas to get her away from her father.

"Can you believe that kid? She had a getaway car?" Cole yelled at me. "She had Peter Tan driving a getaway car! To get away from *me*. No one wants to get away from me! Everyone loves me! Even that little shit Peter Tan!"

I said nothing. Nothing to interrogate why his only child quoted back to him terrible things that Joe Sullivan had said about his own son decades earlier. Or why Peter Tan knew to flee the apartment and get the car. I couldn't ask Cole why two upstanding Cal undergrads, with their 3.8 GPAs studying on a Saturday afternoon, would react to him the way they did, so I said nothing and did nothing. I stayed on the ride.

8

Dr. Chen, riddle me this: Why was I fertile the night that Sigrid was conceived? How, at the age of thirty-nine, after being told my whole life it wasn't possible? Why? While my fingers and feet grew into gnarled tree roots, while my skin stretched like I was made with Lycra, while my neck hurt all the time and the weight of my own head felt like it was crushing my shoulders, why was there a ripe and ready egg there to receive Cole's corrupt genetic data?

I can see you wincing from behind your surgical mask as I write this, as if to say without saying it: *The better question here, Nina, was why Cole wasn't using a condom?*

I don't know, Dr. C. Impending death seemed to justify slipshod contraceptive usage.

The urgency of our waning days dictated that Cole and I had sex in the most grandiose style possible, as if our sexual pageantry could bring about our last breaths, and a condom suggests care for the future. A condom cares about what happens tomorrow, and we simply didn't.

Cole was, after all, my death god. He was Eros and Thanatos in equal measure. Had he not appeared to give me a good time before it was time for me to go? Had I not signed up to close my eyes under the weight of his body and feel what I hadn't experienced before? Cole wasn't a partner so much as a facilitator of forbidden feelings and experiences. Ones that my nonstandard body had not been able to receive until its very last days. Why would two nearly dead people waste a thought on a condom?

Driving back to Los Angeles from Berkeley after watching Bryn run for the hills, we took the long way home. The route that winds precariously close to the cliffs above the Pacific Ocean. The ocean, angry, crashing and wailing, much like Cole. And in the parking lot of a beach I couldn't see in the dead of night, Cole dragged me out of his van, out and over its still-hot hood, hiked up my favorite skirt that I had worn to celebrate the day I got to meet Bryn, pinned my head down on that still-hot hood so I could smell the heat and the exhaust, and fucked me from behind.

"Don't move," he repeated. "Don't move," he barked when I flinched, stilling me with an elbow to the small of my back.

I didn't move. I couldn't. I was a fish plucked from the sea, gasping, knowing death was my only way out. I mean, really, Dr. Chen? Why not die then and there?

I viewed that night, that act, as a dress rehearsal for death. There was nothing good on the other side. Only a sore vagina, a stuffed-up nose from crying, and my eardrums ringing after Cole's two-hour tirade in the car on the way home about what a monster Bryn's mother was. How she spoiled Bryn and turned her against him.

I didn't move, Dr. Chen. Cole emitted what sounded like a rebel yell when it was done, and then he smacked my ass and laughed.

***

From the Eddie-Addie videos, December 21, 1988

ADDIE: (voice only) Tell Nina about her brother, Evan.
EDDIE: (sitting at the kitchen table, his hands folded in a tent shape in front of his face) That is a *shanda*, Addie. A *shanda*.

ADDIE: That he died?

EDDIE: Yes, that he died.

(long silence)

EDDIE: But God did not turn his back on me. He gave me Nina, and for that, I am grateful.

ADDIE: So do you want her to know that you didn't raise him or what?

EDDIE: Sure, she can know that. Ruth's second husband adopted him. Changed his name. I always hated that he did that. Took away Blattner and gave him Cohen, which is a very boring Jewish name. Ruthie couldn't have found a man with a last name like Zipazooski or Fifferfeldsteinerman? Cohen? Put Smith on the birth certificate and forget about it. I'm kidding. Fred Cohen is a very nice man. Frank? Fred? He's an optometrist in Rye, and everyone loves him. A real mensch.

ADDIE: When was the last time you saw Evan?

EDDIE: Oh gosh . . . Evan graduated from Cornell, same as his mama, in 1966, I think? I attended his graduation in Ithaca. Ruth called me up later angry that I had shown up drunk and made a scene. She really chewed me out. That was the last time I spoke to her. A few months later, he and some friends flew out to Los Angeles, probably looking for jobs in the film industry. You and I took him to Musso and Frank—remember that? He ordered six rum and Cokes.

ADDIE: *That* was the last time you saw Evan? Eleven years before he died?

EDDIE: Jeez, Addie, you trying to make a man feel bad?

ADDIE: You were . . . you had that actress you were dating along, and me, and he was with that friend and you . . . never mind.

EDDIE: You know . . . you want to tell me I had my head up my ass? Fine. You wouldn't be wrong. You want to remind me that I never put family first, that I should have told those recording execs to kiss off when they told me not to bring Ruthie around? You're right. I was weak. I was a son of a bitch with no balls who lost his wife and son for a few cheap pieces of ass and a couple of records that didn't do so hot. You happy now?

ADDIE: Ed, these videos are for Nina.

EDDIE: What the hell does a *bulldagger* like you know about raising kids? Why you even bring that up? You want Nina to think her old man didn't love his own son? Is that what you want? I loved him. I was weak. But God did not turn his back on me and gave me a wonderful daughter who is more beautiful to me than anything. Anything. I had to lose Evan so there would be Nina. I regret that, but it's the truth and I feel so lucky that . . . (Eddie starts to cry) that I got a second chance at being someone's dad, even if it was too late for me to do a good job. Damnit, I wish I'd have . . . when the handwriting was on the wall, I wish I would've taken Nina out of this joint. Out of Los Angeles. Taken her back to Jersey to live near what's left of my family so maybe she'd have a chance. That's my biggest regret, Addie. Make sure Nina hears me say that, why don't ya? Make sure she knows that I knew Tracy wasn't going to do so great with a kid like her. Tracy doesn't know what to do with those type of problems. And here I am, seventy-two and full of cancer, can't do nothing. . . .

ADDIE: (long pause) I didn't mean to upset you.

EDDIE: (crying, coughing, turns away from the camera) Turn that thing off!

(video ends)

***

Cole lay naked on the bedroom floor at the Eddie house. Bruno had worn himself out by licking every molecule of tikka masala sauce from the take-out container that Cole had left open on the floor. Cole had been grouchy since our drive up to Berkeley. More than grouchy. Volatile. Unkind. Unwell.

"So," I said, trying to hide my gobsmacked-ness. "Now we know Eddie felt bad about his son and Addie knew it. And bad about me."

"*Bulldagger*? Who says 'bulldagger?' I bet Eddie railed her anyway."

"Nah," I said. "Addie was taller than him by a lot."

Cole's single ball was slung over his thigh and lashed down with medical tape. He lay on the floor playing with his dog. Cole really loved his dog. He looked at Bruno with the eyes he used to look at me with.

"Hey, Cole? Can I ask you something?"

He looked at me blankly.

"Do you remember when Mr. Hooper died on Sesame Street?"

"Of course," Cole said.

"And Big Bird asks when Mr. Hooper is coming back "

"Yeah."

"The day I saw that when I was, what, four years old? That was the day my father died, in my little mind. When I put it together that the only thing old people do is die, and that Eddie was old and that he was going to die, and then he did."

Cole reached for his boxer briefs. "Was Eddie ever more to you other than the old guy on the album covers who had his spinster lackey take you to the Apple Pan after he died?"

"He was my dad."

"Was he?"

Startled, I said yes.

"Did Eddie do more than blow his load inside Tracy's hairless pussy and then slap you with the name of a woman who was on the right side of his Madonna/whore complex?"

"Yes, I mean, he was old and obsessed with his career and up his own ass by his own admission, but he took me places and told me I was pretty and taught me to bowl. And he named me after Nina Simone because he loved her."

"He bowled?"

"Yeah, at Pinz in Studio City once a week, and he'd get the gutter bumpers for me and everything." I was shaking.

"That's the thing with you Hollywood Good Thumbs. You all have these men who were monuments to their own success. Joe Sullivan, flawed as he was, was actually a father. To nine goddamn children, and maybe by the time my closest-in-age sister, Laura, and I came along, he was done and tired and wanted to be left alone, but at least he showed up, tired and angry, at the end of a long day of work and told us all how much he hated us. Especially me. But he was there. You had these men who had some victory sex with women young enough to be their daughters and called it fatherhood."

"Don't ever say that to Sylvia," I said.

"I'll say whatever I want to Sylvia," Cole said, reaching across his dog for his underwear. "For being your alleged best friend, you always sound afraid of her. Whatever, she's boring and a lousy lay." Cole slid into his boxer briefs while Bruno wandered off down the hall.

"Wait, what? You did not."

Cole laughed. "Don't worry. She banged Nick Sullivan. Years ago. Before the great name change. She got nailed by a totally different person. You got Cole in your hole."

I ignored his dirty quip. "She wouldn't, though."

"Wouldn't what?"

"Sleep with you," I spat.

He laughed. "Oh?"

"You mean you want to hear me say that Sylvia Notley would never, ever get with a . . ." I dithered on whether to say it. "A broke, overbearing, loudmouth white guy. Because I know her type and you ain't it. You're messing with me."

Cole cackled so big and loud I could see, for the first time, the spots where his molars were missing. He raised his voice up to a falsetto and spoke in an exaggerated Irish brogue. "Me father only drove the stinky old garbage trucks of Western Pennsylvania. He wasn't smart enough to work in the steel mills, but we made do. We only had potatoes to eat, and me sisters all shared the same dress. Want me to say in Polish, too?"

"We Hollywood jizz trophies can't compete with your blue-collar upbringing that built your character, as evidenced by your admirable professional success and loving connections with your family, especially your daughter who totally didn't have her friend whisk her away in a getaway car."

He narrowed his eyes.

"Oh, you can dish it out, but you can't take it, huh? Parental neglect with money doesn't feel any better than parental neglect without it. If you hate Chris and Syl and me so much, why do you hang out with us?"

He seemed sincerely shocked. "I liked you. You were different from those two."

I winced. "*Liked*, as in past tense?"

Cole shrugged, looking beyond me. "You were different from the others. Especially Sylvia, but you're never going to quit bowing down to her. It's gross to watch and makes you unattractive."

"You've seen very little of my friendship with her, but okay. You hate Sylvia."

"I don't hate Sylvia."

"You just said she's boring."

"Why are you friends with her?" he yelled. "When you hang out, does she trap you in a beige furniture store in Orange County and force you to listen to Harris Notley recordings until you pass out?"

"You didn't need to be mean to me after watching my dad be fucked up on the video."

"You can't see the difference between love and your dad using you to not feel bad about abandoning his son."

"Did Joe Sullivan love you, Nick?"

He paused to think about it. "No."

"Okay," I said.

"Only my sister Laura loves me. Maybe a couple of those women who used my busted A12 corpus for pleasure on one or more profound, forgettable nights. I'm a nobody. Unlike you,

Nina Cakemaker Blattner Luciani of Connecticut," he sneered. "Talk about being a winner."

***

For a month, I quit going to Good Thumbs meetings. It wasn't good for the cognitive dissonance. Sitting across the table from Syl and Jorie grew menacing. Sylvia could smell some admixture of shame and self-destruction on my collar and was not the type to keep her feelings to herself. Syl would judge. If it was true that she had slept with the former Nick Sullivan back in the day, then it all made sense, though I thought maybe Cole had made it up to bait me. Jorie, if I told her, would look at me with pity. Wanting none of Cole's nonsense had earned Jorie his respect. Her sense of detachment was admirable in some ways and made her seem cold in others. I believed Syl was better than me for being Harris Notley's kid, because Harris Notley was a great American legend and Eddie Blaine was a joke. Sylvia would argue that a dead daddy was a dead daddy, and it didn't matter if his music was kept in the Smithsonian or in the dollar bin at Goodwill.

But we hadn't had that argument since Bondurant.

It only lived in my head.

***

Cole was not at my house when Tracy paid a call. I had taken Bruno for a walk up and down Hillhurst, dazed but present enough to get myself an iced coffee. I treated Bruno to a handful of turkey necks from the fancy meat store.

Tracy hated Eddie's Los Feliz house. She was not permitted to live in it, as he had loudly declared it a No Women

Allowed Zone. When she left Texas and moved to LA to be with Eddie, he rented a house on a bland, middle-class street in Burbank, which pissed her off. The house was white with a dark green trim and a square patch of grass out front. It looked ordinary and was down the way from several other members of the Mike Watson Productions latter-day game show family, and those people did not like her. To Tracy, the Los Feliz house remained a mystery. It was not an appropriate house for a toddler, what with the mirrored walls and the Saltillo tile floors and the ridiculous bathtub that anyone, but especially Cole, would call a Sex Bathtub, but Eddie very specifically said in his will that she couldn't have it, that up on his death, it would go to Addie, and then to me. This served as evidence that Eddie had been terrible to her.

Tracy was still a tiny little thing. I think of all the carbs she had refused over the decades that allowed her to keep herself in size 2 jeans. She had had her hair cut into a tousled pixie cut. She wore an orange tank top that showed off her crepey decolletage, and a pair of jeans with butterflies embroidered on the back pockets.

"Breakfast," she yelled at me, banging on the rusty screen door. I opened it. She waved a paper bag from Canter's in my face. Canter's Deli had been Eddie's favorite restaurant.

I was still in my pajamas. "You brought me bagels? You don't eat bagels."

"I brought you one bagel. I don't. I had yogurt. You haven't been by to see me, so I came over to the Eddie Blaine Memorial to see you."

I looked in the bag—poppy seed, two schmears on the side.

"Do I get to come in the famous Blaine house?"

I gestured toward the two '70s-style outdoor chairs on the porch where Addie and her partner sat and smoked cigarettes for decades. "Nah. We can sit here."

Tracy frowned. She wanted to get in the house.

"This ugly house is probably worth a lot of money by now," she said, staring up at the house. It needed new windows and fresh paint. "What is it now, two mil? More?"

"Do you still live in that creepy house in Malibu?"

Tracy shook her head. "I live in Santa Monica in Justice's condo. He's working in Sacramento during the week, so I have the place to myself most of the time. Hunter is coaching football in Calgary, so I don't see him much. You, though. You still live in that cute white house right next to Bondurant in Teagarden, Connecticut?"

"Not anymore. They kicked me out."

"The town? The whole town can't kick you out."

"Clearly you haven't lived in a small town. Different rules."

Tracy laughed her trademark little laugh. "The Teagarden people must have read that book of yours. So much anger. I'm surprised you still have friends after writing that."

It felt a little rough hearing that, even if it came from Tracy. "Are you shitting me? Everyone who's read it loves *World War You*. Words like *brave* and *unflinching* are used to describe that book."

"My Tri-Delt sister Susie Gelland—do you remember her? You played with her daughter in Dallas a few times when we were visiting. She found it at some bookstore in Austin and sent it to me. She thought it was terrible of me that I hadn't seen it. I read it."

"It was a small press book that sold maybe ten copies to college kids, Tracy. Literally no one cares about that book."

"What if I care, because you're my kid?"

I shrugged, trying to recall some of the lines in my poems that would have put Tracy on the defensive.

"You left Paul, and you live in this house and . . . what else? You have a dog?" she asked, pointing at Bruno. "Since when do you like dogs?"

"Since always."

"You hated Duke," she said. Duke was the Hodges family beast, a crude Great Dane who Greg let head-butt me and piss on my bedroom carpet.

"I hated Duke because he was Greg's dog and Greg hated me."

"Duke was our family dog," she argued. "Dogs don't hate people. You wouldn't pet him. You were hardly around the house!"

"Please don't defend Duke," I said.

She looked around my dry front yard with the near-death cacti to find her next subject for criticism. "So . . . no more making fancy cakes? You were good at the cakes. You won awards. What about the cakes?"

"I'm retired from cakes, as well as cookies. And breads. Flour gave up on me. As did butter. It was a painful breakup, Tracy."

"I suppose you've taken your retirement because of what that awful Tabitha Chen at UCLA has been telling you all these years. Death by forty."

I gestured toward the two bags of trash sitting on the porch. I had been too tired and lazy to walk them to the bin. "Pretty much."

"I'm sorry. I know this apology is long overdue, and that you have been simmering on your anger toward me for a very long time, and that I had a hand in . . . in your choice to not see me much. Or talk to me. Or put your angry-sounding Brooklyn-accent husband on the phone to lie to me about where you were."

"How many times do I have to tell you that Paul's from New Haven? The same town as Yale. You don't listen to me."

She shrugged. "I run into Sylvia Notley once in a while. She goes to the same acupuncturist and she's always so cold. She side-eyes me and doesn't say hi."

"Twenty years with that man. New Haven! Not Brooklyn, not New Jersey. New Haven, Connecticut."

"Sylvia is *rude*," my mother continued. "What a failure I must be for you to choose that snotty woman as your best friend. Ice cold."

"She was there for me when you let your husband do what he did. Syl being cold to you is the least of your problems. Do you even have any female friends?"

Tracy looked away. "We're divorced now. Greg left me," she said, a trill of gravitas in the pronouncement, as if anticipating my pity.

"Of course he did. You got old, little lady! Old! O-L-D old!"

Tracy winced. "You could try to be a little kinder to me."

I forced a laugh. "I'm glad he left you. He was mean. And look, you finally got yourself a body that your football player didn't want to look at, just like me. How does it feel to have a body no one wants to look at, Tracy? Tell me what it's like to not be pretty! Tell me about being *invisible*. I want to hear you say it."

Tracy's jaw clenched. She didn't know which character to play—the loyal wife, the former beauty queen, or the beaten-down sixty-something woman who was living in her child's guest bedroom. This was true: Greg Hodges was mean. To me. And she let him be mean. I think she felt I deserved it. My body and my father displeased the most important men in her life, her husband and her father, and that was that. So now I was mean to her. And she was mean right back. But she had been mean first and never stopped anyone else from being mean to me. That was our family.

"You didn't grow up to be a very nice person," she said.

"My character isn't the one that deserves judgment here. You made me stand up in court and defend that man, who made the case that he only molested hot girls and I wasn't one. You chose that rapist over your own daughter, so no, I'm not nice. To you. And holy crap, you can't even stick the landing of an apology, Tracy. You came here to apologize, right? And now you're whining about Sylvia ignoring you and calling me not nice."

"You called me old!" she said, whimpering like a child.

"You were born in 1958, that makes you, what, sixty—"

Tracy shouted me down before I could finish. "I came here to talk to you about your health and . . . about Kailey Elwood!"

I raised both of my middle fingers. "Another rich blonde you'll choose over your own daughter. She can't take a little heat on social media? She started it. Weak."

"Okay, I see how it is." Tracy stood up from her chair. "I'll go. You don't want me here."

"No, not really. You chose everyone but me. You did nothing while people treated me less than. You conveyed to me that I was unattractive every day of my childhood. You laughed at

Eddie, the most decent man you were ever with. You sided with the bullies so Daddy Jesse would love you the way he loved your sisters. I'm spending the time I have left with people who treat me well. And this dog," I said, gesturing down to Bruno, who lay at my feet licking his paws. "This dog treats me very well."

She began to dig around in her handbag. As she was about to go, she stopped and made a scrunchy face at me. "Why did you leave Paul? He was the only man!" she yelled at me.

I had to laugh at this one. "The only man? I think there are other men."

"That's not what I meant!" She stamped her pink Keds on the cement.

"The only man who'd fuck something as ugly as me? Is that what you meant, Mother?"

She stomped again. "No!" she yelled. Some found this behavior cute, but was I wrong to not be a little peeved that Tracy, senior citizen, still stomped her feet like a kid when she was frustrated?

"Because even the California judicial system recognizes me as unfuckable. Right?"

She stomped again. "No! No, no, no! Stop it!"

"Then what do you mean by 'Paul was the only man'?"

When I married Paul and became slightly more human to my mother, she started sending me little pastel-covered gift booklets on forgiveness. *Open your heart! Family is the most important thing! Love is forever!* Cheesy platitudes for wine moms who were miserable even though they had done everything that they were told to do. Inside, she would write personal inscriptions like *You should be a college graduate! Reapply! I'm so glad you found Paul. What a saint! That restaurant of his looks amazing, but don't eat too much pasta ha ha! Send me photos of those wedding cakes you make!*

When I wrote *World War You,* I had those saccharine booklets in mind. How mindless they were. How guilty they seemed, like they knew they were hiding depressing truths and that I, Nina Simone Blaine, had been called to serve as harsh reality's samizdat. How ineffectual, knowing that a collection of corny sayings didn't undo the mental assault her husband perpetrated against me. But that didn't even matter because he didn't matter. What mattered what that she backed him up at every turn.

In some ways, her behavior was understandable. It was all she knew. No one really treated Tracy like a complex human being, if I thought about it long enough, which I didn't.

She had said many times she couldn't relate to me, so she wouldn't even try.

"The only man who has the patience to understand you!" she whined.

I nodded. "That's not . . . that's not better than the other one, Tracy."

"I see," Tracy said. "I don't know what I'm supposed to say to you. Everything I say is wrong and you're convinced you're going to die soon so you're being rude and surly. You abandoned me and your brothers, so they don't even know you. And maybe that was fair. Maybe I should protect my sons from your negativity."

"I abandoned *you*? My *negativity*? Protect *them*? You couldn't look me in the eye in that courtroom that day. You know what you did. You sold me out for some man who treated you badly, too."

She nodded. "And you flunked out of Yale. Who flunks out of Yale?"

"Fuck you. I was supposed to be some beacon of strength and go back to school as if nothing had happened? 'Your Honor, if it may please the court, I am too ugly for Greg Hodges to molest.' You think that didn't affect me?" Tracy would argue that the statute of limitations on me being angry about that had long since run out. She hadn't changed and would not change and that was the most painful part of seeing her. She would never stop being Jesse Westervelt's least-favorite daughter.

"Oh, and for what it's worth, probably nothing, but I'll say it anyway: I didn't flunk out of Yale. I was given a mental health leave of absence, and I never went back. But go ahead and tell yourself the version of the story you like best."

"You really made some bad choices."

"No, you did. I think you and your stompy old lady feet should go."

She stopped to turn toward me with her index finger raised. "You need to apologize to Kailey Elwood and tell that Nicky Six Six Six creep to back the hell off of her."

I walked my mother down the driveway to the sidewalk, pushing her by her tiny, bony back. "I will do none of that."

"Okay. Well . . . when it comes time to pay that bill, be ready for it."

"Wow, my own mother is threatening me! On behalf of someone she doesn't even know. Someone she likes better than her own daughter because she's pretty and rich." I looked up at the row of palm trees down the street; my next-door neighbor was out getting his mail and he waved at me. "What a beautiful day!"

"I said what I said," she said. "I have to wait for my Uber. Unless you want to drive me home."

"You want me to drive you all the way to Santa Monica?" I asked as if she hadn't lived in LA long enough to know that a ride of that distance was simply not requested here. "No way."

"I usually drive Justice's car, but he has it this week."

"Hodges left you so broke you don't even have a car? In LA? And you're still defending him?"

"This conversation is over." Tracy hoisted her bag over her shoulder. "I wish I had a nice daughter. Some people call their daughters rays of sunshine. You're the opposite of a ray of sunshine."

I laughed at that one. "Well, you're the opposite of a mother."

Tracy started her walk down Wayne Avenue toward Los Feliz Boulevard. Then she stopped and turned around to drop her final bomb.

"Nina? Get over yourself."

***

Later that day, Nicholas J. Sullivan received a letter from a lawyer in San Jose instructing him to cease and desist publishing "compromising" photographs of Steven K. Elwood. He waved it around for me to snatch out of his hands as we sat eating tacos.

"For a guy who is technically homeless, it's amazing that they found me."

Technically homeless?

The letter was printed on heavy cream-colored paper and although it was only two sheets, the letter weighed more than you'd think it would.

"Whose address is 50000 Playa del Carmen Road, Malibu?" I asked, holding up the envelope.

"No one's. That was my last known physical address, and the landlord texted me to tell me to come get it since it looked serious."

"You can't afford to live in Malibu, my dude," I said. Playa del Carmen Road was the windy road that rose from the cliffs above the ocean where the wealthy kept themselves isolated from the general public. Greg Hodges's hateful box of metal and glass was on Playa del Carmen Road.

"That was a house share with some unsavory bondage and flogging enthusiasts. You can't put a full dungeon in a two-bedroom apartment in Encino, lady."

"Still. How did you afford that rent?"

He smirked. "I ran their sex party in exchange for free rent. Promoted it. Cleaned up the bodily fluids afterward. Cash under the table, plus a small room to keep my pallet and note-books filled with my memoirs."

"Gross," I said.

I sat at my father's vinyl 1970s breakfast table—brown and red swirly vinyl chairs next to a round yellow resin table, plowing into cereal I couldn't taste with milk that was probably a little sour. Cole snuck up behind me and pulled my ponytail down hard. Something snapped in my neck.

I reached back to grab his hand. "Stop it! You're hurting me!"

Cole cackled. "You'd be a lot more fun if you liked a little pain with your sex. All those years of that fat man fucking you in the dark and never making you cry. Or come, probably."

I reached up to touch the spot in my neck that throbbed with pain, and he swatted my hand away. "A lot of women like this sort of thing. For a girl with a dead daddy and a stepfather who declined to molest her because he only got hard for perfect tens, I'd think you'd be one of them."

With every ounce of resolve I had, my body full of adrenaline, I said what I meant, even though I knew there would be punishment. "Get your hands off me."

He let go of my ponytail and stepped back. "As you wish, Miss Blattner."

"I didn't ask you to do that," I said, the room spinning, and my eyes filled with stars. "I didn't *consent*," I hissed.

"I'm going to go play with someone else. Your house is boring and your food sucks and you don't have Super Mario on your Nintendo." He stomped across the tile floor. The front door opened and slammed shut.

"Why do you have to do this?" I asked, but he was gone.

I cleared the dishes, took a shower, and looked up 50000 Playa del Carmen Road on my phone. It was one of those sprawling Spanish-style estates with a circular driveway, perched on a cliff above the ocean. Zillow listed it as off-market. It had last sold for $6.9 million.

Why was I surprised when I looked up the name of the owner? Danielle Delgado Elwood. Online search: Danielle Delgado, Miss New Mexico 1991. The second wife of Steve Elwood.

As I was crafting a few questions for Cole that I wasn't going to ask, I decided it was time to address the absence of my period for nine weeks.

Early menopause, right? Right, Dr. C.? You said I might hit menopause early.

The second line appeared on the stick. I was in my father's house, alone. I hadn't spent much of my life alone. There was always Paul, the restaurant, the noise and drama of life at Bondurant. But here, with this stick telling me my fate, I felt it.

"Dad?" I said, like he was right down the hall in a terrycloth robe listening to Bing Crosby on the hi-fi. Like he'd come flying down the hallway and ask from a step outside the bathroom door what was wrong.

Sylvia didn't pick up her phone or answer my barrage of urgent texts.

Jorie responded to my text with "LOL COLE'S BALL," which . . . I expected better from her, to be honest.

"Addie?" I said out loud. Addie would have been a champ about this. She would've driven over with a gallon of matzo ball soup and half a chocolate cake and told me she knew every abortionist in LA County. She would have adopted my baby, even at age eighty-nine and unable to walk.

"Daddy Addie?" Daddy Addie was what I called the two of them in those videos Addie insisted on making for me. They were a dreadful interviewer/interviewee team. Cutthroat and unfunny. They made Dick Cavett and Norman Mailer look like sporting chums.

Who else did I have? Chef Paul? *Hey, sweetie, remember that time I left our marriage because I didn't want to raise your niece and nephew, and you were being a jerk? Well, guess what?*

Tracy? As grandmother? Please.

My phone rang. Sylvia.

"Um . . . I can't believe I'm about to say this?" I said, my California upspeak cranked to the moon. "I'm pregnant."

"Blainey."

"Cole's fault," I said. "Of course."

Sylvia was silent.

"I don't want to tell Cole."

Syl coughed into the phone. "I wish you hadn't wanted to tell me."

The memory of all the times Sylvia cried on the phone when she had miscarried—she had wanted a child more than anything and to be the one A12 female who successfully carried a pregnancy and didn't die of an aortic dissection or collapsed lungs because of it—had gone offline in my shock and horror. Syl married the first chucklehead she could find right out of college in hopes of having a child as young as she could. Dr. Chen, I know you told her no and not to try a hundred million times, and I know Syl didn't listen. She didn't listen even after that chucklehead, a dull Stanford classmate of hers who was in law school and barely spoke to anyone at gatherings, left her over it. I don't know the number of miscarriages she had. I wouldn't ask her those things.

"I'm sorry. I didn't know who else to talk to. I had to talk to someone," I said. I understood my mistake, though. Over the last five years, when Sylvia finally gave up on that dream, she and I did not speak of motherhood. It was what kept our friendship going, I realized. She had other friends and many cousins, all of whom she had faded out on over time because they had become parents and she had not. It was why she formed the Good Thumbs: We were guaranteed to never bring up wanting children.

I never wanted to be a mother. Part of it was the horrible instruction I received from Tracy. Part of it was A12. Part of it was the fact that Eddie Blaine was so damn dead, and I would be the same to any child: either dead or soon to be dead.

But in the back of my mind was Cole and his magical thinking. He believed that he was going to live to a ripe old age.

Forty-five was super geriatric for an A12-er but not for him. He had quit going to see you years earlier. He told me you were not as smart as UCLA Medical Center thought you were.

To be Cole and to believe the things that came out of his mouth.

"It's Cole's responsibility to take care of you," Sylvia said. "You think he won't?"

"No," I lied. "Are you mad?"

"Mad at you? Nah. Not enough time for that."

"I sense that I should change the subject. I do need help, though."

"Look, Blainey. If you're going to ask me to take you for an abortion . . ."

"Did you really sleep with Cole?" I blurted out. "Or is he on with his stories again?"

There was a long pause. "Blainey, I'm working. I'm not in the mood for this."

I couldn't breathe. The acid coursed through my veins. She didn't love him. But this also meant that Cole wasn't lying, and that meant something, didn't it?

I didn't respond. I heard a loud, long sigh and then, "He wasn't your boyfriend back then, so I didn't do anything to you. And why the hell are you saying this to me? You never did anything stupid? Anything desperate? You, crying about your horrible family your whole life, didn't mind not being able to have babies but it was never okay with me. My family was wonderful, and I had a lot of love to give. Nick Sullivan was some random guy and maybe he'd knock me up and then go away, like I wanted. By the way, if you breathe a word of this to Jorie, or to my mother, I will never speak to you again."

I didn't speak. I couldn't.

"That motherfucker had no business talking to you about that, but it doesn't surprise me. He doesn't respect anyone's privacy. Nothing is sacred to him."

"You're right," I said.

Her voice grew angrier and more intense. "How dare you even ask me that," she demanded. "How the hell did you think it would be okay to come at me with this shit? The way you talk to me sometimes, I swear. Thoughtless. Thoughtless and stupid." She hung up.

I sat on the toilet sobbing and shaking. I could hear my father's voice from the video: "The happiest moments of my life these days outside of playing with my little girl are in the big bathroom at my house, drinking a rum and Coke on the can...."

I flushed the toilet and lay down on the white, speckled marble floor my father chose for his favorite room fifty years earlier. The cold marble felt good on my cheek. I cried like I had never cried before. I thought maybe the force of my sorrow and fear would expel the fetus straight out of my body. *You don't want to be here,* I said to the clump of cells. I heaved like a walrus, mourning a part of me that I didn't even know existed until that moment. This was an extra death tacked on to my inevitable, physical one.

There was no way I'd survive a pregnancy. Mad respect to all the disabled parents out there, but I wouldn't even be afforded that privilege. I'd just be dead.

I threw the pregnancy test stick down the hallway and rested my head on the fuzzy bathroom mat to cry. I must have fallen asleep because Bruno the Dog had the stick in his mouth when he found me, his owner kneeling down over me kissing my neck, telling me how happy he was to hear the wonderful news.

9

Eddie and Addie video, January 9, 1989
Eddie is seated at his desk, wearing a black, silky shirt.

ADDIE: (sounding pissed—what happened before she hit the record button?) Honestly, Eddie, the most interesting thing about you as a seventy-two-year-old Vegas has-been who tips a quarter on a ten-dollar check at Denny's is that you openly hate Leonard Cohen. What did he ever do to you?

EDDIE: I've never met the bastard.

ADDIE: This amount of hostility toward a fellow Jewish singer is a little over the top there, Ed.

EDDIE: I was told I wouldn't make any money or have an audience if I used the name Sandy Blattner because of antisemitism. I was the toast of the Catskills for years. The happiest years of my life—and not because I was young but because everyone knew who I was. Eddie Blaine? That's nobody. There is no Eddie Blaine.

ADDIE: Why did you put "Blaine" on Nina's birth certificate?

EDDIE: I've been Eddie Blaine so long, and maybe she'd have a better life as Nina Blaine. Tracy and I never discussed it. Maybe all the little kids at Nina's first-grade class are impressed that her old man sang "Somber Mountain." Ha. Tracy and Nina are the only legal Blaines. My license says Eli Sanford Blattner.

ADDIE: I know where this is going.

EDDIE: Ruth—

ADDIE: I'm going to stop you right there, because you bring up Ruth on these videos and you don't seem to understand what it's going be like for Nina to see her old man going on and on about some woman she's never met.

EDDIE: Ruth would be very kind to Nina, and I wish that Nina were being raised by someone like Ruthie. Tracy makes the finger thing a bigger deal than it needs to be. Ruth would point my girl in the right direction.

ADDIE: Nina is your daughter and that's not Ruth's problem.

EDDIE: And I'm a bastard for it, but not as big a bastard as Leonard Cohen.

ADDIE: Ed, it's been, what? Forty years? She's over it. Ruth. She's over you.

EDDIE: Leonard Cohen got to be a Jew. No one told him he had to be Larry McGee or whatever *goyishe* crap those suits came up with. He writes those fruity songs and people think he's great. Same with Neil Diamond. Where are that man's balls, I ask you? (pause) You know who else gets to be a Jew? Fred Cohen, or whatever that mensch husband of Ruth is named.

ADDIE: Tracy is Nina's mother and that's not going to change. You must have liked something about her. (Eddie laughs— here I know he's biting his tongue—he probably wants to make a crack about Tracy's breasts.) Tell Nina a good story about her mother.

EDDIE: (shrugs) For a girl who don't weigh more than a hundred pounds, she sure can fart. She sneaks off to the Taco Bell and puts down a whole bag of those crunchy beef tacos.

I find little bits of lettuce and cheese all over the front seat of my Cutlass Supreme. She thinks I don't know about it. But late at night . . . the Winds of Tracy tell the truth.

ADDIE: Jeez Louise. Do you have anything nice to say about Tracy?

EDDIE: (shakes head) Don't act like you're surprised. She eats absolute crap every day. She gets away with it because it doesn't affect her figure. Nobody in her family can cook. Nina survives on peanut butter crackers and those goddamn crunchy tacos. Tracy can't even open a can of soup. Ruth—

ADDIE: (interrupts) Eddie! Stop! This is for your daughter!

EDDIE: Don't tell me to stop! You try going without home-made soup for forty years! (quiet, then crying, punching himself in the chest) *Yiskadal, yiskadash, sh'mei rabbah . . .*

ADDIE: (yelling) Eddie, stop it! Please!

(cuts off filming)

***

Dr. Chen, I made an appointment to see you after I couldn't get an early enough appointment for an abortion anywhere in Southern California. When I went to see you, I was hoping you'd say, "no problem! I'll take care of it for you right now! Hop on the table!" But you're a geneticist, and you don't know how to do a lot of medical procedures, I guess. Then you surprised me by saying there was no reason I couldn't carry this pregnancy to term, and I asked you if that meant that I could hold out until Little Siggymuffin was thirty-six weeks in utero and then I'd die, and you'd harvest my sweet little booboo out of my dead body, or did you mean that I would live long enough to hold her and feed her and change at least twenty poopy diapers until it was time to hand her off to her adoptive parent? You didn't have a very good answer for me, explaining that medicine was not a psychic practice. But I should not feel that I had to abort.

I had a choice, you were saying.

You said to make sure my will and my medical power of attorney were up to date.

"Sylvia," I said, and it seemed like you couldn't hear me. I had named Sylvia as my medical power of attorney. Sylvia, who was mad at me for getting pregnant and had asked me not to contact her for a bit.

"Sylvia doesn't have much more time than you," you told me, and I wanted to throw your psychic statement out the window and into your face.

***

Who will love me when I'm gone? Not that this matters to me. It must have mattered to Eddie. Eddie in those videos at the end of his life, smoking a Pall Mall and shining on Addie's attempts at getting him to speak to me after he was dead. Thirty-two years is a long time to have someone miss you every day.

Sigrid won't miss me, that's for sure. And that, I knew, was the kindest thing for her.

No torches, no monuments, no memories, no missing me. I could do this if I were merely the vessel. You aren't going to put the name Sigrid on her birth certificate, and she'll never know that I named her Sigrid Alma once upon a time because it sort of sounded like *sacred honor.*

Cole knew about the pregnancy. Hiding it from him would have been a sensible course of action if I had been sensible when I peed on the stick. That's what I got for thinking Cole had left for the day rather than merely gone down to the 76 Station on Hillhurst to get Gatorade and a bag of wasabi peanuts.

"A double A12 baby!" Cole squealed at me that night, lying in my bed, covering my tummy with little kisses. "What a blessing!"

Our sex that night had not been scary or passionless or distracted or with murky consent around pain and power. It had been entirely sweet and even reminded me a bit of what I grew bored with over time with Paul. The news had given me a different version of Cole. Rather than the hilarious, salty, passionate man I'd fallen hard for, he had changed into someone regular, a proto-dad figure capable of missionary style and then a fun group shower with singing and loofah-ing.

"Cole, you aren't old enough to pass on A12."

"But you and I both have it, so the child has a 100 percent chance of being a mutant like its parents!" he beamed. "I want our baby, Nina."

He said he wanted the baby, but I couldn't get him to elaborate on what that meant. If I insisted that he, like me, didn't have more than a year or so of life left, he got mad. He'd say I didn't believe in him. He'd say you, Dr. Chen, were a snake oil huckster who wanted to get your mitts on my money. He'd laugh like a madman and then turn up an Eddie Blaine tune loud and sing along with it, telling me I was disappointing my old man with my negative attitude.

A few days after Cole found my pregnancy test, he showed up at my house minus Bruno, who he claimed could not be accounted for, and with a big blue bruise beneath his one eye.

"Did you sell your dog for money?" I asked. "And what's up with the shiner?"

"No," Cole said, removing his shirt and making himself comfortable on the couch. "Bruno is vacationing elsewhere. I get him back when I get him back."

"That doesn't make sense. Who has him?"

"Bruno is not your problem, Nina. I want to be happy right now." Something in him shifted, and he suddenly got cheery. "I'm so excited to be a dad again!"

"Yeah, this child won't hate you because they won't remember you. Because you'll be dead."

He paused and gave me an icy look. "You are a very Bad Thumb."

I felt the acid fill my veins as I said, "You just turned forty-six. That's 115 in A12 years."

"That, my love, is a garbage approach to major fundraising perpetrated by the UCLA Rare Disorders Clinic, which is a front for Tabby Chen to make money and have a group of people to gossip about. She seems lonely and is kind of a bitch, you know? I'm not dying anytime soon. I'm basically Alobar from *Jitterbug Perfume* and will totally live to be a thousand. I lift weights, do yoga, have lots of sex, and have at least two of those twelve-dollar smoothies with the green stuff in them a week. I'm not dying."

"Lots of sex?" I asked. The cortisol was flowing, so might as well leave no stone unturned.

"I suspect if we discuss that, it will make you sad. Hey, you're going to die soon, so what does it even matter?"

I stared at him. He sat up on my gray IKEA replacement sofa and patted the cushion beside him to get me to sit next to him.

"I only love you, ma chérie, but I am a broke man. Not a broken man, but a broke man. Due to some legal machinations, our friend Steve Elwood successfully sued me for defamation in 2004 and, as such, garnishes my paycheck up to 85 percent. The way around this is to not have a job, right? And that was the deal I had with Hannah—she was the breadwinner, and I made a little money here and there with writing and bartending and, for a while, when Bryn was little, I had a job disinfecting the walls and floors at a seafood processing plant, which was terrible, but it was cash under the table."

"And how long did you last at that job?"

"Two whole months! It was disgusting. I can't have a job because an overly sensitive billionaire takes all my money. Since you are cash poor and won't sell Daddy's ugly bordello and have a death wish, I can't, like, marry you or count on you for the financial support I require."

"Excuse me?"

He hoisted himself off my couch with his cane. "Which is why I run an event called Three Fates. It's what the kids call a sex party. It's so much more than a sex party, but I know you are a prim little scamp who's only had sex with me and the avuncular meat carver of Teagarden, Connecticut, so you would probably be appalled at the public displays of alternative sexual expression we get up to."

"No need to dig at Paul, and I don't get what you're saying."

"It's six hundred bucks a head to get in, maximum fifty people. Full bar, full dungeon, we have a medic on hand. I take 50 percent of the door and split the rest with the medic, the bartender, and the security guard. I need the money, and it's fun. And you know what? If someone wants to enjoy some public sexual expression with an A12 mutant with eight fingers, eight toes, one eye, and one testicle, well . . . glory be to those of us who walk the earth in incomplete bodies, be that through elderly father, industrial accidents, or the grace of God."

Cole was smiling as he told me all of this.

"You and me, baby?" he said, running a finger across my cheek. "We never had a monogamous, committed relationship. You're going to abort our child, so you're not really my favorite person, and once you evict Baby Courchaine from your womb, you probably won't be seeing much of me anymore. I'll be looking around for a younger normie to have another baby with. That's what I want to do with the rest of my life. Have a baby and be a stay-at-home dad."

"You already have a kid," I said.

"False!" he shouted, kicking an empty take-out container off my coffee table. "I have an error! I picked the wrong woman to mother my child and that was always the whole problem. *Bryn.* There shouldn't be a Bryn. I named her Sadie. Hannah wanted to name her Bryn, so we made that her middle name, but we always called her Bryn. Sounds like a grain. *Oat Bryn flakes.* Like a cereal that tastes like ass."

"So you run this sex party and you have sex with whomever at the sex party?" I asked.

"That is correct. Purely for business purposes."

I tried to ignore the ache in my heart. "So you're kind of a prostitute?"

Cole nodded his head a few times. "That is correct."

"All to stick it to Steve Elwood?"

"Pretty much. I have an accountant friend who has given his blessing on this course of fiduciary action."

"And Steve Elwood happened to have an A12 baby after all this?"

"Which is an example of God's mystery," Cole said.

"Okay."

"I'll be running Three Fates Saturday night. Want to come? You could sing for us with your mellifluous Eddie Blaine-ian voice. We could use a little evocative entertainment. Your rendition of 'White Rabbit' at last week's karaoke was luminous. You don't have to be totally naked. You can be in your skivvies. Be prepared to show off your beautiful, deformed body. Revel in its sexual power. And, of course, if there's a bloke or a lady there who strikes your fancy, feel free to do whatever you'd like that is on offer. Consent is king at Three Fates, of course."

Dr. Chen, after all of that I made him an omelet.

***

If my life was a courtroom and Cole was on the bench as its judge, it was not my sexual history that I would want brought before him. He'd make a case. He was always making cases.

Forget that adjudication. I went with him to Three Fates. If I was to be as close to Cole as I wanted to be, even as I knew deep in my heart that was impossible, it seemed there were more than a few craven Angelenos who did not get enough reckless fantasy in their daily lives and chose to succumb to the fictional worlds of dominance and control as facilitated by Cole Courchaine.

The drive toward the Three Fates house in Malibu, on Playa del Carmen Road, of course, took us past the gate to the brutal cement and glass mansion that still belonged to my former stepfather. I didn't tell Cole, who sat beside me in the back seat of a chauffeured black Escalade that the owner of the house had sent for him, as we rode up the hill past the gate.

Jorie, who had made the rounds in the kink scene once upon a time (there is a market for amputees and her missing fingers counted, she explained, and there was a period in her twenties, brokenhearted and a bit curious, when she allowed in the fetishists and found them to be both depressing and selfish), advised me not to go to Three Fates in a text exchange:

JORIE: Nina, I don't think you understand! This isn't the kind of party where there's, like, people tied up in pretty rope formations getting spanked. What Cole does is much, much more sick and twisted and dangerous. And illegal. You'd probably drop dead of a heart attack.

NINA: J . . . I'm going to die anyway.

JORIE: *Nope.* Don't even with that excuse. *Don't go.* He invited me two years ago and I left after five minutes, it was so sick. Remember that movie *Requiem for a Dream*? That, only worse.

Here, I will make a statement about free will.

Yes, Dr. Chen: I did, of my own volition, get in the car with Cole and allow myself to be driven to a Malibu mansion to go to a party that Jorie explicitly advised me not to attend.

Yes, I did, of my own volition, enter that mansion, knowing full well that I was about to see some things I was better off not seeing.

Yes, I did get on the stage and sing "White Rabbit," but I don't remember doing that at all.

The minimum age to attend Three Fates was twenty-five, Cole emphasized, because he wanted to keep out the underage-chasing creeper crowd, but also because he didn't find super-young women all that attractive himself because he likes a challenge, and they are not a challenge.

What?

"A woman who claims to know herself, now that's the big game I like to hunt," Cole told me in the Escalade as the driver pulled into the circular driveway in front of the mansion. The house looked innocent, with Christmas lights strung through the trees. "Older guys who go for the eighteen to twenty-five demographic are cowards. The weakest." He kissed me on the cheek and told me no one was going to hurt me.

***

One of the privileges afforded to you when you handed your entrance fee to Cole at the door was anonymity. Everyone, including myself, had written out a name tag upon entrance, the name of your choice.

Mine said *Alice Roosevelt*.

Drawn upon my name tag was a big red *X*. That meant "I do not consent to anything." I was not to be touched without explicit consent. The other nametag symbols were a green circle, meaning "I consent to anything and everything," which was not permitted to a first-time Three Fates attendee. First-timers, Cole explained, always got the red *X* until they proved themselves worthy of one of the other two tags. The third was a solid black name tag with no name on it at all. Those attendees who could take whatever they wanted from anyone wearing a nametag with a green circle on it. Cole wore a solid black name tag.

I reached up to touch his black name tag, and he swatted my hand away.

"So like . . . rape with permission?" I asked.

"Don't do that. Look, no one is going to touch you tonight without your permission, so don't worry about other people. They know what they've gotten themselves into."

"What are you going to do tonight, Cole?" I asked, noticing the physical cringe when I reached out for him, my fingertips grazing the flesh on his forearms. His eye winced shut. He pulled his arm away from me.

"I'm not Cole," he said slowly, and with the slightest hint of contempt. "And I'm not Nick. I have no name here. It's the greatest privilege to be unseen, and you can't see me," he said and walked away.

***

At midnight, the party attendees gathered around Cole, who stood above them on a stage made from old pallets. "Patrons of the darkness, rejoice, for we have found in this communion of souls the safety inherent in danger! A hearty welcome to my favorite bunch of sick fucks!" Cole changed into a burgundy velvet jacket with no shirt underneath. The shirt was unbuttoned far enough to reveal his series of pink, raised scars from his heart surgeries that curved around the asymmetrical bowl in his chest that resulted from his bowed-inward sternum. I was struck by the offense I took at Cole bearing his bumpy, scarred A12 chest to a room full of people who could never understand it the way I could. The little railroad that ran up the center, down into the dip, and up again. The purple dots, the places where the doctors broke his ribs and put them back together. His own two pearly nubs on his gnarled left hand. The missing teeth and the prosthetic eyeball beneath his eye patch. How could anyone see that as beautiful the way I could?

The makeshift stage had a series of spotlights. Above, a disco ball twinkled. Around the perimeter of the room, which had been cleared of any furniture, were candles—some in candelabras, some the squat, scented kind like I used to have in my bedroom in Teagarden—propped on narrow tables. All illuminated in such a way to keep the light off the faces of the patrons of Three Fates. The room felt like being inside a black-and-white photograph.

"Would you like some absinthe punch?" a woman with black hair in a bun wearing a tight black dress asked me as I lingered in the back of the crowd, watching Cole work the room, giving directions, reviewing the rules, and explaining the penalties he would exact if you were to stray from the rules. The woman had a green circle on her name tag, which read *Ivy*. "Have you had absinthe before?"

"I have," I said, taking the plastic cup from her.

"I made the punch. It's real wormwood absinthe, from France. No fake stuff."

"I'm here with Cole. Cole brought me," I said, regretting it immediately. This was not the high school dance.

"Oh?" she said. I couldn't see her face in the dark so could not register if that sound was meant to indicate that she knew him. But I knew, by the sound of that single, clipped syllable, that she did.

"Well," she continued, "Cole is here with me, too."

"Okay," I said, annoyed.

"He's here," she said, pointing at her heart. "And always will be."

"He's never mentioned you."

"That's because I'm none of your business. And trust, I will continue to be none of your business. I'm Ivy, and this is my house. Let me know if you need anything. There's a quiet room upstairs if you get overwhelmed and need to rest."

"Thanks," I said, and slurped hard on my drink. I thought of what Jorie had told me about leaving the party after five minutes, but nothing gross or sexual had happened. Just that creepy girl trying to make me feel bad.

***

Cole clearly relished being the ringmaster of this gathering of the perverts. After an hour or two of unseen gasps, lengthy cumcries, screams that barely sounded human, and the crack of a leather whip lashing flesh, Cole ordered his revelers to gather back at his makeshift stage. He had his own halftime show, with a microphone and a sound guy and a bowl full of candy to throw at his crowd. The stage had been illuminated with what looked like an IKEA floor lamp, and two men wearing tight white pants set up a small table wrapped with blue plastic.

The room was dark, and I could barely see Cole on his dimly lit soapbox, as I chose not to leave my seat in the back of the room, nursing my second cup of Ivy's absinthe punch, leaning against a shiny grand piano, and thinking my thoughts. A few people had approached me to ask if I wanted to touch their garter snake and assured me they were talking about an actual reptile. A woman whose face I could barely see told me I was beautiful, and I told her I was pregnant, mostly to get her to leave me alone. That rude Ivy came back around to ask if I wanted a bowl of pozole, which was being served in the kitchen by the light of a single candle and would be spooned into my mouth by someone in a Mardi Gras mask, but otherwise the edict of my nametag was respected.

Cole turned down the thumpy club music and took the mic. "Silence! I need everyone to shut up! This is important." Everyone in the room stopped talking. Something in that silence felt like violin strings tearing at my flesh, making me want to weep.

Cole cleared his throat. "Tonight, I stand before you all humbled by your community support of me and my submissive little girl, Ivy. Ivy has devised and consented to a ceremony to show her loyalty to me in front of all of you. If you have a red X on your nametag, I hereby respectfully ask you to head upstairs or outside, as what is about to happen is not for the uninitiated. Love is pain, pain is love, and when a woman like Ivy takes on the pain of the man she is in love with, that is something to be honored."

I suspected that the circus world of Cole's imagination, which he had made real within the confines of another wealthy woman's house, was something he had wanted to show me, right? Cole as large and in charge as he could imagine. Getting other people to pretend along with him? Because he very easily could have hidden Three Fates and Ivy and whatever else he had going on. This was no accident. I was there to see this because he wanted me to see it. Because he wanted me to fight for him. Because he knew me, and he knew that I didn't fight for anything, and maybe I should get around to that before I left the goddamn building.

"Sir, you are the best thing that ever happened to me," Ivy said into the microphone, kneeling before Cole on a pillow. Her face caught a shaft of light, and I could see that she was young, probably not much older than Bryn. "You are the best thing, sir. To ever happen to me." The robotic cadence of her speech made this world sound fictional. Bad science fictional. I thought of the Bondurant student who published my poetry book on her small press, who came by the restaurant once to watch me ice a hundred cookies shaped like the letter *B*, complaining about some horrible sci-fi novel a Bonnie classmate had passed to her for publication. *I know the world is fictional, and maybe I don't know world-building, but I do know bad, and this was very bad.*

Ivy said, "You are the best thing that ever happened to me and what your body lacks my body shall also lack."

The cleaver on the small table up on the stage caught a flicker of light. I looked down at my left hand. I knew where this was headed.

"You are the best thing that ever happened to me in my puny, insignificant life."

"What say you, my love?" Cole breathed into the microphone. Ivy placed her left hand on a small table that was also covered in blue plastic.

"I, Ivy Courchaine, fully and wholeheartedly give . . ."

Cole, with a Joker's gleam in his eye, snapped on a pair of black latex gloves. He held up his hands into the light for all the see.

My heart rate tripled, and I felt like my brain was made of lava.

This could not be good for the baby, I thought, realizing for the first time that night that the drink I was nursing had alcohol in it.

The front doors to the house were shut and there were two tall men guarding them, or what I took to be men, since the darkness didn't allow me to see their faces. Nor would the screams and catcalls of the crowd that had pushed their way up to the stage, to Ivy, whose real name was Ava Elwood, like that other Elwood we talked about all the time, allow me to hear those men's voices. I forced myself up and waddled in shock toward the door.

"You are the best thing that ever . . ." Ivy continued, a bit of a nervous warble in her voice. She stumbled on her words and then started to cry a little bit. A cry of fear, not joy, not sorrow. Cole stood before her, massaging her ring and pinky fingers. "And I give you that which you do not have."

I looked down at my own hand. Three fingers, two nubs. Three fingers, two nubs. I had been born like this, had carried this sense of shame around my hand, but had also never missed those two fingers. They were not meant for me. But this was a thing I shared with Cole. This was my thing with Cole, our shared deformities. Our shared weirdness. Our shared ugliness. You couldn't just take that for yourself. You had to be born with it. You had to fight for your right to exist with it. You weren't supposed to take what we had been given.

Two men in feather boas buzzed around the room handing out champagne flutes. Empty champagne flutes.

My body hurt.

I was forgetting to breathe.

"Be ready, my vampires." Cole lifted the cleaver up and into that thin shaft of light. I looked away. Above the murmurs and gasps I heard the chop, the sound of metal cutting through skin and bone, the blade hitting the wooden table on the other side, her scream and her final cry of "I love you, my sir" before one of Cole's hired goons picked her up and carried her off the stage.

The crowd cheered. Each of those people rushed the stage to take a drop of Ivy's blood into their champagne glasses. Someone I assume was the medic got to work cauterizing the wounds.

"Now we are the same," I heard Ivy say, sounding droopy and drunk as that man carried her through the crowd. The audience clapped and howled.

You couldn't just steal my deformity along with my boyfriend, I thought.

I also needed to be airlifted to a hospital. But I hadn't admitted that to myself just yet.

The next thing I felt was cold. Freezing Connecticut winter blasting cold, though this was August in Los Angeles, and you could smell the wildfires and the smog and the sickness in the hot night air. Then I felt a man with big, muscular arms picking me up off the floor and carrying me outside. Over this man's shoulder, I heard the roar of the ocean down below. And then I heard the voice of Eddie Blaine say, *Nina, my little girl! You can survive anything! You can lift the mountain over your head and throw it as far as it will go.*

What did you forget to teach me, Daddy? There's something I should know, right?

My father replied, *How to make Ruthie's chicken soup. Addie wrote* Somber Mountain *because she was in love with some girl. That's why it's such a downer. By the way, baby, that boyfriend of yours? I hate his guts. Those Catholics are no good. Klinger's had this horsey-looking Boston kid teaching tennis lessons one summer and he had the worst teeth I ever saw in my life, and he still got Joan Leininger from the next hotel over pregnant. Tell people you stood too close to that weirdo, Nina, and that you're a Jew like Mary from the Bible, getting pregnant without that gonif touching you.*

***

"Nina? Nina? Talk to me, Nina."

I was shivering, wrapped in a man's suit jacket, laying on the wet lawn next to the fountain in the middle of the mansion's circular driveway. The moon was full, and I had a pounding headache and needed a drink of water.

"What?" This man smelled like burnt onions and bad cologne.

The man with white hair wearing a tight black tank top cradled me in his arms like a baby. "Nina. You're okay, Nina. We're waiting to see if you're going to need to go to the hospital and then my driver is going to take you there, or to wherever you're staying."

My senses were mucked up and I couldn't focus on this man's face, nor place his voice, though it was familiar in some distant way.

"Nina?"

"Oh my god," I said, placing that voice and focusing on this man's face, now leathery and aged, bolting awake and aware.

Greg Hodges, retired, old, and divorced from my mother, lowered his voice, and spoke directly into my ear. "I know I can't ask you to not tell your mother you saw me here. Maybe you wouldn't tell her you were at a thing like this one. But it might hurt her to hear that, and I don't want to hurt her any more than I already have."

I wiggled out of his grip and did a log roll on the grass to get away from him.

"Get the fuck away from me," I spat.

He reached his hand out toward me. Since the last time I'd seen him, he'd gotten a tattoo of a lightning bolt on the inside of his forearm. "Nina, I'm trying to help you."

"Leave me alone."

Greg nodded. He had blood spattered on his shirt, and I didn't know if that was mine or if he'd bathed in the blood of the evening's entertainment. "You hit your head on the tile on the way down. When you passed out," he said. In my hand, there was a plastic bag of ice. "You have a bruise on your forehead."

I touched the spot. It felt tender.

Greg said, "Let me call my driver to come get you so you get home safely, sweetie."

I started to cry because my head hurt, because Greg Hodges had no business calling me sweetie twenty-some years after he ruined my life.

"You ruined my life," I whispered to Greg. "I left college because of you. And you're a rapist. You raped those women, and you aren't even the least bit sorry you did it."

Greg exhaled. "Okay, Nina. I'm not here to argue about the past. I'm sorry if I did anything to hurt you. Right now, though, you need a doctor."

It seemed Greg had been to therapy or something, probably dragged by the woman he took up with after kicking my mother to the curb.

"Sorry isn't even a word, Greg. Or a thing. You wouldn't know sorry if it raped you."

Greg seemed sincerely aggrieved over this. "Whatever you want to say to me, Nina. I'll take it."

I let out a laugh. "You were never half as cool as Eddie Blaine."

I expected Greg to protest that statement, listing his athletic accomplishments and retelling his tale of woe about not winning the Heisman, but he simply nodded and said, "Okay."

Greg's house was visible from where we stood. Perched on a hill below the perv mansion, looking out at the Pacific. All the lights were on inside. My room, the smallest one in the house, did not have a view of the ocean or the mountains but of a ten-foot-tall pile of dirt, which had been dug up for a swimming pool. Greg, too cheap or too mean to have the dirt removed, had it piled against my bedroom window. I hated that room so much—the metal window frames, the gray cement floors that were ice cold on my feet, the three framed pictures on the wall that I was allowed, because all décor had to be approved by Greg, so I couldn't hang any poster I wanted on the wall. He permitted me a Cézanne print from the LACMA gift shop I had to fight tooth and nail for, the panoramic photo of my eighth-grade class at Campbell Hall, and a black-and-white photo of my mother taken her senior year of high school, when she was voted "Future Miss America" by the male members of the Highland Park High School Class of 1976.

"Nina?" Greg asked. "Are you involved with Cole Courchaine?"

It was clear that yes was the wrong answer. I didn't answer.

"I know I have no right to tell you anything. Did you know about what happened in there ahead of time?"

I said nothing. The shock took over.

"Did he warn you? Nina? Did he tell you what he was going to do?"

I was crying so hard I could barely breathe. "Fuck you, Greg."

"Okay," he said, handing me a wad of tissues from his pocket. I cried harder. "That thing with Ava—Ivy, I mean—has been going on for a while. If you have an open thing with him—"

I shook my head.

"She's his collared submissive, if you know what that means. They had a formal ceremony at the last party."

"I'm not going to listen to you, of all people," I said, pulling away from him. "I know my own life."

"Look," he said. I was shocked at his calm. "You're in shock. This is going to hit you later on."

I felt like I was floating outside of my body. That's a real thing, Dr. Chen. It's too bad we never talked about the medical reason for that. I'm very sorry that I was flooding Sig with cortisol. She might have anxiety later in life because of this night. "The new wife made you go to therapy, huh?" I said.

"What?"

"Is your young new girlfriend here at the party? Does she know you're here?"

He didn't answer.

"Aha! I knew it. There's the guy I know!"

"Nina, I think the right thing to do would be to take you to the emergency room. Let me get my driver to take us down to my house."

I struggled to pull myself up on my feet. "Hell no! I am not setting foot in that house ever again. I should find Cole."

"Nina, no!" Greg's tone of voice changed. "Please don't go in there and look for him."

"You can't—" Even though I was wobbly, I got up on my feet and started walking toward the house.

Greg dove after me and grabbed my arm. I twisted my body to get him to let go. He wouldn't, though, lunging forward and grabbing me around the waist and lifting me off the ground. Greg hoisted me over his shoulder like a sack of potatoes and walked me away from the house. I tried to elbow him in the head to get him to drop me. I didn't care if I died falling on concrete from six feet up. I did not want Greg Hodges to touch me, and I said as much.

"Nina, he's . . . they're having sex in front of everyone. Do you want to see that? Do you?"

I had kept it together so well for so long. The only contracts with others that I sought were that others had to make my life either better or neutral. No net losses. No pain. Wasn't that why I left Chef Paul because the needle was flickering too far in the wrong direction? Wasn't that, compared to the mess I had found myself standing in at this very moment, so little?

This, dear Dr. Chen, was the moment I really died, not today or tomorrow or whenever Stanford Hospital sends me to the morgue. My death was when these the dual sorrows and disappointments collided and I was sandwiched between these two men, these behemoths who decided where I was going and who I'd be when I got there.

These two men had the audacity to think of themselves as heroes.

Did Cole come outside to look for me? Reveal himself covered in blood and semen; his grin so bright it could have illuminated all of Los Angeles?

I don't want to tell you, Dr. C.

Did I know, in my heart of hearts, that there was no one I could talk to about this moment, this reckoning, as if I standing at the pearly gates with Saint Peter laughing his ass off at me, *Oh, dear girl, whatever did you do to deserve this moment, the cruelest trick the universe could have ever played on you?*

Cole, now trailed by Bruno the Dog, stood illuminated by the light of a circling LAPD helicopter, stripped down to his boxer briefs, threw his bloody jacket and pants into the fountain in front of Steve Elwood's ex-wife's mansion (per public records), and walked over to the Escalade that we had arrived in, opened the door to the backseat and let Bruno hop in. "Nina! Nina!"

I was still slung over Greg's shoulder. Greg heard Cole and held onto me tighter and started to walk in the other direction.

"Sir? Sir! I demand you put Alice Roosevelt down on the ground this instant!" Cole yelled when he saw me six feet in the air on Greg's shoulder.

Greg set me down. Dizzy, I careened into Cole. He smelled awful—booze, sweat, and yes, blood.

"Who's that jagoff?" he asked me.

"Greg Hodges."

"Wait, your stepfather?"

I nodded.

"Hey!" he yelled at Greg, lifting his cane as if to smash it into Greg's face, "Greg Hodges, why the fuck are you at my party? I don't let abusive pieces of shit come to my thing, asshole."

Greg assumed his giant powerful man stance. Greg was six four to Cole's scrawny five ten and had about a hundred pounds of muscle on him, too.

"You're that guy?" Cole continued, his voice rising with anger. "The scumbag who went around saying Nina was ugly?" Cole continued. "We do not countenance rapists at Three Fates."

I stood there and watched my bloodstained beloved, who was in some sort of altered state from his violent act moments earlier, reel back his cane and deliver it at full speed to the face of the man who derailed my college education, stole my childhood, manipulated my mother, argued for my irrelevance, and disrespected Eddie Blaine by tossing out a box of his Vegas memorabilia. I, Nina Simone Blaine, with a headache that felt like I had received a similar blow, witnessed justice in real time finally, after so many years.

I promise you that the only way to maintain your sanity at the end of your life is to always know who the villain in your story is. Because when that gets murky, you fall in love with the wrong person. You'll live for a ghost. You'll die for a ghost, too.

Greg reached up to cover his face and Cole gave him a swift knee to the balls. He fell to the ground. Cole kneeled on his chest and spat in Greg's face and said, "That's what you get for hurting an innocent girl, you sack of crap. You were charged with caring for and protecting Nina and what did you do? What did you do? You, self-appointed boss of what counts as beautiful? You took away her *mother* because she didn't look like a goddamn model?"

Greg just lay there, guarding his face with his hands.

Cole had Greg's hair in his fists, pulling his head back and forth. "Give Nina back her childhood, you bastard!" Greg went limp and doubled over and Cole kicked him in the small of his back.

I couldn't hear Greg, but I suspect what he said was, *I'm sorry.*

Cole, a mostly-naked live wire of anger, put his bare foot on Greg's throat. "Don't ever show your face around here again. That's what you get for fucking up a child."

Cole grabbed his cane off the ground and put his arm around me and started to pull me toward the black Escalade we'd arrived in. "Nina? Nina? You're going home, Nina. Get in the car!"

I didn't budge. That grass felt so cold on my feet.

Greg said nothing, and that was for the best.

Cole barked at me like an angry father to get in the damn car.

May you never have to reassess who the villains are, Dr. C.

10

Time for a breather here, after telling you about Three Fates. It was *a lot*, as the kids say.

The clock on the wall here at the Steve and Kailey Elwood Memorial Death Room ticks very loudly! Down. Down. Down.

Three more hours.

Where is Cole? I'm getting antsy.

Let's enjoy a nice story: In 2015, I won a Best of Connecticut award for Best Cookie. The local press that year was absolutely in love with my molasses cookies, which were only available on our dessert menu from Thanksgiving through Easter. We recommended dunking them in espresso. They also paired nicely with a cup of our hot local apple cider. All my idea. During the holidays, I sold them by the dozen out of the restaurant, and every spring, Bondurant would hire me to make hundreds of them to give to students during finals. There was a photo of me on the Stella di Capra website, holding up the certificate, Paul standing next to me with his arm around my waist, while the rest of the kitchen crew stood around us with triumphant smiles. Please tell your daughter that her biological host person was the queen of molasses cookies for a couple of years, and that it was her life's greatest triumph.

***

A few days after that awful night, I woke up alone in my bed from another night of druggy nightmare sleep to a long, nasty email from Chris Kyriakis. He had spent the previous evening writing to all the Good Thumbs to inform them in no uncertain terms what assholes we were for not visiting him in the hospital. Not one of us bothered to even respond to his texts about his surgery. He asked us to bring him food and no one did.

It hadn't even occurred to me to respond. I was too bombed out after seeing what I had seen at Three Fates. I forgot to eat for an entire day. Plus, we understood that, out of all of us, what he wanted most was to die, on his own schedule and on his own terms. That's all he talked about, all we talked about, and if he wanted to be in control of how that happened, and if he wanted to go out on a dramatic bang all pissed off at everyone, well . . . that's what we all thought we were seeing.

Hurt people hurt people.

But there was this: "Jorie told me what that motherfucker did to that girl at his sicko party. That worthless sack of shit not only gets how many girlfriends walking around in an A12 body with no money, but he also levels up to ritual amputation? I don't want to know this!"

Chris didn't need Jorie's gossipy mouth to find out about this, though. The internet, of course, picked up the story of Cole and Ava Elwood and what they were calling *ritual amputation*. I would wager that it was Cole himself who tipped off some young upstart journalist, wanting to raise awareness that in the decades-long beef between Nick Sullivan and Steve Elwood, Nick was up by ten points and two fingers. The headlines were grotesque. Cole must have been enjoying it, pulling some twisted Bonnie and Clyde act for all the world to see.

It was my mother (I called to verify, not talking out of spite here) who supplied my name and contact information to Kailey Elwood, and I am assuming my whereabouts on the

Sunday night a week after Cole's morbid party. I had not left the house in all that time. Cole disappeared on me after using all my lavender shower gel the following day, leaving behind Bruno and his bloodstained boxer briefs.

I was looking forward to another Good Thumbs night. I needed the company. I needed to talk to people so the low buzz in my brain could maybe stop, so I could stop playing over and over in my head the last conversation Cole and I had before he ditched his dog and his bloody undies and skipped town.

"Do you think you're so goddamn special that you get to have a three-fingered hand?" Cole said to me when I confronted him. I sought in his angry face some softness, some evidence that he loved me, that he cared about how what he had done had affected me. My body shivered like it was five degrees outside.

Because you didn't choose yours and Ivy did?

It was tribute!

I happen to think what she did for me was beautiful.

I happen to think what she did for me was beautiful.

My brain couldn't stop replaying that speech. Over and over and over.

I happen to think what she did for me was beautiful.

I happen to think what she did for me was beautiful.

I happen to think what she did for me was beautiful.

I happen to think what she did for me was beautiful.

And for the whole day after that conversation, my body would not stop shaking.

***

Chris invited me, Jorie, and Sylvia to meet him for dinner. He wanted to talk. We were welcoming back and saying fare thee well to Chris Kyriakis, who planned to sell his yacht and move to the Kyriakis family island in Greece for the foreseeable. He said he'd buy us the most gorgeous Japanese food at an izakaya in Downtown Los Angeles where he knew the chef. This surprised me, as I had believed he hated us when I got the email in which he called me a pathetic idiot and spent a paragraph defaming my late father, calling him a no-talent loser and something that a Google search indicated was the Greek word for Jew.

Chris waved me to the back of the restaurant when I arrived, guiding me to the table where the others sat. Chris reeked of cologne. I had to smoosh up against him in the small, padded booth. He had ordered appetizers and green tea.

"Fuck you," I said to Chris, setting the tone for the evening, shaking my napkin open and placing it on my pregnant belly. "Syl and Jorie, if Chris isn't going to apologize after his meanie letter writing campaign last night, then I'm not coming to any more of these."

Chris turned toward me. In addition to being drenched in Drakkar Noir, he blasted me with his hot colon breath. "I wrote an email and that was worse than what Cole did?"

"Nina, Cole's not welcome at Good Thumbs gatherings anymore," Jorie said gravely. "Just so you know."

This news irritated me. Good Thumbs minus Cole? Boring! I looked around at the A12 Stick-in-the-Mud Doom Squad fiddling with their chopsticks and refusing me eye contact. "You know what? Good. Hey, how about we just blow up the whole goddamn group, huh?" I was about to cry. I was hoping for support. I needed a hug. I needed to talk. I had seen some shit.

"About that, Nina. I have done a ton of work on myself, and as such, I prioritize relationships with people who are not personally destructive, so I'm going to make you choose between having me in your life as a friend and staying with your boyfriend," Jorie said. "I hate doing that to you, and I'm weirdly a little sad about losing Cole as a friend myself, but I'm turning forty-one next month, and seeing forty-two is something I'd like to try for as well, so I need to avoid drama and caretaking people who accept shitty treatment. I can feel this horrible energy coming off you. It's Cole's energy. This dark, sick energy. I really hate it and don't want it in my space."

Syl shot me a look.

"How can my energy be Cole's energy?" I asked.

"You need to cut him out of your life," Jorie said. "For your health. Because you can't afford to be walking around full of fear chemicals, puking all the time. You're messing with your baby's brain development. Seriously, your child will have anxiety and health problems and depression unless you knock this off. Listen to me, Nina. He's not worth it."

Just as I was about to interrogate Jorie's friend-eliminating methodology and knowledge of fetal brain development, a too-chipper voice, like way too chipper for my personal insulin levels, stopped by our table and shouted, "Nina Blaine? Is that you?"

This woman had on a baseball cap and sunglasses; her loose green sweater obscured by the baby clinging to her from its sling. I was maneuvering a piece of cooked *hamachi kama* into my mouth (avoiding raw fish as the obstetrician had advised me), trying to deflect the awkwardness of being with Sylvia for the first time since she yelled at me, Jorie's weird statement about energy, and Chris's terrible odors. I hadn't eaten much that week. By the time the seaweed salad and the fried chicken and the metal basket of translucent shrimp dumplings had arrived, I realized I was starving, rushing every bite into my mouth.

I looked up at her and said, with my mouth full, "I'm sorry, who are you?"

"Dr. Chen told me you all would be here tonight. I'm Kailey Elwood. A friend of hers."

"Dr. Chen told you what?"

"Do you mind if we join you? She told me this is your gathering of A12 friends, and Zinnia here is your A12 friend."

Kailey hustled her baby into my arms, passing her little body across the table, cooing about how I, of course, would want to hold her, and ordered a server to bring her a chair. Standing behind her was an obvious bodyguard—a hefty man in a black suit with his arms crossed. I took Zinnia Grace Elwood, junior A12er, in my arms. What else was I supposed to do? She was nearly a year old and had little rolls under her chin above her black-and-pink corduroy dress. My eyes fell on her little A12 tripod hand. I looked into her blue cross-eyes. I pulled on her stretchy skin and touched her tiny absent fingers. I felt like a jerk, giving a baby a once-over like a used car to make sure she really had the Twelve. And then, I burst into tears because I was holding an actual A12 baby for the first, and likely last, time, and that this baby might be the last baby I ever held, and I wanted to hold my baby, but there was no guarantee that I would.

"Are you okay?" Kailey Elwood reached over to rub my shoulder. She was directing all her energy at me, staring at me with an eerie half smile. I wanted to swat her hand off my shoulder but didn't. "You seem agitated, Nina."

"She's so . . . Twelve-y," I said, reaching for a napkin. "Look! This baby is stretchy like us."

"Yes," Kailey said, reaching over to pat down Zinnia's red cap of hair. "She's got her own style. I'm glad you got to see her."

"It's really not that big of a deal," I began, sniffling.

Kailey asked, "Nick Sullivan chopping off Ava's fingers wasn't that big of a deal?"

"What? No, having A12," I said, reaching around Zinnia to wipe my drippy nose with my black cloth napkin. "It's not that bad. Just extra doctors' appointments and maybe a few surgeries. Everyone in our group has had the heart valve surgery. Zinnia will probably live to be in her fifties. Or older."

"My husband and I are looking for Nick Sullivan. I think you know where he is."

"We're eating," I hissed back as I reached around the baby for the shrimp dumplings. "I'm hungry. We don't want to discuss that right now."

"Are you sure?" Kailey continued. "I mean, the incident was picked up by the *LA Times*. You didn't see it?"

"We're trying to have a nice evening out, do you mind?" I said to Kailey, who wasn't listening because she knew she didn't have to. Zinnia grabbed a handful of my hair and yanked it. "No one invited you to our dinner, remember?"

"Excuse me, Kailey Elwood, my friend Nina told you to leave," Sylvia said. Kailey smiled a fake, toothy smile at Sylvia. "You need to take your baby and that big guy in the suit back there and get out of here. You're not invited."

"I'm here to talk to Nina, not to you," Kailey said, talking down to Sylvia. "A crime has been committed against a member of my family. I'm sure you understand."

"I said get out of here," Sylvia said, anger rising in here.

"You should get out of here, Kailey," I said.

"Just answer the question and I'll never bother you again," Kailey said.

"What are you, a cop?"

"I don't want any part of this. I don't want to hear about Cole doing Lord knows what and I definitely don't want anything to do with this bitch," Sylvia said, pointing at Kailey. "I'm out." She grabbed her bag and slid out of the booth and headed for the door.

"Thanks for chasing my friend away," I said to Kailey. "I guess being a billionaire entitles you to ruin people's evenings."

Kailey ignored me and reached for a dumpling, and Jorie smacked her hand away from our food. "Steve and I would like your help in tracking down Nick Sullivan. Steve's daughter Ava is in the hospital. Legally, things are a little murky, as Ava claims she consented to what happened and refuses to press charges against Nick."

Panic rose in me, a combination of nausea, a need to run for the exit, and the wish to just turn out the lights and be done with all of this. My forehead began to sweat. "Here, take her," I said to Kailey, passing Zinnia back, feeling the acid rise in my veins and the return of the body shakes that I thought had passed. "I'm not doing this, either." I started shaking harder.

Kailey, bouncing Zinnia, continued. "Nick wrote some terrible and false things about Steve on his website in the early 2000s and Steve won a defamation suit against him. Steve has never collected a penny from him, though. Steve says they were friends for a time, or at least friendly when Nick bartended at a place he used to frequent. Marrying Steve caused Ava to end our friendship, so exactly how she met Nick Sullivan is unclear to me," Kailey said, looking into Zinnia's face. "Any information you have about that, or where Nick is right now, would be helpful."

"Nina and Cole were dating," Chris volunteered. "She was goo-goo-ga-ga for the guy even before they met in person, and she's been his little ragdoll for the past six months."

Jorie kicked him under the table and said, "Chris? Please don't."

"Oh, I didn't realize. I'm sorry, Nina. Did he dump you for Elwood's kid?"

"He didn't," I said.

"It doesn't matter, Chris," Jorie piped in. "Chris, please don't cause problems for Nina. She's not your enemy."

"She's not my friend, either."

"Then why are you here, Chris?" I demanded, feeling relief in my anger at him. "Why do you continue to hang out with us when you hate us?"

"I have no one else." He shook his head like I was a moron. "Same as you."

"Nina?" Kailey asked. "I understand why you would want to protect Nick, but I think we can both agree that letting the police know where he is would be the right thing to do under the circumstances."

No, I thought. *Why would I talk to the police about someone named "Nick" who doesn't exist?* "Absolutely not. I'm leaving," I said, hot in the face. I grabbed my purse from the floor and ran down the dark, narrow corridor toward the front door, trying to avoid bumping into the servers. My brain was flickering off. Breathing became labored, and my heart raced, and I couldn't judge the distance between me and the exit. But soon I was out in that filthy alley, running toward Spring

Street crying, having some sort of panic attack. Sylvia sat in her car across the street looking at her phone and I screamed her name so loudly and with so much bloodcurdling need and fear behind it that she heard me over the din of Downtown Los Angeles. I fell on my knees when my legs gave out from under me, sobbing. I skinned my knees on a dirty sidewalk and was probably going to get sick from it.

Sylvia dashed across the street and hauled me up to my feet. "Blainey, what's going on?" she yelled above the traffic sounds of Downtown LA. "Get off the sidewalk, it's filthy." She put me in the passenger seat of her car and popped open the glove box and pulled out a first-aid kit.

"Blainey, you can't do this. You have a baby inside you. You can't—"

"That baby! That A12 baby!" I squeaked out, knowing that the sight of Baby Zinnia wasn't the reason I was melting down. "That was real. She was real," I said through sobs.

"Blainey, shhhhh. Shhhhhhh." Sylvia held me to her chest across the center console of her Toyota Highlander. "We need to clean up your knees. That looks nasty. There's literal shit on the sidewalks downtown." I shook as Sylvia put on a latex glove and smeared ointment on my wounds and had me put Band-Aids on them.

"I'm crying because of that baby," I repeated, wondering if Syl knew I didn't believe what I was saying.

Sylvia, with her stocked first-aid kit in her immaculate car, gave me her side-eye. "Where's Cole? Nina? Answer me." Sylvia took this tone with me from time to time, this holier-than-thou voice from on high that said she was right, and I was wrong, and I better let her solve my problems or else. "Nina?"

"I don't know."

"Are you lying for him?"

"I don't know where," I said, which was the truth.

I happen to think what she did for me was beautiful.

I happen to think what she did for me was beautiful.

I happen to think what she did for me was beautiful.

It was the *for me* that really did it, Dr. C.

"Did he break up with you?"

"No."

"Did you break up with him?"

"No."

"He chopped off a woman's fingers, Nina! Where's your dignity?"

"I saw Greg Hodges," I explained to Syl. "He was at that party. He tried to protect me from Cole. He even picked me up and threw me over his shoulder to get me away from him."

"Wait, what? Greg tried to protect you? *Greg*? Nina, what does that tell you about Cole if Greg Hodges pops out of the woodwork and tries to rescue you?"

Sylvia had that look on her face—consternation, confusion, searching for the right thing to say. Just then, Kailey Elwood, with Zinnia on her hip and her security goon by her side, knocked at the window.

"Oh hell no," Sylvia said, flashing her middle finger at Kailey. She started the engine and pulled away. "No fucking way."

Sylvia hit the gas and sped up the street toward the 101. "We're going to my place, and we're going to order some takeout and talk."

"I want to go to my house." My throat felt sore. "Can we go there instead?"

She shook her head. "Your place is a mess and honestly, it smells like garbage. No. The Eddie Blaine House isn't that far from my house, and after we eat and talk for a bit, I'll take you home."

"I have to feed Bruno."

"Who's Bruno?"

"Bruno!" I yelled. "Cole's dog!"

"He left behind his dog?"

I happen to think what she did for me was beautiful.

What Sylvia didn't understand, because I didn't tell her, was that on my phone was a text message to Cole, sent twenty-two hours earlier, asking the simple question, "Where are you?" Which, under normal circumstances, is a question posed to a loved one by a person who cares about that person's well-being. The text went unanswered for twenty hours. Then Cole sent an image of Eddie Blaine with his arm around a Vegas dancing girl decked out in silver and red feathers in front of the big sign at the Flamingo in 1968.

Would no response be worse? Less confusing? Why did he send me an old photo of Eddie? Was he with another woman?

I had to be in my house if Cole showed up or called. Every cell in my body was screaming for him.

Sylvia wasn't the type of friend I could lay out this situation as evidence to. She'd say, "Forget him, he's an asshole" and ask me what I wanted for dinner. Sylvia never had a minute of trouble dispatching a bad boyfriend to the bin. She never let anyone talk to her like she was less than. She was made of stronger stock than me.

I debated asking Syl to take me to the emergency room.

"Okay, we can go to your house, but you're not allowed to bring up the finger thing!" I yelled.

Sylvia kept her eyes on the road, not looking at me. "Nina, we are talking about the fingers. He traumatized you. Look at how you're acting! You were on your knees screaming on a sidewalk with literal shit on it and you're arguing that there's nothing wrong? You know, that man could've easily hidden that whole thing from you. His sicko party and his other girlfriend. He wanted you to see all that. To hurt you."

I pounded my fist on the dashboard. "What did I just say?"

Sylvia remained calm. "Do not hit my car. Tell me why your sense of self-protection has gone completely offline."

"Sylvia, I am begging you—"

"He wanted you to see that!" Syl yelled. "Not just read about it on the internet, because it's so disgusting and over the line that you, as a mostly reasonable person, Nina Blaine, might have assumed he was making stuff up. It's so grotesque and outlandish that part of you wouldn't have believed him. He wanted to mess you in the head. He wanted you to see that and fight for him. To show him what you're willing to accept. To participate in his race to the bottom with some other girl winning because she gave up her fingers, so what are you going to give up, right? You're whole goddamn head? You're in so deep you're not even taking in that he not only has a side piece, but that he would lift up an ax—"

I kicked the dashboard of Syl's car, hard. "Stop it! I'm not listening to you! Stop talking about him!"

Sylvia didn't stop. "You have a baby inside you, Nina! This is not about you anymore, got it? You cannot be making yourself sick over some crazy motherfucker who is probably off with some other woman while he thinks about you sitting around pining for him—"

"I said stop!" I screamed.

"He's playing you." Sylvia shook her head. "And you—you committed to this," she said, pointing at the bump underneath my gray sack dress with a soy sauce stain. "You know damn well you didn't get an abortion to keep his ass around."

We were finally quiet, dragging along Sunset Boulevard in traffic, Syl's car stereo playing a slow, sad tune by the real Nina Simone. She pulled the car over in front of a Thai restaurant. "I'm going to run in here and get us another dinner. Waterfall beef sound good? And noodles?"

I nodded.

"Do you want to come in the restaurant with me?"

I said no. That I wanted to fall asleep.

She pointed at her dashboard and said with a sharpness, "You're lucky that kick didn't leave a mark. Blainey, I'm not playing; you need to calm down right now. I'll be back in a minute." She locked me into the car and walked into the Thai restaurant.

Daddy had Addie and I have Syl. I remembered coming to Los Angeles to see Addie when I was in my twenties, and finally, to her absolute relief, Addie could unload the adults-only Eddie Blaine stories on me. How beleaguered she was all those years, cleaning Eddie's vomit off the vinyl back seat of so-and-so's Cadillac, bailing him out of the clink in Vegas at three in the morning, listening to him cry his baby boo-boo tears about Ruth and his lousy life, and getting treated like a joke after all his hard work.

Like Addie, Sylvia was always the friend who was right, and that made me the friend who was always wrong. I could have asked Syl to text Cole to ask where he was, but I also couldn't. Involving her in this mess was over now that the news of the finger chop was out, and whose fault was that? Mine? Not mine. None of this was my fault and yet I feared that if fingers (still-attached ones) were to be pointed, they would be pointed at me. The night of Three Fates, I stood outside under those Christmas lights around all those perverts and smiled as my boyfriend kicked my evil stepfather in the nuts, serving justice and balancing the universe.

Sylvia returned to the car with a big paper bag full of Thai food. She was trying to be gentle—I could see that she was really working hard not to tell me I was a moron—but all I heard out of Sylvia's mouth on the ride to her house was the unforgivable, *You're no different from Tracy, selling yourself out for some man. Where I have seen that before? Have I not, for years now, snubbed your mother for the same?*

Is it inevitable, Dr. Chen, that we turn into our parents, no matter how different we think we are from them? How lucky it was for Sylvia to turn into her own mother, who I knew as brilliant and loving and above all, protective of her little bird baby. How could it be that I, in this moment, was completely Tracy's daughter, ruining myself to keep a man?

The Uber ride I had requested while Syl was in the Thai restaurant sat waiting for me in front of Sylvia's house when she pulled up. Her driveway was so narrow that she had to stop and let me out before pulling in between her house and the house next door with an inch to spare on the passenger side. In the time it took her to execute her troublesome parking practice, I walked to that car with the bag of Thai food in my hand, drunk on my own sense of freedom and ingenuity, and told the driver to step on it. I went in my house and locked the door, dumped two scoops of kibble in Bruno's bowl, and stashed my phone in the refrigerator next to the carton of milk Cole had bought weeks earlier. I devoured the entire container of *pad kee mao* and half of the steak salad before passing out on the couch, dreading an eventual trip to the bathroom and having to deal with the pounding on my door, which came sooner than I thought. Sylvia kicking it and screaming my name, Bruno defending his temporary master, barking back at her, Sylvia screaming that if I didn't open the door, she'd break it down, she'd have me put in the hospital, I needed help, I was having a nervous breakdown, which yes, Dr. Chen, yes, I absolutely was and I'm glad that Syl called you instead of the mental health people because you at least plucked me from the floor and held me and let me cry and shake.

And yes, I lied to you about what happened. Lied straight to your kind, concerned face when I was on the floor of my father's house having a meltdown because I didn't want you to think this was about Cole. I'm so sorry for that, Dr. Chen. I'm so sorry for scaring you. What happened that night at his terrible party had nothing to do with me, though. It really didn't, Dr. Chen. Sylvia may have felt otherwise but it wasn't cheating. My suicide mission pregnancy meant I didn't have to worry about what it meant. Nothing meant anything, and that was the gift you gave me. In the cold fright of my brain turning itself inside out I knew I could just sit tight and wait some more, wait for him to come back, wait for things to be different, for my body to stop hurting, for that love to return, because it absolutely had to.

11

My father's grave at Forest Lawn was a few yards to the south of the replica of the Old North Church, not that far from his supposed buddy Telly Savalas. Addie could never verify that and got annoyed when I asked, like there was a story there—a really juicy story, maybe with fist fighting—but she'd zip her lip and change the subject every time.

Graves are hard to find at Forest Lawn—it's a gaudy, hilly place in which to rest, and the Blattner family was angry that my mother planted Eddie Blaine at a flashy cemetery in Glendale among acres of strangers instead of sending his body back to New Jersey to be buried in the Jewish cemetery with his parents.

I had nothing to do except sit in Eddie's house, throw up, and wait for Cole to call me, text me, show up, anything. The silence on that front was deafening, so I went to Forest Lawn, figuring this would be the only time I'd ever see Addie's and Eddie's graves side by side.

After about an hour of searching, I found my father's headstone, which reads (he wrote it, I am told):

EDDIE BLAINE
legendary American singer
born ELI SANFORD BLATTNER
October 31, 1916–May 16, 1990
from Klinger's to Hollywood to The Grave

Two years earlier, I had handled Addie Chambers's burial and end-of-life affairs, after I got a call that she, along with twenty-two other residents of the elder care facility in Thousand Oaks, had died of the virus. Eddie Blaine, long ago, had bought two burial plots at Forest Lawn, one for him and one for my mother, but when my mom married the football guy, she gave the plot to me, and I, picturing my final resting place among the oaks and maples of western Connecticut, gave it to Addie.

I had them write on her tombstone:

VERA ADELINE CHAMBERS
Brill Building songwriter whose songs made you cry
Beloved Aunt, Friend, and Manager
April 25, 1933–September 7, 2020

"Vera Chambers was Eddie Blaine's manager," said the woman sitting on my father's grave when she saw me kneeling in front of Addie's stone with a handful of daisies, yelling above the recording of my father singing "For You Are My Only Love" blaring from her phone. "For over forty years. She went to work as a secretary at the Brill Building in 1955. In 1956 she was given a chance to write a song and, months later, was threatened with getting fired for failing to produce a hit. Eddie Blaine hired Vera and she wrote his hit song, 'Somber Mountain,' which is my favorite song."

I nodded, not looking at her, fighting my impulse to correct her. Since arriving back in Los Angeles, I had been dreading this errand, going to check on the graves because I'd run into the woman Addie called Loony Bird whom we both hated, and we knew she deserved our hatred because Tracy hated her as well. Addie had a history with this woman—phone calls, orders of protection, a private security company that sat outside our house when I was a child—even after Eddie passed. Even a few overnights in the county jail did not compel this woman to give up seeking the attention of Eddie Blaine's heirs.

"Nina Simone, is that you?" the woman shrieked, her stringy white hair catching the wind, blowing in her wrinkled face. "Is that really, really you? Little girl all grown up?"

I pulled my sunglasses off my head and covered my eyes.

Her smile grew wider. "Not Nina Simone the Black lady singer. Nina Simone Blaine, Eddie's daughter! It is you! Your hand! I remember your hand with the missing fingers because you have Bell's palsy!"

Kill me.

She rearranged a set of purple plastic beads around the perimeter of my father's headstone. "It was such a blessing that you were born after Evan died. What a tragedy for your poor father. He was so young. It would have been so wrong for your father not to have any living children."

I trained my gaze on Addie's stone. She would have liked the font, I thought. The stonecutter did a nice job.

"Did you ever have children, Nina? Nina Simone *Lucy-Annie*? Your married name? I never saw anything in the papers about Eddie Blaine being a grandfather. Believe me, I would've noticed!"

My ticking time bomb fetus rested comfortably in my womb. I would not tell this woman that I was pregnant. I'd hoped that my round belly would be chalked up to eating too many cinnamon rolls at Primo's and not some divine blessing upon the earth that required me to deliver Eddie Blaine's grandchild for the pleasure of his dwindling fan base.

This woman, with her heaps of plastic garbage that she'd decorated the ground above my father's powder blue casket, wasn't talking about actual people. That's what it sounded like, and what Addie had said when she'd casually complain to me over the phone. For decades, my dad's numero uno fan had been playing with paper dolls in her head, only the dolls were my family.

"Addie, not Vera, because no one ever called her that, came down here and bawled you out several years ago, I heard, for being here when you were not wanted, and staying after you were asked to leave. Then you got into deep doo-doo with the Glendale PD for refusing to leave my father's grave after Forest Lawn security told you it was time to go, and you spent some time in county for resisting arrest, and when you got out you came back and did the same thing again. I don't want to talk to you."

She beamed. "I want to talk to you, Nina! Because I love Eddie so much!"

"I don't want to talk to you. Leave me alone."

"You're so lucky to be Eddie Blaine's daughter," she said in her childish singsong. *No, I'm not,* I thought, but I didn't need to offer the Loony Bird a flake of my life.

"I said leave me alone. Get out of here."

She took a step closer, and I instinctively moved away from her. "He made eyes at me from the stage at the Flamingo in 1969. The way he hit those high notes in 'Somber Mountain,' kind of like yodeling but not? So talented. I have been in love with him ever since."

"You need to get the fuck away from me," I said, shocked and thrilled by my own newfound capacity to be cruel. "You're in love with a persona. An idea of him. He was a real person, and trust me, you wouldn't have liked the real man, Sandy Blattner. The person you say you're in love with isn't real. Not only because he's been dead for thirty-two years but because the famous Eddie Blaine was fake as hell. Fake, and he knew it and he called himself a phony. He hated himself for leaving his first wife and kid so he could be a D-grade Hollywood hack instead of a Jew and a family man. If he hadn't been the fake bastard he was, I wouldn't be here."

My insides clenched with how badly I wanted to put hurt on this ridiculous person. How I wished she'd evaporate, disappear, leave me alone to what was rightfully mine. Eddie and Addie were my family, my caretakers, two people who loved *me*, and how dare this interloper not only invade what was mine against my explicit wishes but act like she was the victim when I told her to get lost.

"How sad, the way you talk about your wonderful father. When you were born, I sent your father a card and a little stuffed bear. It was so cute. I was hoping to hear back from him, a little thank-you card, but nothing."

"That's because he hated you," I began, clenching my fists, then unclenching them to drop Addie's daisies on the ground. "You were just some stalker who tried to destroy my family."

"How dare you speak to me like that!" she hissed, her sing-song little girl voice making me hate her even more than I thought possible. "You don't understand how much your father means to me!"

"You're a stalker! He hired security to keep you away from our house!"

Dr. Chen, if I told you this story face-to-face, you'd probably say most Americans misunderstand fame. What a strange byproduct of media, of history, that we think we know a stranger because we've seen them in a film or heard them sing a song thousands of times.

I didn't have to respect this woman's delusions. For hadn't my entire life, from the cradle to the grave, suffered from respecting the delusions of others?

The idea that Tracy actually loved my father, that my father's absence from my life wouldn't matter because he cut a few albums that ladies who wore curlers swooned over sixty years earlier. The idea that a whiskey-pickled pisser of a man could be a father to a little kid at the end of his life.

The idea that Nick Sullivan could change his name to Cole Courchaine and suddenly be good, holy, unblameable, a god who could take whatever he wanted with the expectation that it would be given to him without complaint.

The idea that I could hide away in Teagarden for my entire life and never have to feel my feels about any of it. The idea that if I were out of sight, living a small and circumscribed life with a man who owned upward of three hundred knives, then none of these people could hurt me anymore.

The Loony Bird picked the wrong day to show up at Forest Lawn.

"I had planned to leave the other half of these flowers for my father, but it looks like you've taken up every inch of space with your tacky shit," I yelled, feeling only slightly bad when I saw her face fall. She had really gone to town—a pot of bright pink tulips, plastic Mardi Gras beads, two gold foil balloons in the shape of the letters *E* and *B* flapping on their red ribbons, a plastic child's king crown, a handmade sign that said "To Eddie with Love," surrounded by little red heart stickers left over from

Valentine's Day, and the same faded, framed eleven-by-fourteen color photograph of him that she'd been carrying around for decades, the photo lifted from the back of *The Very Best of Eddie Blaine,* featuring a flirtatious thirty-five-year-old Sandy Blattner in goyim drag gazing wantonly at the camera.

"I can move some of it," she offered, grabbing a handful of plastic junk in her hands.

"I want all of it gone," I said, the rage rising in me that I hadn't felt since Greg Hodges lifted me six feet off the ground to save me from Cole and myself and whatever else was lurking in Malibu that night. "Most of this shit is against Forest Lawn's rules anyway. I want you gone. This is the last day of your pathetic life you're going to spend sitting here. I'm having you banned from Forest Lawn and you'll be arrested if you ever come here again."

"You wouldn't do that," she said in her baby voice. Seeing a tatty old woman act like a child made me ill. "That's so mean!"

"I'm not dealing with you ever again. Get out of here, now."

"No, please no," she cried. "Eddie . . . I love him . . . please don't take Eddie away from me. I don't mean to bother you."

"I hate you," I said. "You'd park your car in front of our house, and he wouldn't come home because of you. You stole what little time I had with him! I only had seven years with him, and you think you get to be part of this? Of my family? You don't. You're not a fan, you're a menace. Get out of here," I said, yanking my phone out of my pocket. I got on my feet only to smash her plastic trinkets underneath my boots. She howled as I kicked her candles, stomped on her plastic beads. and popped her stupid balloons.

I snatched her framed photo of my father and held it close to my chest, I had no intention of handing it back to her. "You have two minutes to pack up and leave before I call security and have them take you away."

"Please! Please!" she shrieked. She tried to grab back her photo, but I held it above her head and told her I wasn't giving it back. Her screams were louder than what I heard the night Cole did what he did. She lay on her back in the grass, kicking and begging, grabbing handfuls of the offerings I destroyed. "Eddie! Please! No!"

I walked behind a mausoleum and called Forest Lawn security and, hugging that old photo of my dad, watched from yards away as they stuffed her in the back of a police cruiser.

She didn't get to lay any claim to my father. I didn't care if she had nothing else in her life. I didn't have time for another delusional, selfish person. I didn't have to share him, and I wouldn't.

Eddie was mine, Dr. Chen. She couldn't have him.

12

A few days later, after taking those pills you prescribed, drinking the lemony magnesium drink you sent over, opening the door for the nice person delivering those healthy microwaveable meals you ordered, and doing little else besides crying, sleeping, and watching television, I got this text from Syl:

Chris K died last night. Funeral in a few months in Greece.

Damn. So sorry. I responded.

I'm booking a flight to Athens. I assume you can't travel. If I'm wrong, let me know.

I looked out the window of the SUV I had rented, across the rocks and brown, dusty mountains and low, scrubby vegetation of New Mexico. The shimmering hot parking lot of the Love's Travel Stop in Lordsburg, off Interstate 10, lay before me. I was five months pregnant, and I had spent an hour in a truck stop bathroom shitting and puking my guts out. It was so loud and gruesome that a woman knocked on my stall door and asked if I was okay.

I was sitting in the SUV with a thirty-two-ounce bottle of red Gatorade, a spotty banana that had cost two dollars, and a plastic bag full of tissues I'd been using to wipe the vomit from my lips along the drive from Los Angeles, and with Bruno the Dog next to me panting, sticking his snoot out of the cracked window, not drinking the water I set out for him. Bruno occasionally let out a single whine, as if asking me when he'd finally see Cole.

Small memorial gathering tomorrow night at my place.

Sorry, I won't be there. I'm in New Mexico, I texted back.

NM? Why?

I'm so sorry about Chris.

A pause. *No, you're not. You barely knew him and didn't care for him.*

Another pause, then *Why are you in NM?*

I didn't respond.

Does Tabitha know where you are?

Blainey? Answer me.

Sylvia rang my phone. I let it go to voicemail.

***

Cole greeted me at the front gates of Galatea Ranch, a shabby, hippie-ish hot springs resort in Silver City in a pair of hot-pink swim trunks printed with palm trees and flip flops that showed off his gnarled tree-root feet. He had gone to New Mexico to "clear his head," he explained. He had "a lot to prepare for." He "needed time to meditate and get in touch with God," so he started driving across the desert, stopping only at a Jack-in-the-Box to pee and eat those greasy deep-fried tacos. A shady guy at a roadside motel in Arizona stole his wallet off the counter in the lobby, which was just as well, as it only contained seventeen dollars, eleven Pennsylvania quarters (he hoarded Pennsylvania quarters for some reason), and his PetSmart loyalty card. He had called me late one night because he missed Bruno. Did I have Bruno? He couldn't remember where he left his beloved dog. Could I bring him his dog, please?

I added that he couldn't remember where he'd left his Nina, either.

Galatea Ranch was a cluster of pink Southwest-style buildings surrounding in-ground hot tubs of various sizes and temperatures, shaded by cottonwood trees. When I pulled off the dusty two-lane road and into their gates, Cole was just inside the gates jumping up and down and clapping. Cole leaned into the driver's side window of my rental car and kissed my cheek and told me I'd have to pay the thirty-five-dollar day use fee, as I was now a day user, and opened the back door to dive onto Bruno, who licked the face of his master as if he were a giant ice cream cone.

"You, my delicious woman! You, this beautiful, sacred vessel of the divine! You! My lovely, unseen daughter! And you, my majestic canine! My loves!" He laid a slobbery kiss on my mouth when I climbed out of the car, unsteady on my swollen feet, which hurt like hell because I was pregnant and probably malnourished because I couldn't keep any food down. The sun in New Mexico was closer and meaner than the sun over Southern California and it broiled and mocked me. As I stepped out of the car onto the gravel, Cole bent down to kiss my belly through the spilled-on green cotton dress I wore for my entire drive out to New Mexico.

"I feel sick. I'll hurl in the hot springs," I said.

I followed Cole through the double doors and into the outdoor tub area, which was surrounded by a rickety wooden fence. Galatea Ranch, for being a "health spa," reeked of chlorine and mold. The smell was so strong it was like someone was holding a musty sponge up to my face.

"Please! Hurl in the hot springs. I will bathe in your vomit as tribute to you and our child."

I clutched my stomach. I hated the word "tribute." Why was there so much tributing going on? My belly quivered. There was a living, breathing person in there, and you, Dr. Chen, had jellied my belly and told me it was a girl.

"Chris Kyriakis died," I told him as I pulled off my dress and lowered my naked self into the coolest temperature pool available at Galatea Ranch. Ninety-two degrees Fahrenheit. The bottom of the pool was a little bit slimy. The sun was setting, and the strings of Christmas lights overhead and wrapped around the cacti lit up.

Cole had taped his long scrotum to the side of his left leg with a large amount of masking tape. "Look, it hurts all the time, and it helps to not have it dangling. I might as well get it hacked off, right? Maybe let Ivy have a swing at it? Oh, sorry. Too soon?"

My stomach lurched. I didn't want to talk about Ivy-slash-Ava. If I was to occupy my place in the fantasy world of Cole, he had to concede that there wasn't an Ivy and there hadn't been a finger chopping ceremony which hadn't been the most disgusting, disgraceful display of . . . whatever it was supposed to be a display of.

"Chris died," I said again. "Did you get Sylvia's text?"

He looked at me as if I had said something in a foreign language.

"I guess his heart stopped and he died?"

"Okay? I'm sorry? He and I were not friends and he thought you were a stupid bitch for being in love with me."

"Well . . ."

"You *are* a stupid bitch for being in love with me."

"I thought you should know."

"Did he get the death experience of you, Syl, and Jorie giving him the four-way he so clearly deserved?"

"No."

"Well, look who was the selfish one!"

"Sorry I brought it up."

Cole shrugged. "He hated me. Nobody hates me. I'm extremely lovable."

I thought of Bryn. *The waste of space. He thinks he's John F. Kennedy.*

"If anyone hates me," he continued, "I guarantee it, bad things happen to them."

"Excuse me," I said, crawling out of the pool to vomit into the trash can I had been eyeing since we got there. I clung to its sides while I emptied my stomach of the spotty banana and gas station granola bar I had gotten on my drive.

"Don't let that mean old man in the green cap see you do that. He'll kick you out, you unsanitary wench," Cole shouted as I wretched.

"Where's the bathroom?" I asked.

He paused before answering, to laugh to himself. "Go through the double doors right there and go to the right. You'll see it."

I dried myself off with a towel from a stack next to the trash can and put on my dress. I grabbed my bag—it had my underwear in it, and putting those back on required me to be sitting down—and headed inside to the bathroom, where I rinsed out my mouth in the sink and then sat on the toilet. Rummaging around in my purse for a mint, my phone lit up with a new text.

Hi Nina, it's Kailey E. I have some new information I'd like to discuss with you. This is my private number. I trust you won't misuse it. Please call or text.

While I was sitting on the toilet, trying to decide what to do about Kailey, there was a knock on the bathroom door. "Hello?" a high-pitched man's voice called.

"Yes?"

"Are you Nina?"

"Yes."

"I'm Reggie, the manager," he said. It sounded like a growl. "When you're done in here, could you come to my office next door? There's something I need to discuss with you."

I figured I was in trouble for throwing up in the trash can. Vomit near a hot tub was probably a health code violation, and I assumed he was going to fine me or ask me to personally carry the bag to the dumpster or something, which would have been a little punitive, but fair. I flushed the toilet, put on my undies, checked myself in the mirror, and headed into the narrow, windowless office, where the old man with a mustache sat behind a generic-looking desk.

Reggie wore an orange Hawaiian shirt and had a terrible sunburn on his face. "Mr. Sullivan told me you would take care of his bill," he said matter-of-factly, with some sort of East Coast accent.

So he was Nick, not Cole, at Galatea Ranch. "What?"

"When he got here, he said his wallet got stolen and he told me his friend Nina was the daughter of Eddie Blaine the singer and she could cover it." I hated being referred to as Cole's friend. Had Cole called me his *friend*? The man pushed an itemized bill across the desk for me to look at. Cole had been there for eight nights. He tapped the total at the bottom, circled in red pen: $1275.

I pushed the bill back. "Okay, why did you let him stay here if he couldn't pay for it and he told you someone else would cover it?"

"Well, the last time he was here, he was with a girl who paid the whole bill. She sprung for the deluxe suite and everything. I thought that was you."

"I've never been here before."

Reggie narrowed his eyes. "Look, he said you'd be good for it."

"I'm not paying his bill," I said.

"I can take a card or if you have cash . . ."

Sigrid kicked my stomach. I wasn't done puking up everything I had eaten that day.

"Did he tell you he's running from the law?" I asked. "He chopped off a woman's fingers."

His eyes widened. He recomposed and said, "Didn't say nothing about any fingers. You sound crazy, lady. He wouldn't do that."

I mumbled something about Cole leaving behind his dog.

"This matter isn't up for discussion. You need to give me your card," he said icily. "Or cash."

"You don't believe me?"

"He warned me you were going to say some crazy shit and here you are, saying crazy shit." He held his hand out for the card I wasn't going to hand him. "Sounds like that man's had more than his fair share of crazy women in his life. Listen, we need to start up your tab, missy, so give me your card."

Missy?

A wave of sickness washed over me, and the food still inside of me flew upward and landed on the floor.

We looked down at my mess.

"You shouldn't be going in the tubs if you're sick, Miss Blaine. And I'm gonna have to charge you for having to clean that up."

"I'm pregnant. Cole's the father."

He shook his head, like he couldn't believe what an idiot I was. "Whoever Cole is, he's a poor son of a bitch. I'll be right back with a mop." He yelled Nick's name as he fled the scene in his office. My head began to hurt.

Dr. Chen, I fished in my bag for the key to my rental car. Cole thought he was smart, but he was not so smart as to steal my car key or my wallet or my phone.

My shoes were another matter. They were still out back next to the hot tubs.

Between me and my rental car were about twenty feet of gravel, pebbles, rocks, sharp little bits of New Mexico geological products. Some smooth, some jagged. A large sign at the door instructed visitors to not walk outside without shoes under any circumstances because of the scorpions.

I ran out the door and into the heat, abandoning a very nice pair of leather sandals.

My vision began to fade when I got into the car. I pushed my foot on the gas. My foot felt slippery like there was something between my foot and the pedal. I looked down and saw the dirt and blood smeared all over the floor mat and the pedals, and then, a scorpion about the size of a house key clinging to the bottom of my foot.

I pulled off the scorpion and threw it out of the window of the car, wincing from the pain. My slippery foot slammed on the gas as I peeled out of there.

When I walked back into the Lordsburg Love's Travel Stop and smeared blood from my feet on their very clean floors—here I must commend this Love's location's stringent cleaning protocol—I apologized to the woman working behind the counter. I cried as I paid for a pair of black plastic flip-flops, a first-aid kit, and another Gatorade. Then I went to the restroom to wash the gravel out of the cuts on my feet.

I had to get the hell out of New Mexico. Cole was going to be mad at me for fleeing and not paying his bill. Interstate 10 was mercifully light on other drivers. An hour later, feeling like I was going to faint, I pulled into another Love's Travel Stop (again, very clean). As I was sitting in the parking lot catching my breath, waiting for the white spots in my eyes to calm down, so I could at least make it to Tucson and check into a hotel, my phone rang.

"Nina?"

"Who is this?"

The woman mumbled a name, and I thought I heard her say Sylvia. I had my glasses off and couldn't read the name on my screen. Executive functioning had gone offline.

"Where are you? I'll come get you."

"You'll come get me? You're going to drive all the way here from LA? Sylvia, I'm in New Mexico somewhere. Cole's at some hippie hot springs place here. It's called Galatea Ranch in Silver City off Interstate 10—"

"Oh yes," the voice said. "I know it. Ava and I used to go there together. Is Ava there with him? That's her spot."

"Ava? Syl, who is Ava?"

"Nina, this is Kailey Elwood."

Oh shit.

"Damnit! I'm sorry. I thought you were my friend."

"Nick's at Galatea Ranch, huh? I'll let Steve know. Thank you for being so helpful, Nina."

I clicked the red button on my phone, realizing what I had done. Then I either fell asleep or passed out. I can't really say.

***

"Is this a hospital?" I asked, looking around a small, white room. The window shades were drawn, with a shaft of bright light making a triangle on the floor. My feet were wrapped in bandages, and I had an IV drip in my right arm.

An older man with a white goatee sat on the chair in my room looking at his phone. "You're at UCLA Medical Center. I had you airlifted here. Don't worry about your rental car. I had it returned for you."

"What? Who are you?"

He nodded. "I may have sent some of my employees to look for your car in case Nick was with you. They found you passed out in a parking lot about a hundred miles east of Tucson. That scorpion bite did a number on you. Very dangerous for you and your fetus."

"Who are you? The doctor?"

"I wish. No. I'm the famous Steve Elwood. CEO of Exegesis."

The Steve Elwood?

This guy?

Steve Elwood must hide from the press because I had never seen a photo of him beyond the twenty-year-old ones Cole had shown me. A pasty nerd in his sixties, he was as unremarkable as they came. His hairline had crept back pretty far, but he was still hanging onto what was left of his stringy, graying hair. He had a gut underneath his Death to the Pixies T-shirt. On his feet were a pair of camo-print Crocs. Next to his feet was a purple JanSport backpack, exactly like the one I'd carried in junior high. For being so rich, you'd think this guy wouldn't dress like a kindergartner.

"It looks like you were expecting someone more handsome?" Steve Elwood seemed warmer than I imagined him. "Whatever Nick Sullivan's been saying about me must be good if you were expecting me to look like Brad Pitt."

"Who told you I'm pregnant?" I demanded.

"Tabitha Chen told me. She's a new friend of my family."

You and your big mouth, Blabitha Chen.

"I want to talk to you about Ava. My daughter. Who I obviously failed miserably, judging from this entire situation."

"You want to get Cole arrested, don't you?"

Steve smiled and pressed some button on his phone. "You mean Nick Sullivan, my nemesis? Sure do. Thanks for the tip. He seems to have fled that resort in New Mexico that Ava used to take Kailey to when they were at Pomona together. Any chance you can tell me where he is?"

Steve Elwood wasn't the cops, but I had accidentally called the cops on Cole.

After an awkward silence, Steve said, "Ms. Blaine, he maimed my child," in a louder-than-normal speaking voice. "She claims to have willingly participated in that?" His hands were clenched in fists, trembling. "I mean—Sullivan writing mean, untrue things about me—I don't really care about that. Plenty of people have said worse things about me over the years. But going after my daughter—that's like—does this man have any sense of humanity or does he get his rocks off on hurting people? Like, that's his entire deal now, hurting people. Shouldn't he be dead by now, from having A12 at age forty-six, or does he lie about that, too?"

I shrugged. As hurt as I was, I was not, nor would I ever be, Team Elwood.

Steve clearly needed to talk. "You know, Nick's harassed me for over twenty years now, and I get that he's pissed about that lawsuit from eons ago, but I haven't collected a dime from him in all these years, nor do I care to. His animus toward me makes no sense. It's tired and boring but he seems to get a charge from it. I ignored it for years and then this insane *thing* happened with my child and now I'm being forced to wonder how a man this low, this heartless, exists among us."

Steve Elwood, a wealth hoarder with a below-average record of charitable giving, had no business calling anyone heartless. I smiled. "He said you were secretly a rich kid who pretended to be poor but went to Stanford and knew everyone in the Silicon Valley."

"He can say whatever he likes about me, Ms. Blaine. As far as that goes, he's the one who preys on wealthy women. Multiple women at a time," he said, pointing a finger at me, "but he needs me to be the rich kid? My parents had five kids to put through school. My father worked for a logging company. I'm a graduate of the University of Oregon. Go Ducks! But there's always been this rumor of how I lie about having gone to Stanford, when actually he lied about going to Harvard. Nick started that rumor, back when he had that blog. Nick was always projecting. And he loves spreading around those doctored photos of me in the nude at a party. He photoshopped that years ago and still shows them off like anyone cares."

"Oh?" I asked.

Steve Elwood pushed his glasses further up his nose. "I will not say I have been 100 percent faithful to my partners, Ms. Blaine, but I will say that I haven't been to a party that wasn't a fundraising event or a wedding since college. I'm very boring and a workaholic."

"Okay, not sure what that has to do with anything."

"I'm telling you he's a liar, Ms. Blaine, and not a very good one."

"Okay."

He must have sensed I was not in agreement with him. "Seducing my daughter Ava and doing what he did. Sure, that's sick and, yes, Ava hates me for marrying Kailey, and obviously what you should do to retaliate against your old man is to jump into bed with the cretin who has made it his life's work hating your old man and spreading lies, especially all those lies about me garnishing his wages. Boo-hoo, he can't hold a job, Elwood is such a meanie. That stunt with my daughter was beyond the pale." Steve paused to blow his nose into a tie-dyed handkerchief that he pulled from the backpack. That Steve Elwood looked and acted like someone's jokey dad kept confusing me. I expected a slick Bret Easton Ellis villain, and he was the biggest dork, like he wandered out of a Magic the Gathering tournament into my hospital room by mistake looking for the restroom. He stuffed the hankie into his backpack and pulled out a giant green water bottle covered with stickers. He took a long sip.

"But you're the real girlfriend, right?" he shot at me, the straw part of his water bottle still in his mouth. "Ava's some side piece. Stand by your man and all that."

"I don't want to talk to you about this."

"No offense, but how did he manage to knock up a forty-year-old with A12? Like, how is that possible?"

"Ask your new bestie, Dr. Chen. She's here somewhere," I said.

"I will, if you don't mind."

We were quiet for a while. "It really hurt to read what Kailey had written about your daughter having A12."

Steve nodded. "I apologize for that. You can understand that we were shocked and saddened by her diagnosis."

"Don't have any more children," I told him.

He laughed in that uncomfortable way men laugh when you tell them something they're going to disregard, because you are smaller than them, and how stupid you must be to say words they don't want to hear.

"You're too old," I plowed forward.

"Don't you think you're too old?" Steve asked.

I said quietly, "Not like you."

"I am too old. Old rich men do old rich men things like make babies with young women who are way out of their leagues, right? Maybe Kailey did marry me for my money. She sure as hell didn't marry me for my looks, though that doesn't explain how it is that a man as revolting as Nick Sullivan gets the hot chicks, but some things in life transcend explanation."

"I have A12, too. I'm no different from Cole."

"Yes, you are. You really can't see how? How unattractive he is?"

I took offense to that, really. "If he's unattractive, so am I."

"No, no. That is categorically false, my dear. Other than your three-fingered hand, I honestly can't tell that there's anything different about you. He looks like a freakish, misshapen horror show. You look like a pleasant, attractive girl who is missing a couple of fingers."

What about my bulging eye, I thought but didn't say. I didn't know if I should thank him for this. I'd been walking around assuming I was a circus freak for decades. The opinion of Steve Elwood, tech billionaire, shouldn't have mattered. He was not my friend. But he was now one of a handful of men who called me attractive.

"If Cole is ugly, then so am I. And so is your baby."

Steve Elwood ignored the ring of his phone to continue his soliloquy. "But yes, Nina, I know that I likely won't get to see Zinn as, say, a thirty-year-old, the way I get to see my older daughters be adults. And that is absolutely a disservice to her. Deeply unfair. Now some people will say it doesn't matter because Zinn will never have to work a day in her life and can take her inheritance and buy her own island and sixty-five Lamborghinis, so what does it matter that her dorky old man isn't around? But I know she'll probably argue that it does matter. If I'm lucky. I'm sure I have put Zinn in an emotional lose-lose situation the way your father did, yes?"

I wasn't going to cry in front of this guy, but I knew I was going to anyway. "The only other person, besides Cole, to ever express that to me was my father's first wife."

"I know what I did, Nina. You don't need to explain it to me. Zinn is loved and she will continue to be loved whether I'm dead or alive. Maybe you weren't, though, which explains why you have your knives out for men like me. And if that's the case, I'm very sorry."

I nodded, wondering to myself what his voluntarily mutilated daughter might say about being loved by her father.

"What are you going to name your baby?" he asked.

"Alice Roosevelt," I lied.

"I hope she is able to transcend her lineage," Steve said, standing up from his chair and reaching for his purple backpack. "I'm not the monster that Nick claims I am, or at least I hope I'm not. There are those who look at their lot in life and aren't happy with it, and either they fight for better and grow into a more evolved soul, or they, like that scumbag boyfriend of yours, do the opposite. It was nice to meet you, Ms. Blaine. I hope you stay in touch with Kailey. She's a good mom to our little octopus. Let me know if you need anything."

"Thanks, but I won't," I said. "I'm going to die right after she's born. A12."

"Oh? I hope that isn't true, but if it is, I'm so sorry. Who will take care of your baby?"

"That's a secret," I said. He nodded and said he understood.

Selfishly, I didn't want you to take Sigrid to the Elwood mansion for play dates, Mama Tabs. But maybe that's wrong of me—maybe Siggy should have an A12 friend her own age.

13

ADDIE: Look whose here!

LITTLE NINA: (yelling, happy kid on Eddie's lap) Nina!

EDDIE: (in his velvety singing voice, now raspy and weakened)

> *What do you mean-uh*
> *That I'm in love with Nina*
> *So in love with Nina*
> *The best girl in town!*
> *She is never mean-uh*
> *Because she's my Nina*
> *Adorable and polite*
> *She keeps us up all niiiight!*
> *No need to explain*
> *Nina Blaine is the most*
> *Beautiful girl in town!*

ADDIE: Daddy has a great singing voice, doesn't he, Nina?

LITTLE NINA: Yes!

EDDIE: Your aunt Addie is too kind. She also believes she gets paid extra for praise like that.

LITTLE NINA: I'm the most beautiful!

EDDIE: (gives me a big kiss on the cheek) Yes, you are, baby doll. Yes, you are.

ADDIE: Nina, sweetie, do you have any questions for your father? Before—

I slammed the space bar on my laptop to pause the video. I could never watch the last video past this spot, where Addie catches herself on the word *before*. Like *before he goes. Before he dies.*

Because he was going to die.

That old leathery man there, coughing above my head. How could he leave me?

*****

"Why didn't you ever have children?" sounds different when you pose the question to a renowned medical researcher and physician with an office wall as bejeweled with diplomas and awards as yours, Dr. Tabitha Y. Chen, MD, PhD, Wellesley, Stanford, UCLA. That you and you alone can map my DNA, know me and mine on a literally cellular level, and then go into semi-retirement to take on your belated pass at motherhood, depriving the new generation of A12 babies of your services.

"I am a human trash sack," never really got me off the hook with my lack of fecundity and lack of remorse over that lack. I'm not bitter or anything. I'm just wondering if being a doctor twice over got you out of performative femininity.

And yes, Mama Tabs, I'll assume you'll want me to answer the question that goes, *So wait a minute . . . Cole hacking off the ring and pinky finger of a woman he was having sex with, mostly because she was the daughter of his nemesis, didn't make you fall out of love with the guy? It was that he tried to stick you with a check?*

Listen to me, I say, emulating my father's old-timey New York accent that he couldn't hide when he drank or got tired.

Listen to me, Doctah Chen!

You know me on a cellulah level, Doctah Chen! But do you really know my haht?

And here, since we're doing a bit, you would say:

Nina! I've been studying your haht for thirty yeahs! Lookit, these MRIs! It's so big! It's enlahged! You got a big haht!

And the laugh track not only plays, it *sings.*

***

This is all to say that after Steve and Kailey Elwood saved me from dying from a scorpion bite, I began to miss Sigrid.

She was in there, sitting on my bladder. I knew her. Felt her. I didn't want to love her with that connective, deep love. But she was inside of me, my unexpected end-of-life bestie and living proof that sometimes you, Doctor, are full of shit.

I tried so hard not to think about her that way. I tried not to talk to her. I tried not to wish for things in her future.

I thought that I would die and you would have to ghoulishly remove her from my corpse, like Abe Kruse himself came back from the crypt and made my life into a movie.

Remember how I'm a human trash bag? Human trash bags aren't supposed to want things. I'll get shamed for wanting things, up to and including the love child I made with Cole the night his daughter told him to fuck off.

I sneak peaks at Bryn's internet presence. Like looking into the future at what Siggy might be like when she grows up.

Allow me to kvell about Bryn a bit:

Did you know that Bryn was third in her class at Lowell High School, one of the most selective high schools in San Francisco?

Did you know that Bryn served as her mother's maid of honor when she married Carlo Robinson, acclaimed tenor, in 2018?

Did you know that she turned down Princeton, Williams, and the University of Chicago, and chose Berkeley to stay close to home?

Did you know that she got into Stanford Medical School? Yeah, you probably had something to do with that.

Did you know Bryn called me a "stupid cunt" that one time I met her? You have to really love that younger generation for saying stuff like that.

***

When I returned to my father's house on Wayne Avenue, empty and cold and a little funky smelling because I left town with an unflushed toilet (California water crisis always at the fore, right?), there was a message from Sylvia waiting for me. Typed up, sealed in a goldenrod Notley Vineyards envelope, taped to my door.

Dear Nina,

You're not answering your phone and I don't know why or what that means. I assume you're avoiding me on purpose. I called Tracy. She said she didn't know where you were.

My mother and I are leaving LA for a few weeks starting tomorrow. We are the subjects of a documentary about my father, and they are filming us traveling to Washington, DC, with my father's piano, which we are donating to the Smithsonian. We'll be on a road trip for the next two weeks, with no privacy. I'm not looking forward to this—I've been dreading the day I send the piano away, but here we are. My mama is turning eighty during the trip and we have a huge party planned for her in Memphis, with some Notley relatives and scholars in attendance. And I'm turning forty very soon. As are you.

There is a real chance we may never see each other again. I want you to know that I love you and that having you as a friend, not only as a fellow Twelver but as a Bonnie and an Angeleno and a person who always picked up her phone until now . . . I am grateful to have known you, Blainey.

What happened with me and Cole nine years ago is none of your business and the fact that he told you to make trouble between us or to stop you from aborting . . . well, I hope I'm wrong about his intentions but that's what my gut is telling me. I owe you an apology—I shouldn't have conveyed to you that Cole was a nice person to date. I get why you like him—Twelver, he's cute and funny and he says the things you've spent your life wanting to hear. But he's also kind of mean. Not because of the Elwood thing, but he was deeply unkind to Chris K. I get why Cole wouldn't like Chris as a person, but we were a support group, and he was anything but supportive toward him.

But also I wish you weren't pregnant with Cole's baby. I feel like he did that on purpose to be evil. How he pulled it off I can't understand. But from where I sit, that was an evil thing to do to another human being, especially to one who loves him as much as you do.

I will not contact you any further, as I sense you don't want to talk to me, and I don't want to be the friend who comes at you hard with things you don't want to hear. You aren't well, and I worry about you, but that kid's due in February and after that, I don't imagine we'll have much time.

I'm going to direct my energy to my mother and our documentary and to myself. Thank you for everything. You are and were a very important part of my life, dear friend. Love and blessings to you and your child.

xo, SMN

***

I sent a text to Jorie asking her if she had seen Syl before she left town.

Hi, who is this? Jorie's text reply read.

Nina

Sorry, could you tell me more?

Jorie, is that you? It's Nina Blaine

This is Jacqui, her ex-wife in Colorado

Hi! Is Jorie okay?

Jorie passed away last Friday

What? I had no idea. I'm so sorry.

Yes

May I ask what ended her life?

We had plans to be with her at the end of her life, I texted.

A few minutes passed.

No offense, but she was miserable in LA. I wish she'd never gone back. She was in a support group with a bunch of spoiled brat idiots. I was her only family. She came here two weeks ago and got very sick. She went peacefully. Her mom died a few years ago, and her older sister is ninety and has dementia. She had no one else but me.

I'm very sorry, I texted.

Me too. Poor Jorie. What a waste.

***

One of the reasons I fell in love with Cole was that he shared my indifference toward family. Cole's family, per his stories, had done him dirty. Of the nine Sullivan children, seven were still alive, and he only spoke to Laura, child number eight, born when their mother was forty-six.

Laura loved Cole more than anyone else. She would tell anyone this. Cole was her baby, her "Little Nicky." She carried him around the house and fed him with a bottle and pulled him down the street in a red wagon that she'd turned into a little bed with pillows. Cole loved Laura because Laura loved him no matter what. Even as an adult, she still called him her Little Nicky and doted on him.

The rest of the family had an investment in his behavior, which he couldn't understand. He was mostly a good kid—he got good grades and stayed off drugs. He attended a private high school on scholarship, where he charmed teachers and won academic awards. He got a scholarship to the University of Rochester but left after a year because everyone there, he insisted, was stupid.

Cole fought with his parents after Sullivan child number seven, Michael, died of a drug overdose. His mother was ashamed, and she'd yell at him to not be like Mikey. There was no real language for grief in their house. Cole's father died a few years after Mikey did, and his mother didn't cry when she lost him either.

Cole and Mikey were never close, as Mikey couldn't be bothered with Cole's existence. But Cole appreciated that his brother showed him that there was a way out of the family, out of expectation. All you had to do was break a rule and poof, you were gone.

The older six Sullivan siblings found fault with Little Nicky. He was a liar, a cheat. He bragged and acted superior. He lived in a fantasy world that made no sense and would get nasty if you questioned his version of reality. Over the years, each sibling found a reason to cut their littlest brother out of their lives.

But not Laura. Laura was only three years older than Nick. Nick would ask his mother why Laura wasn't his mom. Laura was better than his mom. She gave him more hugs. She let him play with all her toys.

Why, he asked me once in a voice so small I could barely hear him, couldn't I love him the same as Laura?

***

Forgive me for being discursive, Dr. Chen, but my clock is running out.

A history lesson:

Teagarden, Connecticut, was a hamlet in Litchfield County that consisted of a boarding school for privileged runaways, a quaint bed and breakfast, Chef Paul's Michelin-rated Italian restaurant that shuttered during the pandemic, and a Sunoco gas station with a Subway inside. For miles on all sides, there are farms, houses, rolling hills, trees, and a few other gas stations. In fact, the Village of Teagarden exists because Ethel Hale Bondurant (1880–1949) once wrote a (failed) fantasy novel called *Teagarden*, so she renamed the twenty-five acres that she inherited from her dead husband "Teagarden," basically after herself, and somehow it worked out that Teagarden got its own zip code.

Ethel Hale was the precocious and lazily beautiful daughter of a Hartford doctor who quit Smith College in 1900 to marry a man named Lawrence Bondurant, who was a Gilded Age financier who owned several hotels and office buildings in Manhattan. Mr. Bondurant had inherited the land in Litchfield County that sits underneath the school, Stella di Capra, and the Sunoco station (the three Ss of Teagarden). Lawrence Bondurant was very good at earning money, but not very good at being a husband, and they had no children. When he politely died when Ethel was thirty-seven, she sold off his assets, and built a beautiful, whimsically designed school for girls who "had more to offer the world than what their hands or breasts could produce," which, yes, Dr. Chen, you can buy a T-shirt with that slogan on it in the bookstore. (Put down the deposit for your daughter's Bondurant education now!)

Campus legend had it that Ethel, a lesbian, had very cannily decided that if she was going to have a passionless marriage, it would be to a millionaire. Fair play if so, but I think she merely loved money and her own mind far more than she could love Lawrence or anyone else.

Lawrence Bondurant was rich, but he was not a good-looking man. Ol' Larry was forty years old when he wed young Ethel quietly at her family's church in Hartford. She was his first and only wife. Tintypes from 1900 being what they were, their wedding photo, widely distributed on Bondurant admissions literature, shows a smirking young woman in a white lace gown standing beside a grumpy, anxious, stone-faced man in a suit and top hat, looking not like he had just taken a bride but a huge shit. (I can't take credit for that—that's Sylvia's comment from junior year—it got a lot of laughs in the dining hall during Taco Tuesday.)

The Bondurant School was studied by architectural historians frequently because it had, on purpose, cobblestone paths that lead to nowhere. The terminating point of the path out of Old Main is a patch of ferns in the woods. The red brick pathway out of Seelye Hall went to the dumpsters behind the dining hall. At the time of the school's founding, Ethel would place *objets d'art* of her own making in those spots. Her hobby was sculpture, and the elaborately built stone paths were a stunt to get people to look at her funky statues of big-breasted women assuming positions that a human body could not achieve.

It isn't lost on me that I spent my teenage years in the real-life fantasy world of a wealthy, artsy woman. I claim strong emotional attachment to the place because, for me, it represented safety. It was far from the ice-cold house my mother saw as her just dessert for being so darn pretty, and the stepfather who would have put me in a bag on the curb on pickup day if he could have. Bondurant was bright and warm and fun, and there were books, and I sang in the choir and performed in plays. It was all well and good until it was over and then and only then did I feel what Sylvia felt at night when she would pine for the comfort of her mother and spend hours curled up on her bed with the beige, curly phone cord wrapped around her feet, crying, wishing she could be with her. Sylvia wasn't running away from anything at Bondurant—her mother was in Ghana on a Fulbright her first year there, and Bondurant was a short drive away from her uncle and his family in New Haven.

Bondurant was the only real home I knew, and how sad is that?

I can picture baby Nicholas Sullivan alone on the couch in a narrow house at the top of a hill on Anaheim Street, Pittsburgh, in the winter of 1977. The walkway to the door is badly shoveled—there is ice and a pile of old boots on the porch. Up the brick steps and through the front door, the TV is on, there is dinner on the table, and the air smells of cigarettes and mashed potatoes. There are nine other bodies in the house, but no one is minding Nicky. Maybe Nicky has a Cookie Monster doll he puts in his mouth, or maybe his brothers come in the room and throw him on the floor so they can watch the TV.

Laura hovers over the couch and wants to hold him, reaching out her hands to grab his little body, but someone always stops her. No one lets Laura hold baby Nicky.

Rosie yells at Cindy, now the oldest girl in the house as the eldest sister has married and moved out, to please give Nicky his bottle. Cindy doesn't hear or forgets. He shrieks for hours until Rosie comes and sees her starving baby boy with a full diaper, begging to be fed. She is too tired to notice his hunger and discomfort and falls asleep on the couch while holding the bottle to his mouth. Her hand slips, the bottle falls out, and his screams do not wake her.

At some point, Nicky gets older and starts taking this type of treatment personally. If only Nicky was more——, his mother would feed him on time, his father would notice him and smile at him, his older siblings wouldn't pry him from Laura's arms, and he wouldn't clown around at school, needing the teacher to praise him and tell him how smart and funny he was.

If he could make himself into someone worthy of love and care, he would receive it.

People toss around the term *daddy issues*, as if it's a girl's responsibility to take one on the chin for her father in perpetuity. All Eddie Blaine ever did was die when I was a little kid, but from that experience, what was I supposed to do? Mature into a grief-proof little oak tree with endless grace, a complex understanding of human relationships, and the ability to rise above every ball of shit that was ever thrown at her, as if able to fly? A tall order for a seven-year-old girl who watched her old man die while he garbled the name Ruth over and over.

It took me until now, knowing Cole, to recognize what Eddie was crying over during the last minutes of his life.

Eddie Blaine was a character. Maybe not as pathological as the pretend Cole Courchaine, and maybe antisemitism and the way Hollywood worked had more to do with Eddie Blaine forsaking Sandy Blattner and becoming a human shiny bauble singing over soaring strings.

Per Tracy, I knew my father could be mean and boring. He could crack a joke, but he couldn't take one. He would laugh and laugh when he took a stinky old man dump and left the bathroom door wide open to upset my mother, like that was the pinnacle of domestic comedy.

But my father was so loved in his life. By so many people—from Ruth to my mother to his ghoulish grave-sitting fan who, I believe, was responsible for throwing eggs at the house, which I only noticed when my pregnancy-enhanced sense of smell registered the odor of sulfur near the front door.

Someone threw eggs at the house.

I was extremely pregnant, had a throbbing migraine, could smell the dust in the couch cushions, and couldn't keep dry toast and lemon La Croix down. I thought it meant that someone cared enough about me and/or my father to throw those eggs.

Maybe it was Rosie Sullivan's forgotten baby boy, trying to get my attention.

If you, sequestered in your own madness, take apart this story, strip it down to its foundation and check it for termites, you'll note that Cole never actively loves anyone. He is always on about his debts—what he should have, what others owe him, who wronged him. Nothing was ever his fault.

Throughout all of this, I missed Cole.

He was, like Ruth had said of my father, "the sun and the moon and the stars."

Because he was, in stillness and in lust, the human manifestation of the absence I felt by my family.

Read that again if you must. Make sure Sig never knows what I mean by that.

Eddie Blaine, the deadest dead guy who ever died. Tracy, bad at math, always smiling for the camera. What more was I supposed to be?

***

Two months before I gave birth to our little binky-boo, I went to the courthouse, threw down some cash, and scratched Nina Simone Blaine from the record and became Nina Ruth Blattner. I didn't want my name to be a reminder of my father's fictional self, and I didn't want to bother the real Nina Simone any more than I already had. I had been meaning to do this for years. Everyone around me had changed their name, so why not me?

I sent my mother a text so she could update her records.

"Okay, sweetie," she responded. "I hope that brings you peace."

*****

The package sitting on the front porch of the house seemed normal. A normal cardboard box. Had I ordered anything that would have been mailed from Cranberry Township, Pennsylvania?

Inside, there were packing peanuts and a ball of bubble wrap taped up with blue painters' tape, about the size of a soccer ball.

The note, handwritten on the back of an Andy Warhol Museum postcard, read: *I'm the only man to ever give you what you won't admit you want.*

There was a cold pack inside the box.

I held the cold ball of packing material in my hand.

There was a strange antiseptic odor to the ball in my band.

Iodine?

I undid the tape slightly, but I knew. I knew what he had sent me.

When you sign a contract when you mail a package via the United States Postal Service, where you say there are no aerosols, weapons, explosives, or human body parts, and now, the father of the little kicker sitting on my bladder had lied to a postal worker to mail me this completely unsubtle package, like I had never seen *The Big Lebowski.*

This is the thing, Dr. C: Your mental landscape becomes a nonstop lie audit machine after a while, after extended contact with a guy like Cole. Evidence provided: He lied to a random postal employee. He packed up Ava Elwood's severed fingers and lied to the buttons on the little machine when it asked if his box contained human specimens. This violated my sense of integrity. Civil servants deserve respect. Of course, he had lied to me plenty of times, but you don't immediately see those lies when that same mouth tells you your biggest truths, the smallest little hidden bits of your very being, the bits you've held in the dark for so long they don't even exist as words.

The arrival of the fingers added extra vomiting to my already packed schedule that day, and, finally, I was angry.

Cole? I texted. *You suck for abandoning me during my pregnancy*

I waited a few seconds and added, *I'm in a lot of pain please come home and help me I need you*

For the first time in two months, he texted back immediately. *I suck?*

Yeah, you do, I replied. *And WTF with that package? That's disgusting*

I ABANDONED you? I didn't do anything to you

A few moments passed and then, *If you've told anyone that I've abandoned you, you can go leap off a tall building. Do not say my name to anyone. I mean it*

And then, *Your father abandoned you. I did nothing!*

And then, *Are you even really pregnant? Seems like something you'd lie about to get your hooks in me*

And then, *Eddie Blaine's little girl can't say thank you for the nice gift? Put it in the freezer and forget about it, then*

Wow, I hit back. *Why are you being so hurtful?*

I'm not being hurtful. You're being rude and spreading lies about me. I'm blocking your number. You're way out of line.

I'm out of line? WTF is wrong with you?!? I texted back.

No response.

Sigrid gave me a good hard kick, and I crawled to the bathroom to puke again.

14

I suppose you all had a meeting. The Siggy Squad, let's call it. You, Dr. Chen: newly radicalized by those screenshots of my final text exchange with Cole. Steve Elwood, hot to turn Cole in to the fuzz and rich enough to make it happen. Sylvia Notley, arbiter of justice, fixer of my mistakes. And my mother, because why not? Tracy's always down to clown, especially if wealthy types are involved. Maybe Steve-o flew you all to Gdansk in his private jet to Make Plans and you toasted my death and the privileged, miraculous life of Emily Lucille Chen (You back-stabbing, betraying, overused name-giver, Dr. Chen! I told you *Sigrid Alma* and you were like, no, she's going to be *Emily Lucille.* Half of the girls in my class at Bondurant were named Emily. *Sigrid Alma Sacred Honor*!) Then you all got drunk on currant wine and sauna-ed, then you flew home on his private jet. (That nurse put something very special in my IV drip! Drugs! Light and feathery, I am, I am!)

I really wanted to go to Gdansk. It looked so cute in photos. Chef Paul hated to travel. The furthest he and I ever traveled was to Florida for his grandmother's funeral. I wanted to see Poland someday. My paternal grandparents immigrated from Poland. Now I am out of somedays.

You could have warned me that shit was about to go down, Dr. C!

There was a knock at the door of the Eddie Blaine manse. Syl was gone. Jorie was gone-gone, as was Chris. Cole had made me his number one enemy. That left only one person besides yourself and Chef Paul who knew where to look for me.

I hadn't left the house in over a week and crawled from the living room to the front door. On the other side of the door, my mother banged away, screaming bloody murder, "Nina, let me in!"

Piles of take-out containers and flimsy plastic bags from 888 Vietnamese Deli covered the living room floor. The only food I could eat and keep down was their #10, beef pho with brisket. Every day at four o'clock, their delivery guy dropped my soup container on the porch. I crawled, my belly heavy with child, to retrieve the bag, crawled back, and sipped on the broth until it was cold, and I spent what felt like hours chewing the bite-sized bits of beef and the cold, stuck-together clump of rice noodles, because my baby needed the nutrition. (I also ate the turkey meatball dish you sent from the fancy food delivery place, but the pho was the only thing I could count on to stay down.)

Tracy stepped right over me. Her toenails were painted the same shiny gold as her sandals, which she wore even though it was November. "Holy hell, this place smells like a horse's ass!" She carried a bright pink bouquet of flowers in a glass vase. "For your birthday, Nina. Happy birthday." She moved aside a pile of pho empties on the coffee table to set it down.

My birthday had been two days earlier. That great big birthday. Forty. There had been no celebration. No one called. No one even sent a damn card. My fortieth birthday cake was going to be an enormous monument to my longevity as a Twelver. Italian meringue icing. Edible glitter. Three tiers. Dark chocolate cake made with the highest-quality Ecuadorian cocoa. The cake I'd fantasized about for years never came to be. It was just as well. The thought of eating cake made me ill.

My mother nattered about, trash-talking Eddie Blaine's house. Had she failed to notice that my stomach was engorged with a giant baby, and I was crawling like a tortoise behind her back to the stack of pillows on the living room floor where I had made my nest in front of my laptop? I was rewatching season seven of *The Office*. The best season, in my opinion.

My mother looked around the house. "Oh, Eddie. What was so damn special about this ugly-butt house?" Her Texas twang had returned. "Addie never did anything with it since the seventies. How we suffered because your father wouldn't let me have this house, much less live in it when we were broke after he died."

Would it matter if I pointed out to Tracy that we weren't broke? My mother had a job: She did make up for the actors on the set of the CBS soap operas. She was good at it, and it paid the bills. But she had long screamed from the mountaintops that Eddie Blaine should have set her up good. It was easier to be mad at him than to mourn him.

"Mom?"

She was in the kitchen, opening and closing the drawers and cupboards. "Give me a minute. This ridiculous house! I can't breathe!"

"Neither can I."

"This house, my lord! My eyes hurt!" she said, touring the bathroom. "Mirrors on the ceiling? Really? The wallpaper in the bathroom is really something. That harvest gold stove still works?"

"It's my ugly house now," I shouted.

"What was the big deal about this place?"

"Mom?"

"Nina Simone? Sorry, Nina *Ruth*. Ruth like Eddie's first wife?"

"Ruth because it rhymes with truth. Could you come in here, please? Bring me a seltzer from the fridge, too."

My mother slid off her sunglasses. "What, you can't get your own seltzer? Oh my god, what the hell happened to you?"

"I can't get my own seltzer, no," I said softly. "If I could, I wouldn't ask."

"You look pregnant," she said.

"I am."

"How?" She sat down on the couch and hunched over me, squinting like I was algebra and she had five seconds to solve me.

"Unprotected sex."

Tracy sucked in her breath. "That guy . . . the guy who harasses Steve Elwood like it's his job. He did this to you? I heard what he did to Steve Elwood's daughter."

I clutched my belly to protect who was inside. "Did to me? Like I didn't participate?"

"Why didn't you get an abortion?" my mother said, louder than necessary.

I shrugged. "I exercised my right to choose."

"You look terrible!"

"I feel terrible. I'm at the end of my life and everything sucks."

Tracy sat back on the couch. "I'll kick that son of a bitch's ass for knocking you up. You're not supposed to be pregnant, like, ever! Especially not at forty. He isn't here, is he?"

"Could you get me a seltzer from the fridge? I'm in a lot of pain and it hurts to move and I'm having trouble breathing and if I sit up, the baby shifts onto my bladder and I pee my pants. Please?"

She sighed loudly. I wasn't supposed to ask Tracy for favors.

"Where's Sylvia?" she asked. "She's not here helping you?"

"In Washington, DC, with her mom, filming a documentary."

"You and your stuck-up friend!" Tracy groaned. "Aren't you mad there's no Eddie documentary?"

"Mom, she's not stuck up. You hate her because she's my friend and she sticks up for me. And you're racist. A confident Black woman makes you uncomfortable."

She made a pouty face at me. "That's not true!"

"Look, no one cares about Eddie Blaine. Except me and his lunatic fan who I got banned from Forest Lawn."

"Oh, that poor woman," Tracy started, clutching her heart. Years earlier, she was signing onto Addie Chambers's protective orders and now she was defending her? "Feel sorry for her, Nina. Don't get her banned from the cemetery."

"She's a menace," I said. "I don't want her sitting on Dad's grave every day."

"You're a mean little girl, Nina. She's a poor, probably mentally ill, old lady with nothing and nobody in her life and all she's doing—"

"I'm going to ask you to leave if you don't *shut up*, Tracy. And can I please have my seltzer?"

"That's how you solve problems, you get rid of people. Like you got rid of Paul." Finally, she went to the kitchen and came back with a can of fizzy water, and I took a much-needed sip.

"Paul got rid of me. Just like Grandpa Jesse got rid of you. *You looked like a two-dollar whore on that television program,*

Tracy Jane, making eyes at that Jew," I said in my grandfather's deep Texas drawl, parroting Bryn and her impersonation of Cole's father. "*Why can't you be more like Julie and Wendy? Why'd I get two regular daughters and one circus clown hooker?*"

I clutched my belly. Throwing up wouldn't have been the worst thing, especially if I aimed it on Tracy's shiny exposed-in-November gold toes. "I wish Cole were here. He'd destroy you before picking you up and physically throwing you out the door."

"What would that classy man say to me? The man who cut a girl's fingers off!"

I went full Bryn: "That your father was right! You're a circus clown hooker who sold out her own daughter for some sex offender slab of beef because he was a football player. Because he made you look good to your shallow parents."

Tracy winced. "No, that's what you'd say to me."

I smiled to myself. Telling off Tracy to her face was one of the advantages of A12 and this death-sentence pregnancy. "You couldn't face yourself and you needed a man around to give you your sense of worth. No man and you were nothing. It didn't matter if that man treated your daughter, and *you*, like shit. Your only daughter owed you a favor and that was to pretend to not exist. And way to go, getting yourself a couple of manly men sons who wouldn't embarrass you by being disabled and reminding you of that time you were young and stupid and you married that corny old guy. Finally, the third Westervelt sister married a real man and Big Jesse would stop telling you not to come to Dallas unless you have on dark sunglasses and pretend to be the housekeeper! Hell, maybe he even let you drive his Cadillac after Greg put a ring on your finger and finally made Daddy love you."

Tracy didn't have a comeback. She looked at me with her mouth open.

"You didn't even show up for Eddie's funeral. You told me to lie to everyone and say you were sick."

"I . . ." She had nothing.

"Well, there it is, Tracy. You can see yourself out. I'm not in any shape to fight with you. This is probably the last time you'll ever see me. My baby has an adoptive mother. You are very legally not allowed to have this baby. All taken care of with lawyers and everything."

"Wow," she said. "You are awful."

"I'm doing you a favor. The baby could have A12. She could look like me. Can you imagine raising two ugly children? What would your family say?"

Tracy's cheeks reddened. "I don't want to raise another child, kiddo! The way you've rejected your brothers, I reject your baby! I'll save myself a ton of worry by not being grandma to your little bastard."

I said nothing.

"My father thought I was a circus clown hooker? Well, Big Jesse thought you were a monster! He asked me once why I didn't put you down like a junkyard dog when I had the chance!"

I began to shake. "Do you not hear yourself?"

"What do you and Sylvia and Paul and that nice man who knocked you up say about me, huh? That I'm so nice and pretty? That I'm the best mom in the world?"

Sigrid shifted and I held back the acid crawling toward my throat. "It isn't the same. You were the adult." A trickle of warm pee dripped down my leg. "You spend your whole life calling me a monster, and you wonder why I'm not happy to see you?"

"I tried to help you—"

"You paid thousands of dollars for fertility treatments so you could have a do-over kid with ten fingers who wasn't half Jewish."

"You're not Jewish, Nina! Eddie never went to temple. He never said anything about raising you Jewish."

"That's not what he told me!" I was thinking of the Addie-Eddie videos that Tracy didn't know about. "I'll be dead in a month, Tracy. You're mad that I'm the only person who doesn't give you a pass because of your looks. Which, by the way, are gone now because you got old, like Eddie Blaine."

Tracy sat on the edge of my couch. "You're lying on the floor pregnant by a man who chopped off some girl's fingers, and you think you're better than me? Who the hell are you?"

"That man punched Greg in the face! He's the love of my life! How wonderful that I lived to see a man punch that fucker square in the nose and give him a sharp kick to the balls. My hero!"

"He what?" Her voice went up two octaves. "When did he see Greg?"

I didn't answer. She didn't need to know.

Her voice got grave. "When the hell did you see Greg?"

I shrugged. "Not telling."

"Goddammit, Nina, where did you see Greg?"

"In hell, with Grandpa Jesse."

She shook her head and sighed. "Nina, I did the best that I could with you. You could have gotten those plastic surgeries. You didn't want to. You're a monster because you choose to be one. Maybe the best way I knew how to love you was to make sure other people loved you, too. You thought you could change the world, but you hid from it. Maybe that makes me a bad mother—"

"It does," I said.

"You had every chance and every privilege. You wanted to be ugly, and you wanted to be angry. You hid in a tiny town in the middle of bumfuck nowhere for how long and you blame me for doing what I had to do to keep a roof over our head—"

"They're called jobs, *Tracy.*"

"—and pay for that fancy school in Connecticut."

"That fancy school saved my life."

"I had to make choices to survive, Nina, because unlike my sisters—"

"You don't get it, do you?" I yelled, with my remaining precious energy. "I didn't choose this. I didn't ask for this. You did this to me, and you won't even accept it. You did this but you've always made it my problem. I'm not a monster. You're the monster, don't you see?"

Tracy was quiet for a while. I didn't expect an apology or some other evidence that Tracy was prepared to reflect on how she'd treated me for so long. It would have been nice, Dr. C!

"What do you mean, I did this to you? You could have gotten an abortion. You have half of UCLA Medical Center at your beckon call! You did this to you. You chose it!"

I was crying. "I don't mean the baby. I mean my body."

"You could have gotten your eye and your nose fixed." (I want to point out that my nose was merely large and Jewish, not affected by A12!) "And you could have gotten a prosthetic for your hand. You didn't want to. Like it or not, as a woman, looks matter. You had a nice husband all those years, though, so I did something right. A nice man who overlooked your missing fingers and your anger."

"You had a baby with an old man. You're the one who gave me this body and this death sentence."

She seemed sincerely surprised. "I will never accept that!"

"I'll never accept that it isn't true."

"I loved Eddie and I wanted to be a mom when I was young. That's all there is to that. I can't help but be mad at that awful Dr. Chen at UCLA who stuck it in your head that you have A12 because Eddie was old. That's like saying I should never have had you and I don't like that. She ruined your life that day when you were a kid, telling you you'd be dead by forty. And she made parenting you even harder. If she hadn't told you that, you'd have had a completely different and probably happier life. All I ever tried to do was to get that garbage out of your brain. But she won! You love her more than you love me."

I thought about this. It had never crossed my mind to see what you said to me when I was eleven and you were a second-year resident as the pinball flipper that sent my life careening in an entirely different direction.

"No, Tracy," I said, quietly. "I would have had a happier life if you had tried to protect me."

"I did try to protect you. From Dr. Chen and her garbage."

I gestured at my belly. "You know what? Forget it. I have more important things to focus on."

"Like when that good-for-nothing crazy man comes back wanting to be that kid's daddy?"

I smiled at the thought. "Cole would eviscerate you," I said.

"Cole has already eviscerated you, Nina Simone."

"It's Nina Ruth."

"No."

"Get the fuck out of my house," I hissed.

Oh, to be so close to death, to know that there would be zero consequences to the choices I made from here on out. I had but one mission left in this life and that was to deliver, to you, a healthy infant who would live so differently from me, even if she was born missing two fingers or all ten. You, Dr. Chen, would love this baby the way I would love this baby, the way I did love this baby, and the way Tracy would not/could not. She lacked heart and imagination. Maybe that wasn't her fault, but being my mom didn't change her mind about anything. True, I could only pray that my Sig/your Emily would never call you a circus clown hooker, but that is for you to sort out, dearest Mama Tabs.

"If you weren't pregnant, I'd slap you."

"Go ahead," I said, hoisting myself up. "Slap me. Do it!"

She considered it. I could tell. But I was in a pitiful state, and she knew it.

She smiled, suddenly and eerily, like that conversation hadn't happened. "Do you have a beer in the fridge? I need a drink."

I was pregnant and could barely move from the living room floor, but she thought I might have a beer. "Anything?" she persisted, getting up to move toward the kitchen. She wasn't used to not getting what she wanted. "Wine? Please say you have at least wine. Doesn't your friend own a winery?"

"I'm pregnant."

"I need a drink," she shouted, stomping her little feet like that would manifest a bottle of booze.

"Addie loved White Claw at the end of her days. They're in the pantry. Take the whole box."

"Addie was a drunk," my mother opined. Pot. Kettle.

"Tracy, I told you to leave. Take the White Claw and go." Tracy banged around the kitchen, opening all the cupboards.

I heard her open the freezer. "Ice, Nina? Why don't you have any ice? You have an automatic ice maker that you don't even turn on. What is this shit in your freezer? Why are you eating this? What is this—Bananas Foster ice cream? You're forty years old and you're still eating that unhealthy trash. What is this wrapped up thing?" I heard her say, and then she appeared in front of me, holding a dusty can of White Claw in one hand and the package from Cole in the other.

Dying at this moment wouldn't have been horrible, except it would have deprived you of a daughter and Cole the excitement of pissing on my corpse. I took as deep of a breath as I could. "Put that back," I ordered.

Tracy held Cole's bundle aloft with her manicured hand. "Is this drugs? Are you doing drugs?"

"Put it back! What is wrong with you? Put it back!"

Tracy scolded me. "I'd believe it if someone came to me and said you were doing hard drugs. I would totally believe it."

"You were on cocaine the day you met my father!"

I heard the squishy pop of bubble wrap and the whine of packing tape being ripped from where it was. "Don't!" I tried to hoist myself up off the floor, but I moved the wrong way and a shot of warm urine streamed out, soaking my leggings. "Will you please, just this once, *fucking listen to me*?"

Existing was a delicate physical act for me at this late point in my pregnancy. One wrong move and I would pee my pants or get lightheaded. I could barely breathe if Sig moved the wrong way.

Her scream let me know. My original name, ripped and bloodied, fled from her throat.

In tears, blanched, frightened, Tracy sat on the floor beside my head. I rolled to the other side so I wouldn't have to look at her.

"I told you not to open that."

She lay beside me on the floor, shaking. Her bracelets clanked against the Saltillo tile.

"This is what happens when you don't listen to me," I said, as calm and collected as I could be. "I said don't open that and you did and when you disrespect me like that, you get what you get."

Tracy looked sincerely shocked at me. "Nina?"

"You didn't listen to me, Tracy. Again. Disrespecting me is a real problem."

Tracy cried, "How could you?"

I tried to fluff the pillow beneath my head. "How could I what, *Mrs. Greg Hodges*? I'm a monster, remember? Also, you're lying in my pee."

She hopped up off the floor. "Nina. I'm not the one with two—oh my god—*fingers* in the freezer left there by her psychopath boyfriend!"

"How was Greg Hodges not a psychopath?"

"Oh my god!"

"He ditched you for a younger woman and you're still defending him?"

Tracy's hands shook. "Who—what happened to you? He didn't leave me for another woman, Nina!"

I remained calm. "I told you not to open that and you did."

"Why are those in your freezer?"

My head felt like it was about to burst. "I don't owe you an explanation. Please leave."

"Nina?"

"I have to stay alive to push this human being into the world and then I'll be off the coil, enjoying umbrella drinks with Eddie in the Grand Ballroom in the sky."

"You've always wanted to die. And now you're abandoning a child."

I managed a loud cackle. "You weren't sad when Eddie died! You never gave Eddie abandoning me a thought."

"That's not the same."

"Yes, it is!"

I didn't have the energy to fight her. Tracy was winning because I was immobile on the goddamn floor and I had nothing to say that I hadn't already said many, many times before. I didn't want to say who was going to be Baby Sig's adoptive mama, but apparently, she already knew. Tracy wouldn't lawyer up—she was more into whining and complaining and less into action, especially in her Pilates-and-gold-toenail dotage. But I could hear her words without her saying them out loud: *Dr. Chen is a busy doctor! She must be sixty herself by now! How is that any different than Eddie being in his sixties?*

And sure, Mama Tabs, it's true: You are fifty-five years old. Too old to be taking this on, probably. No one would bat an eye if I left my child to Tracy, and she has ten years on you. But you should be mother. I see that. I want you to know that I see that.

"Eddie loved you," Tracy said, sounding winded.

"Great," I squeaked out. "So did Cole. Tracy, I need you to put that package back in the freezer, please."

Something clicked in her head, though. "Get up! Off the floor!" she yelled.

"I can't."

Tracy was a strong little thing—all those years of Pilates—and she hoisted me up off the ground and caught me when I thought I was going to face plant.

She got me up on my knees. The weight of my belly shifted. "Please leave me alone."

Tracy fought off my attempts to swat her away. "You need to be in the hospital."

"Mom, there's pee on the floor," I said, pointing at the puddle next to my pillow nest, as she hauled me up on my feet. I began to fall forward; she caught me by the shoulders. "Dr. Chen is coming tomorrow."

"Oh, fuck her!" she yelled, grabbing my purse off the kitchen table, digging through it looking for who knows what. She opened my wallet, squinted at my drivers' license, and muttered *Connecticut* under her breath as if the Nutmeg State had done her dirty. My mother threw my wallet back in my purse and then grabbed my purple blanket off the floor and forced me to step into my truck-stop flip flops, which were sitting on the porch by the front door. She walked me to her car, a black Audi Q5 with tinted windows—very much her taste. "I know she's getting your baby. She called me."

"What?" I murmured.

"Where are your shoes?" she yelled in my face as she pushed a button that moved the car's passenger seat back all the way. "Real shoes? You're upsetting me. You can't lie there on that hard floor in a puddle of piss, Nina. I won't allow it."

I reached down and hit the button that made the seat recline and covered my eyes with my forearm. I did not have the energy or the ability to walk back into the house under my own power.

Tracy leaned into the open car door, her fuzzy tennis ball face inches above mine. "I do love you. I don't want to see you suffering, and I don't want you to die."

I didn't answer.

Tracy went back into the house and returned with my black sneakers that no longer fit on my pregnancy-bloated feet, my denim jacket, a stack of T-shirts, my one clean pair of maternity yoga pants, a towel (for me to sit on), two cans of lemon LaCroix, and my keys. She looked at me with disappointment and started the car. A Taylor Swift song came banging out of the speakers.

I reached for the volume control to turn it down. "How come anytime anyone affirms and validates my feelings about my body or my father, you say they put poison in my head?" I asked her as she drove north on the 5. "That includes Addie, who was the closest thing I ever had to a grandmother, all the doctors at UCLA Rare Disorders including Dr. Chen, and literally every one of my friends, plus the counseling staffs at Bondurant and Yale, plus my therapist in Connecticut, plus Chef Paul, who married me and spent all day, every day, with me for two decades. But your opinion and that ignorant football player's opinion are somehow the only ones that matter."

"He didn't leave me for someone else!" She pounded on her steering wheel. "Stop saying that!"

We hit traffic, and my mother took a tube of bright pink lipstick out of her center console and applied it while looking in her rearview mirror. "Where the hell are you taking me? Why are we in Burbank?"

"I'm taking you to a hospital. I didn't say which one."

"That is messed up, Tracy Jane."

"This whole thing is messed up, Missy Miss."

"Speaking of messed up, Greg also attends an underground sex party in Malibu where certain daughters of billionaires get their fingers chopped off. He was there that night."

My mother threw her lipstick back in the console, pushed her sunglasses up, and merged into the carpool lane.

My mother turned up her Taylor Swift.

"I dare you to crash this car, Tracy!"

Taylor Swift presciently advised us to look at what we made her do.

"Do you remember that time we drove up to Sacramento for your school's state capital field trip and we stopped at that Swedish buffet place? You were maybe eight or nine. You ate probably six scoops of mashed potatoes. You were really in love with their soft-serve machine, too."

"Where are you taking me?" I asked. We passed the exit for the Burbank airport and the IKEA and were still going north-ward, nowhere near any hospital I'd ever been to, far into the Valley. "Tracy, why are we driving up the 5? UCLA Medical Center is on the West Side. Answer me. This is bullshit. You're kidnapping me."

She fixed her eyes straight ahead, channeling her energy away from me like when she used to drive me to LAX to fly back to Connecticut. The hostility lay in the silence. We crossed over the craggy, gold-colored mountains into acres of dry Central California agriculture. I noted when we drove past the almond orchard where Cole had tossed his In-N-Out Burger cup the day Sig was conceived.

I fell asleep for a few hours. When I awoke, we passed a billboard for Harris Ranch, and the car began to stink like rotten meat.

"Remember the time my parents came to California, and we drove up to Harris Ranch? You wanted to order the pasta, but Big Jesse made you get a steak and you cried?"

Tracy continued talking while I suppressed my nausea. "You stuffed that package in your bag without ice, didn't you? You didn't keep it cold?"

Tracy pressed a button on her steering wheel, and Steely Dan began to play.

"The car smells like decomposing flesh, Mom."

She slugged back the Diet Coke she'd gotten for herself from the fountain at the first bathroom stop we'd made, and popped the lid off the cup, which was filled halfway with ice. She held the cup out to me.

"I'm not touching those," I said. "I told you to leave that package alone. And turn off the goddamn Dan, Tracy!"

"Take the cup."

"No!"

Sigrid kicked me in the ribs, then my stomach lurched, and a puddle of white, chunky vomit landed on my lap.

"Paper towels in the back, sis," Tracy said as all four windows came down at once.

***

When she stopped for gas and the last toilet break, Tracy pulled my clean yoga pants and a fresh T-shirt out of the back seat, handed them to me, and then walked ahead into the gas station food mart.

She came in the restroom and waited for me as I took off my disgusting yoga pants and kicked them underneath the stall door. Tracy picked them up and told me they were going in the trash.

I saw her gold sandals pacing underneath the stall door. She was fidgeting. When I was a kid, this meant that I was about to catch hell from her. Then I heard a wail. Tracy was wailing. She sounded like Bruno the Dog when Cole and I shut the bedroom door on him, and he felt left out.

"Are you crying?" I asked through the stall door.

"Yes."

"Why?"

"Because my daughter is dying. Or at least throwing up every ten minutes."

Tracy's sobs echoed off the red-and-white tile walls in the gas station restroom. I realized I had only ever seen my mother cry once, in front of Grandpa Jesse, when he was dressing her down for marrying my father.

"Pass me some TP, would you?"

I handed her a wad underneath the stall. She blew her nose and asked for more.

"Dr. Chen didn't make you get an abortion? I spoke to her the other day, when she asked me to drive you to the hospital today."

"Obviously there will be no abortion, so I'm not sure why you continue to bring that up."

Tracy was scaring me. She could never feel her feelings and accept things. I wished that she could be gentle and love me through this.

"You don't get it. . . . I'm so mad at her! That Dr. Chen! I have been for years."

"Mama Tabs? She's great. Don't blame her for anything." My voice seemed louder as it bounced off those gas station bathroom tiles. "See, I liked knowing the truth about my life, Mom," I yelled at her as I struggled to get my legs into the clean pants. "That A12 would shorten my life. I don't think—I know I wouldn't have done anything differently. I like to live an honest life. My life wasn't easy, but it was never a lie. If I had pretended nothing was wrong, how would that make my life better? It hurts to know that you didn't believe I would die around forty and were mad at me for believing it. Is that right, Mom?"

She seemed to cry harder. Was this the first time she ever actually believed I would die at forty after all? For all these years, had she pretended otherwise? Or because she wished I were the type of person who avoided truths where they were painful or inconvenient, like her?

"Sometimes we need to hear things we don't want to hear. And it's hurtful to me that you've been mad at me for all this time because I listened to a doctor. You've never been able to put yourself in my shoes. I was the one walking around Los Angeles with eight fingers and a buggy eye, Tracy. Not you."

"I'm not mad at you," she said through her sobs.

"It always seemed like you were."

My belly weighed me down on the toilet and I knew my knees would give if I tried to get up on my own. "Could you pull me up?" I asked. "I'm having trouble standing."

She opened the door. Red-faced, she hoisted me up like a baby. She caught me in a hug as I pulled up my leggings, her arms pinning mine down as I tried to shimmy up my pants.

Tracy sobbed into my shoulder for a while. "Can we go outside? A gas station bathroom isn't where I want to have this conversation." We walked slowly to the car. Tracy hesitated to unlock it. She was buying time, looking for words.

"Is something wrong?" I asked.

She placed her hand on my belly and cried harder. "Yes," she said. "You're . . . really going to die." Her wails were jarring. "And leave your baby with that doctor." She shrugged. "That's what you want. I'm not interfering. I'm helping, in fact."

"Mom? I don't want to fight with you, but do you think you could accept this situation? Acceptance would be the most loving thing you could do for me right now. Accept my body and my choices and, you know. Me."

She nodded. "This is all so sad," she said as she rubbed a circle on Sigrid with one hand and wiped her tears with the other.

I waited for her to say something else. An apology, maybe, or some shred of something I'd long given up on hearing from her.

She stood in front of me, only sobbing and rubbing. I pushed her hand away. "I don't think it's sad at all."

15

Which is how I came to spend the rest of my life in Steve's tricked-out suite at Stanford Hospital.

I knew this but I didn't know this.

I also didn't know that if my mom hadn't dumped me off at the hospital, even a hospital five hours away, bad things would have happened. My oxygen level was at 92 percent and that was dangerous for me and for Siggy.

I was scared.

Chris was dead. Jorie was dead.

Addie, too.

Sylvia was not returning my calls.

Cole had blocked me on all channels, but I suspected he was the one who had texted "are you dead yet?" from a different number, along with a photo of the University of Texas Tower, which was either a reference to Tracy's alma mater or the Charles Whitman shootings.

I had to have my baby at Stanford Hospital, because you, Dr. Chen, were in on the kill. You sent Tracy to deliver me to Steve Elwood's personal hospital wing so Steve could use me to trap Cole, to exact the vengeance he craved. He didn't give a rat's ass about me or the baby. He was using me. He was using you, too, and he expects you to eradicate A12 all by your itty-bitty brilliant self. The pressure must be unbearable!

Why didn't you tell me ahead of time? Because you thought I'd make a run for it if I were in LA? Out the front door into Cole's waiting van, just like old times?

How much, may I ask, did Elwood pay you for my bounty?

It was hard, at this point, trapped in that hospital room painted a pale blue with recognizable prints (Wiley's Obama portrait was a nice touch), that view of the Stanford campus, with that sweet nurse Annie coming hourly for my vitals and to refresh my lemon water, and with the periodic visits from the new best friend I didn't want, Steve Elwood, to be anything but depressed. Trash television and the pho Steve Elwood sent over daily were kind of it for diversions outside of my new bed rest lifestyle. Steve, being Steve, had access to very rich, flavorful pho (very star anise–forward broth) and he even provided a big ceramic bowl to eat it out of instead of the plastic take-out containers like the ones that littered the house in Los Feliz, which I would never see again. He told me the name of the restaurant in Palo Alto where he got it, and I quickly forgot, but it wasn't a punny name like Pho Q. I accused Elwood of keeping an eye on me in his own personal hospital suite because he wanted to steal my double-A12 baby for research purposes, or maybe to serve as his Twelver kid's personal servant, and he laughed and told me he honestly wasn't that smart.

Someone—you, Elwood, my mother?—must have told Nurse Annie that although I was functioning as the sacred vessel to deliver Sigrid to the mortal coil, my remaining time on this planet was short. When she told me about her daughter, she must have seen something cross my face because she pulled back and asked me if I had chosen an adoptive parent.

I asked her if she had heard of A12 Fibrillin Deficiency Syndrome and she said no. I gave her the quick version ("It's basically Marfan on steroids"—she hadn't heard of Marfan syndrome, either) and told her that it's the disorder of the children of delusional rich geezers.

"Your dad died when you were so young?" she said. "How sad!"

I was relieved when Nurse Annie went home and another nurse took over the night shift because that meant Annie got to go home to her daughter and be a mom.

There I was, late at night, looking out that giant window, over the Stanford campus, where Sylvia had gone to college twenty years earlier. I thought of us sitting on the hot pink rug on the floor of our shared room on the fourth floor of Collier Hall at Bondurant—we had the coveted suite with both a private bathroom and balcony—filling out our college applications together.

And in that memory, mundane as heck, but those are the moments that stick to your soul, a dark gray wave hit me in the face so hard as I looked down at my belly underneath the pink blanket and realized what I had done. I had Eddie Blained my own child.

I could blame you, I guess, as I asked for a tubal ligation many times. Chef Paul was about as fertile as a mile of Astroturf, and I never asked my doctor in Connecticut for one, but you told me the likelihood of my conceiving was slim to zip.

You were wrong!

I must have been screaming because the night nurse gave me a sedative and I woke up to Nurse Annie stroking my head.

What was in that sedative, Dr. C.? I gulped a cup of orange juice and then went on and on to that young nurse about my life and A12, and about car seats.

"There's no way that I could put a child, especially a toddler, in a car seat. Like, lift a thirty-pound body and twist my own body forty-five degrees and then click all the buckles and everything. I can barely carry my own groceries. My muscles are all but gone. I used to be able to stand at a counter in a commercial kitchen for hours and work with my hands and about two years ago, about the time my marriage started to fall apart, I couldn't work anymore. I worked for my husband. He was a chef. I did a lot of his baking and there came a point when I couldn't help him stack the flour bags anymore. And then after about an hour of work, I was so exhausted and in so much pain that I had to stop. We were fighting about other things so he thought I was being a brat, but I told him I couldn't do it and he didn't believe me and I passed out after pulling a bunch of pans out of the oven and ended up in the hospital and you know what I found out after? Paul wasn't the one who dialed 911. It was one of his staff. My own husband left my lying on the floor next to a hot oven in a busy kitchen. He thought I was being dramatic.

"If I somehow lived through this, I wouldn't be able to lift my child into a car seat, even if I had a minivan. Does a minivan make it easier? My boyfriend has a minivan. What happens when the baby kicks me in the chest? I have delicate bones and she'd probably make my heart stop once she could put some muscle behind kicking my busted sternum.

"I'd have to hire a nanny and I don't know if I could afford that since I don't think I can work anymore, at least not in a kitchen, which is all my résumé reflects.

"I wrote a book once, so I am also a writer. Chef Paul never saw me that way. Cole read my book. He praised it even though I don't think he really understood it. There were some dirty lines he liked. Or so he said—dirty lines? Maybe? He might have been making that part up.

"Here's the thing, Annie, and I don't understand this but maybe you do? My ex-husband, Chef Paul, and yes, I always called him Chef Paul, was a nice guy. He got grumpy and distant toward the end, but he was nice. But he couldn't take care of me. Cole, who can be a clown-ass jerk sometimes but also hilarious and strange and deep, saw me. Or I felt like he saw me. Maybe because we both have A12.

"I have never been one to really want things because I have never believed that I could have the things I wanted, but now? Right now? I have never hated my body, even when it failed me and even when the shallow LA people that my mother had around made me feel like a monster. But now, knowing I could never put a toddler in a car seat because you have to lift the child and twist yourself into a pretzel and click all the things in place, and you need a minimum amount of muscle and strength to do that every day for years and years, and I would be winded before all those things were done and I might collapse next to the car and that would harm the baby, right? I couldn't drive after all that. Does that disqualify me from being a mom? Are there special cars and special car seats? Could I rotate a baby?"

Nurse Annie, Queen of Compassion, listened to all of this. Give her a pile of money, Steve.

She sat there and watched me cry because I had not anticipated the loss and dread I would feel toward the end. I don't get to help Sig apply to colleges and I don't get to see her with friends, much less make applesauce airplanes with a little rubberized spoon fly right into her precious, Sacred Honor mouth.

I could have asked Nurse Annie to up my sedatives, but instead I asked what she thought of the name I chose.

She scrunched her nose at the name Sigrid, like I'd offered her a stinky fish.

Her daughter's name?

Tabitha.

***

"Cole is going to show up here, right?"

Get over me, Steve, I thought as I figured out who was hovering over my hospital bed. I was the oven in which the baby baked, barely alive, yet Steve Elwood had become my biggest fan. He patted my head like I was a lap dog, and smiled at me like he was the age-appropriate dad I never had. He was creepy and sweet, and I have some dirt on him: He *smokes*! Dude reeked of cigarettes, like Eddie. Steve Elwood is either sneaking American Spirits behind Stanford Hospital, or he is the human manifestation of Eddie Blaine's ghost, complete with smells.

"I don't know," I said. "Did you bring me pho?"

Steve waved the brown paper bag at me and set it down on the bedside table. "Pho you? Anything."

"Are you going to pour that into a bowl today or—where's the bowl?"

Steve slid his huge Android phone across my hospital tray toward me. "The bowl is in my backpack. Call him."

Steve's cellphone was the size of a trade paperback. How he got such a big phone, I couldn't say. "Bowl, Steve."

His shoulders fell. "Patience, my dear," Steve said. He got the bowl out of his backpack and arranged my pho noodles first, broth second, and sprouts and basil last. Before he brought over the bowl, he drew a Sriracha heart on top.

Steve held the spoon while I took my first spoonful of broth. "You're trying to get his number."

"I have his number," he said, and chuckled. "I own the world's information."

"If you want to talk to him, you call him."

"I brought you pho," he countered. "I am handfeeding you pho when you have nurses on staff to help you with this."

"You don't have to do anything you don't want to, Steve. I didn't realize you weren't bringing me pho out of the goodness of your heart."

"Nick's other girlfriend won't tell me where he is. It's on you. Bring him to me."

I mentally flipped him the bird. Raising my hand to do it for real took too much energy. "Call the cops. Call your lawyer," I offered, taking another bite of soup.

Steve sat on the vinyl chair next to my bed. It reminded me of the UCLA Rare Disorders Clinic chairs that Sylvia and I had sat in thirty years earlier. "Why do you like him? Nick?" He asked, as if asking why I like diarrhea smoothies.

I wouldn't answer Steve Elwood, Dr. C. He didn't deserve to know what wells up and dances around the space between my head and my heart. He doesn't get to know about the hours of phone calls and pages of emails that sounded like they were written by me because there was only a perforated line between me and Cole and I made it the entirety of my final act to tear it away. Elwood and his thirty-four-years-his-junior third wife and his sloppy outfits and his money could go to hell. Elwood wouldn't, in a hundred million years, understand *lefty or righty*, so what was even the point?

Mostly, it was that Cole, like me, was a mutant, a bent twig, a Time Travel Baby, and because we shared those rare qualities, I could see in him my own story and my own beauty.

But, if you're a careful reader, and I know you are, with all those medical awards and fellowships, Tabs, you'll see that I am not talking about Cole as a human being with character, faults, and flaws.

Read closer.

Closer.

Still not close enough.

I wasn't going to tell Steve, or anyone, this but being with Cole, even when he wasn't the most loving of friends, always felt like placing the star on the top of the Christmas tree. Shiny. Crowned. Bright.

But these are just words and underneath them, I know, and you know, because you showed up at Stanford Hospital, imported by Mr. Elwood on his private jet, to wrest the baby into the third dimension and see me off.

What are we going to tell Sigrid the Sea Monster about her daddy?

We should have our stories straight.

I really like my star on the Christmas tree metaphor, so let's stick with that.

"He's not going to be present for the birth of his child?" Elwood continued, scratching his belly underneath his Pixies T-shirt.

I swallowed my broth and laughed. "Do you ever wear a shirt that is not a Pixies shirt?"

He shook his head and looked down at his shirt. "I bought three hundred of these in 1998. Two hundred larges and a hundred extra larges, preparing for the inevitable. Frank Black himself asked me not to wear them in public but he's not the boss of me."

"What?"

"Yeah," he said, laughing. "I have the email framed in my office."

This guy was really something. "How's Ava?" I asked.

He coughed and said, "I even wore one to a Pixies show and stood right in front of the stage."

"Did my mother give you Ava's fingers in that cup of ice?"

His face turned pale. I thought to offer him my "emesis receptacle," a long green bag hanging from a plastic ring with little measurement marks printed down the front. It brought me no peace to watch him curl over like a pill bug, nauseated and ashamed.

Steve was dissociating. Leaving his body. His eyes weren't focused. This was how I got through Greg Hodges's court extravaganza when I was eighteen. I detached. I pretended I was in heaven with my dad, onstage holding hands singing "Sparrow in the Treetop" with Harris Notley on keys. It was hard for me to muster any compassion for yet another bad man who had happened into my life.

I was expecting a soliloquy, badly rendered, spoken from some dark corner of his heart about the love he had for his child, or what a burden on his psyche Cole had been for years. Steve Elwood walked over to my room's gigantic window and screamed like a child, banging on the panes with his fists.

"Yes, Nina! She gave me the fingers!" he yelled at me.

"I told her not to do that. She never listens to me. She gets off on defying other people and she's rude—"

Steve emitted a high-pitched scream.

"I don't know, man," I continued. Lord knows I'd seen worse in my life than those gray, decaying fingers. "You're worth how much money? You can have anything you want, and you have to use me to get to Cole? Don't you think that's kind of weak, Steve-o? Don't you have access to, like, the CIA?"

He continued to scream. I pressed my nurse call button to summon the kindest Nurse Annie.

"How can you?" Steve struggled for breath, his voice high and hoarse. He stood above my bed, clutching those railings, shaking my bed, sweat appearing on his forehead. "How can you say you love him? That horrid, disgusting man? How can you want anything to do with him?" he shrieked.

The nurses arrived as Steve stood propping himself up on the bed rail, his madman eyes bulging and his spittle landing in my pho bowl. "Where is he, Nina? Where is he?"

Nurse Annie yelled, "get a gurney" and three other nurses got him off the floor and I'm pretty sure I got some extra sedative in my IV after they hauled Steve Elwood off, strapped to the bed, wailing like an animal. As punishment. Or mercy. Nothing but pleasant dreams. Soft, elated, cloudy dreams.

Tell Steve I had two hearts: one that saw Cole and understood that the pain he caused me was wrong, and another that loved him for all the reasons I have explained.

Tell Steve that he would be so lucky to be loved like that in this life.

16

Six weeks of bed rest in one of the best hospitals in the country was not what I had in mind for the end of this journey—I was perfectly happy lying like a beached whale on the Saltillo tiles of the Los Feliz house, even though Cole was AWOL, two Good Thumbs were dead, and Sylvia was not reachable. I could have hired a nurse or asked you, Dr. Chen, for additional help, but you had just done me the solid of offering to adopt Siggymuffin and I didn't want to overextend your kindness.

At least there was the house. My house. The small, dated, garbage-and-pee-smelling house that had finally come to be mine. Eddie, finally, left me something to remember him by other than a few discarded copies of his albums and an old, moth-eaten sweater that smelled like onion rings he'd eaten in 1971.

Honestly, Tracy was right—it was starting to smell ripe in there. I hadn't been able to take the trash out in weeks.

The truth was, I still wanted Cole back, to come home and take care of me. Or at least take the trash bins to the curb.

I cried for an hour when I realized I'd never see the Bondurant School again, that I'd never have Chef Paul's chicken marsala ever again. I'd never bake a Stella di Capra cinnamon milk cake again. Or walk across a frozen pond, drive a car, or try a new haircut. I'd never read another book, watch another movie, have sex, or see the ocean again.

And definitely no trip to Gdansk.

I mostly cried about not knowing Siggy.

But also, Cole.

Whatever was in that IV drip, Dr. Chen, allowed me to do something I'd always wanted: time travel.

Blame Eddie Blaine and our stretch of years for that.

There was an ad on the back of a Metro bus about oat milk that—I realized one day driving down Los Feliz Boulevard—Eddie Blaine wouldn't understand. Beyond "Jesus Christ, what the hell is oat milk? How do you milk an oat? Why do oats have titties in the 2020s?" the advertisement also assumed that you knew how to use a smartphone, what an app was, why you should have an oat milk app on your phone. Eddie would have hated smartphones. Give me a dumb one, he would have said.

What if I could have him back for a day? What would we talk about? Where would we have lunch?

He loathed Ronald Reagan, so we'd have to talk about what a tragic world Reagan's policies created. So much poverty and prejudice. Eddie and I would drive around Downtown LA and see the homeless encampments on every street, and he'd point and say that Reagan did that. "He was a terrible actor who made terrible pictures," Eddie often said when he was still alive.

I'd get him an acai bowl, an avocado toast, and a charcoal frozen yogurt. But he wouldn't eat any of it and would tell me to take him to Canter's for a sandwich like a normal human being, please.

Eddie would be 106 years old. Other than me, and maybe Tracy, he'd have no one around here to see—all his friends have died.

What was in that IV drip, doctor?

Whatever it was, this happened: I was seven, and Eddie was newly dead, and I was wandering around a giant house looking for him, calling his name, frustrated but also knowing he was dead and wasn't going to answer me. The IV drip may have unlocked the part of my brain where the painful memories were stored, and I found myself reliving the old one where I was looking for my father and knew I'd never find him.

But this time, Cole came out of the shadows to rescue me. He had the upper body strength to pick me up so he could run away with me. How much did I want someone to show up out of nowhere and take me away to some better place? Cole and I were somehow in the corridors of LAX, except they were crooked and crowded, and he lifted me up and put me on a luggage cart and sprinted down the hallway as I held onto the cart and screamed like we were on roller coaster or at a rock show having the best time. He screamed, too.

Nobody chased us. He was all I had.

I didn't want to wake up.

In another dream, I was on a city bus in Pittsburgh. It was the 1980s, and I had my eyes on a boy in a plaid jacket fiddling around with a plastic walkie-talkie.

The bus stopped, and the driver turned around, and it was Cole's father, yelling at Nicky to come to him. But Nicky saw his father and bolted out of the bus and onto a snowy street, crashing through puddles in his too-big shoes, hiding between those old, heavy-looking parked cars. And I, in the dream, followed that little boy into the cold Pennsylvania twilight and then, his father, pushing seventy and still working ten-hour days, ran after his boy like an Olympic sprinter, screaming *Nicky!* at the top of his lungs.

I felt myself go underwater. When I came up for air, I was in the future watching my baby girl, now a teenager, press her gold Bondurant School name plate to her dorm room door. I saw her teenage face, or maybe my own. She looked excited and sweet and had blonde hair like those sunny Westervelt girls from the photos on Grandma Arlette's mantle.

Inevitably, the dream ended. Being back in reality made me want to cry, but crying wouldn't do anything to help matters, and it exhausted me. I could barely breathe as it was and did not want to be put on a ventilator.

On Christmas morning, I awoke to find Bryn, clad in black scrubs, sitting in the chair next to my bed, looking at her phone and sipping from an orange travel mug.

"Did you see what I did to the mommy elephant?" she asked me, smiling like her father, pointing at the largest member of the elephant stuffie family that you had gifted me when I arrived at Stanford Hospital.

I looked at the elephant. "You cut off her toes."

"Yeah. Look. I gave her A12." Bryn passed me the mommy elephant. She had lopped off the poor animal's cloth toes on her front left foot and whip-stitched the wounds closed with red thread. I held the elephant to my chest. I felt bad for the poor thing. No one else around here needed the Twelve, least of all Mommy Elephant.

"That was sweet of you," I said softly. "To disfigure her like that."

Like father, like daughter.

"I also brought you a Christmas gift."

I strained to turn my head to see her.

"I can open it for you," she offered.

"Okay."

"These are for my sister," Bryn said to me, unwrapping the shiny green paper with a surgeon's precision, neatly folding the paper, and setting it down on the side table. She pulled a stuffed hippopotamus and a pink blanket out of the box and set them down on my chest. "The blanket was my baby blanket. That's a gift from my mother. Hippos and elephants get along, I think, so that works out. Dr. Chen told me about your pregnancy. I'm why you're at Stanford Hospital. Or part of why. I'm in medical school here."

"Oh?" As confused as I was, I was overjoyed to see her.

"I have no reason to lie to you, Nina. People who don't say what they mean upset me. Here's my Stanford ID." She waved her badge in front of my face. "With your permission, Nina, I'd like to be present for the birth. Not only because the baby is my half sibling, but for medical education purposes. I'd like to observe the only known A12 female geriatric birth."

"You want to watch me die?" I asked.

Bryn said, flat as a board, "No. Honestly, I don't. Medical interest, also a little family solidarity."

"You called me a stupid cunt."

"That wasn't personal. That's about Nick, not you. I'm sorry if I hurt your feelings. Listen, if all goes as planned, I'm going to be the heir to Dr. Chen's work," Bryn said, pulling the chair close to my bed. "The Elwoods are paying for me to go to Stanford Medical School to study the A12 genome. In ten years, I'll have her position at UCLA Rare Disorders. And, if Elwood gets his way, then A12 will be eradicated and old farts like him can make babies until they're one hundred."

"That's unethical. Even if the baby has no health complications, it's unethical."

"You don't need to lecture me on ethics, Nina. I know."

"How do you know?" I asked. "Your dad isn't some Hollywood prune."

"No," she said. "But Nick's a pretty selfish guy. He bailed on me and my mom and then got offended when we told him that was, you know, wrong."

I didn't want to plumb the depths of knowledge about Bryn's former relationship with Cole. It was none of my business.

"Hey Bryn? What's your mom like?" I asked.

Bryn placed her hand to her heart. "Hannah Maes Nakamura Sullivan Robinson? The best mommy in San Francisco?"

"Yes."

"She had a great life until Seiji, her first husband, died. As a grieving widow, she answered the stupidest ad *Wired* magazine ever ran. But she was really a mess back then, so we can't hold it against her."

"Okay."

"Other than that poor lapse in judgment, of which she would argue that it gave her me, so it was a good thing, she's a lovely person. She's a very tiny Belgian lady," Bryn made a rectangle shape with her hands to denote how tiny. "Five feet tall. Black hair. A little bit of an accent. She smells like perfume all the time. She retired a few months ago from teaching French after thirty years. She married husband number three not long ago. My stepfather's an opera singer. They're happy. They're moving to Marin, which makes me sad, but I live in a box in Palo Alto, so whatever."

"Is he good to you?" I asked. I wanted to hear that she was okay. "Your stepfather?"

She nodded. "Oh yes. He worships my mom. And he's good to me, too."

"That's great," I said.

"What's your mother like?" Bryn asked.

I laughed. "She's . . ."

Tracy was no one to cry over, but I began to cry.

Bryn handed me a box of tissues. "She cares about appearances, and I never appeared well to her."

"Internalized misogyny," Bryn said. "It's everywhere, really. All the women in my program, at least the ones who are straight, talk about how no man will want them if they're the more successful one. But I think even my mother had a bit of that the day she opened that copy of *Wired*. I'm sick of that shit. Here's a parable for you: A couple of years ago I was walking around a fancy neighborhood in San Francisco and saw a toaster on top of the trash cans in front of a giant house. An upscale European toaster, this chubby, shiny thing and it looked brand-new. I grabbed it and thought, *score!* Peter, my housemate, and I, didn't have a toaster at all and then suddenly, we had this expensive one.

"The first time I used it, the bread got scorched. The second time I used it, the whole thing caught fire. I blamed myself. I thought maybe the bread had oil on it or the voltage on the outlet was too high. I used the toaster three or four more times, and it wasn't until the entire kitchen cabinet above the toaster caught fire that I accepted that the toaster was on the street because it was broken. There was nothing I could do, up to and including blaming myself and obsessing over every interaction I had with that toaster, that would make the damn thing not catch fire. That's how I explain why I don't have anything to do with my father. Because he's that toaster."

"He's a toaster," I said, and it made sense.

"You aren't ugly," Bryn said, grabbing my three-fingered hand and looking at my pearly nubs. "This is the magic of the human body as a functioning system. You're, what, forty? You've made it this far. And you're seven months pregnant and alive."

"I'm on oxygen and whatever's in that bag."

"That's your nutrition. Electrolytes so you don't dehydrate. You should be on bed rest, so it's good you're here."

"Dr. Chen told me not to get pregnant when I was eighteen. That a full-term pregnancy would kill me."

"You could've, though," she said. "You might have died, but you also might not have."

"Can I survive this?" I asked Bryn.

She didn't respond. "I'll be there for her, Nina. Let's focus on that. Your baby has a family. Maybe not a perfect one, but she has Tabitha and her family, and she has me and my mom and stepdad, and my friends. She has aunts and uncles and nineteen cousins in greater Pittsburgh. She even has Uncle Steve and Aunt Kailey, although I know how you feel about them, and I get it." Bryn took a long swig from her travel mug. "I blame my father for this death wish of yours. He makes all the women he gets involved with want to die. The ones I met after he divorced my mom are all dead now, and I don't mean to be rude, but . . ." Bryn swept her arm around the room and pointed at me like *duh, you're next, bitch.*

I didn't hear what else she said, but when I woke up, there was a nurse standing over me with ice chips in a bucket. I asked for Bryn and the nurse said she didn't know who that was.

17

A week ago, Steve came by my room with pho, shrimp spring rolls, a belated birthday cake (white chiffon with raspberry and marzipan, not bad), and three lawyers who fanned a stack of papers across the wheeled table that reaches across my hospital bed. I signed an affidavit saying that Steve Elwood and I shared a night of passion seven and a half months earlier and that he was, without a doubt, the father of the child I was about to give birth to, and that he and I agreed to give the child up for adoption to you. My mother, affirming my mental competence for the first and only time, served as my witness. The papers were then notarized and dispatched forthwith.

I had to hand it to Steve—I expected him to be wink-wink about it, but he took it very seriously. He apologized to his wife, Kailey, and was prepared to go public with the news of their open marriage, to fight against any untrue rumors if Cole decided to take this to the media. While the baby was going to be adopted by a close friend of the family, Steve and Kailey were pleased to have Zinnia's little half-sister in their life and would take financial responsibility for her education.

After the paperwork was signed, Steve leaned over the bed rail and kissed my forehead. "Team us!" he shouted, triumphant, before turning his back to me to answer his phone.

It was a terrible story. After all my huffing and puffing about old dads over the years, the idea that I would have gone to bed with a sixty-two-year-old man, especially one who wore camo Crocs and the same Pixies T-shirt every day, was beyond the pale. My feelings on the matter were written out in my small press book that only a handful of people (including Kailey Elwood) had read. But you knew, and I knew, that detail would get lost. No one had my back on that anyway.

Not even you, Mama Tabs. You say what those old men want to hear all the time.

***

And then it was five in the morning on January 2. Five weeks before my due date.

Nurse Annie wheeled me into the room with the big lights. Monitors were beeping and someone placed a mask over my nose. Next I knew, Sigrid, that tiny miracle, was crying. The attending nurse placed her on my chest and that, my beloved friend, was the first time I died on my daughter's birthday. I was in full cardiac failure, but I didn't care. I watched as the nurse lifted the baby from my chest and gave her to you while the other doctor got to work stitching me up.

Did I want to hold her? More than anything I've ever wanted in my whole misshapen life, Dr. C. But per our plan, I didn't. I saw her shape, through my wet and unfocused eyes, when you laid her down on my chest for a few minutes and when you lifted her up again. Little frog legs, covered in that white pasty stuff, a cap of brown hair. She cried and so did you.

Second death. There was not enough liquid in me to cry. Hopelessness is more of a vomit feeling, anyway, and it has been at least a week since my last solid meal. But yeah, I can be a hypocrite like everyone else.

***

Your tabulations were correct, Dr. C. It took Cole exactly seven hours to arrive at the hospital from his flight from Pittsburgh.

When he barreled into my cozy hospital suite without knocking, throwing open the door, yelling my name, my body flushed with dread. My body was too weak for this. This sick feeling, acid in the veins, was for younger, healthier people. As much as I longed for him. As much as I rehearsed this moment in my head over the last months. The Cole I adored wasn't the one who would show up today. Maybe he'd be Drunk Cole, or Mean Cole, or Aggressively Boring Cole. He wouldn't be Nina's Cole. That person was gone forever. We Zoomed with that therapist who explained it to me like I didn't already know.

Cole held up one of those six-dollar daisy bouquets I used to grab at Trader Joe's on days when I felt unloved. He looked around the room and sneered, "Good job not fucking this one up, Slugger."

Cole turned his back to me to look out the window. His black T-shirt was sprinkled with dandruff. His cargo shorts and rainbow socks were dusted with dirt. His hair had grown past his shoulders, and half had turned gray. He'd grown a stupid-looking mustache, too.

A chill came from him. He was playing his game. He wasn't going to tell me what he was angry about, but he was going to punish me for it, and to him, I deserved it. I was a pathetic, sniveling loser who was so weak and needy that I thought someone as great as Cole Courchaine could love me.

I was still in a druggy haze. My heart hurt seeing him. Rule number one: Don't act happy to see Cole. But also, don't act mad to see him.

"Where have you been?" I asked, my voice feeble. For a second, I hoped he would wink at me and say, *You and me, babe? Let's get out of here.*

He shrugged and sat down in the teal chair that Steve Elwood always sat in. "Around. Austin, to see a friend. Pittsburgh. I went home to see the love of my life, my sister Laura. I gave her the other love of my life, Bruno. They'll be happy together. I had to do right by my good boy before I take up the duties of fatherhood again."

I said nothing.

He turned around. "You know who called me when I was visiting my sister? Sylvia. Sylvia told me you were here."

You must have told Sylvia to call him.

"Sylvia told me that you're planning to claim someone else is the father on the birth certificate. After you told everyone I *abandoned* you."

I hadn't shared that with Sylvia, either. But I knew who had.

He slammed the flowers down at the foot of my bed. "Because I'm too old and going to die soon, like the others. And because you're such an insufferable low-class trickster harpy who thought she could pull one over on me."

"You're not the father," I said, following orders, lying to myself and him and everyone else. He knew it was a lie, but Cole wasn't the most truthful person, and you made me promise to lie. Still, it killed me to speak these words to someone who, despite what he had done, I still loved and wanted. I caught a whiff of his sweat and noted, with sorrow, my last-ever erotic experience. "We didn't have a monogamous, committed relationship. She's not yours."

He cackled. "I know who you've fucked! Chef Boyardee and yours truly and that's it. Don't even with that pathetic bullshit, you." He knocked my plastic bucket of ice chips onto the floor. "Why the hell have you been talking to Elwood, of all people? How did you—Sylvia told me you and Steve are best friends now? You're giving him my baby?"

I stayed silent.

Cole leaned over the bed rail. He kissed my lips and then pressed shut the two oxygen tubes that terminated in my nostrils. He began to laugh. A sick, shivering laugh, complete with tears pouring out of his eye. "Can I tell you why you and I have to break up?"

"What?" My throat hurt from the tubes.

"You're so embarrassing. That 'Somber Mountain' song? Is that the best Eddie Blaine had to offer the world? Besides bringing the most mediocre of the Good Thumbs into the world? You and me? Those were pity fucks, Nina. I thought it would be fun to bang a fellow Twelver, but you got attached and it was pathetic to watch."

I had no fight.

"Where's the money for the baby? You sell the Eddie Blaine Mansion, where does the money go? I need the money. From the house. For our baby. I can't expect my new wife to pay for our kid."

"What?" I said, my voice small.

He laughed. "New wife. A beautiful little sassafras who is young enough to make a baby and not fuck it up. Don't worry—not Ivy-slash-Ava. Her daddy put her away in some rich person's mental health spa. I can have whoever I want, anyway. Nina, what happens to Eddie's mansion? I'm asking you a serious question."

"Paul gets it," I said. Cole had asked many times before. "I'm still legally married to Paul."

He walked over to the window. "That was the whole point of us being together. I fuck you; you give me money. The way of the world, sweetheart."

I didn't answer. You told me not to beg him, not to plead, not to ask him for love or kindness or anything. You told me to be cold. I tried to be cold.

Cole delivered a swift kick to the bottom of the bassinette that sat empty by the window. It went tumbling over with a crack.

"Where's the baby, Nina?" he said, my name escaping from his mouth as a five-syllable shriek. "Where is she?"

In my hand, underneath the blanket, was my call button. He was kicking the ice all over the floor, expecting a nurse or a security guard to rush in to rescue me, making the floor wet so they'd slip and fall.

He laughed. "I've come to take my daughter home. I'm not leaving without her."

"I signed the adoption papers," I said. "I no longer have a legal claim on my baby. My baby, not yours."

Your orders. Step two: Anger him. It wouldn't take much to set him off. He kicked the bassinette again. The plastic sides cracked.

"Why do you even care, Cole? You broke up with me."

"Yes. Because there was a line in your book that made me fall out of love with you," he said. "I'm not going to tell you which one."

Nobody told me that, at the end of my life, I'd forget I'd written a book.

"Let's play a game," Cole continued. "You guess which line in your sad little book made my dick go limp and if you get it wrong, I get to pluck one of these lines out," he said, tugging at the tube connected to the IV needle in my hand. "Loser gives up her right to oxygen. Winner takes home the little double A12 poop machine before Tabby Chen starts experimenting on it."

He stared at me waiting for a reaction. I was barely conscious.

"Nothing? You don't want to play?"

"You're pathetic," I whispered. "I didn't see it until now."

He ripped off the strip of tape covering the line in my hand. I couldn't feel the needle as he slid it out of my hand. A droplet of blood appeared and trickled down my wrist.

"Page 68, Nina. Come on. You don't have all day. I do, but you don't." He fingered the heart monitor attached to my index finger.

"Stop," I whispered.

"No, that's not a line in your book, that's a single word. You lose." He removed the clip from my finger. The machine flatlined.

There was only one more line in me. Morphine.

"Here we are," he continued, his voice rising like a carnival barker. "Look at you, poor pathetic Nina Blaine. You're no better than Eddie and Tracy, bringing a kid into the world that you're never going to spend a day of your life with. Good thing she'll never know you. You're so embarrassed and horrified by Tracy, well, imagine what my daughter will think of you, you hideous thing."

Cole leaned over my bed rail again and put his hot, sweaty face near mine. He moved his attention down to my left hand, which held the morphine line. He ran his finger up and down that narrow plastic tube like a lover.

"You love that baby more than me, and you'll never even know her," he said with an edge of sincerity, like he'd finally, for a second, put down the act. I shut my eyes. I couldn't bear to look at his stupid mustache or his angry face. Cole yelled, "I thought finally, someone who gets me. Someone who isn't like the others. But you love that baby more."

He turned toward me and slowly slid my morphine line out of my hand. Millimeter by millimeter, relishing every second of the passage of that needle. Another droplet of blood slid down my arm. "What's the line in your book, Nina? Say it! Say it!"

I was too exhausted to speak, but I said it: "There isn't one. You're just being mean."

In this small and desperate room, I saw in Cole something I didn't want to see: a bit of my father. *Gross.* What part of me—my mind, my spirit—knew without a doubt that Cole held within him the cures to all my various and sundry traumas, from A12 to an old, dead father, to a rejecting mother, to this very moment he'd engineered. Cole was a grand showman, a Potemkin Village, the Wonderful Wizard of Oz. To demand my salvation from *this fucking guy* made me an idiot, and yet I could not accept a world in which he did not hand me back the magic kernel that would make me whole and happy. That he was both the sickness and the cure was my undoing.

Cole wants to be remembered as a Christlike figure, so let's take a few moments to sing, in his honor, "I Don't Know How to Love Him" from *Jesus Christ Superstar.*

You first, Dr. Chen.

"You're so stupid," he said, a schoolyard bully.

"Steve Elwood," I squeaked out. "He fucked me so good."

Cole held up my morphine line like a trophy. "That's not even a good lie, Blattner. I expect better from a published author."

"He's amazing," I whispered, noting the beeping machines, and the silence between the beeps. "Best sex of my life."

"You're embarrassing yourself," he sneered.

"Did you fuck him back in the day, *Nick*?" I said between gasps for air. "Did he pay you? You worked hard to get him to hire you at his company, and then he didn't, because you're not that smart. But you wanted more than a job. You wanted him to love you." I paused. "Like your father didn't."

Cole leaned down and spat in my face. "Lying, disgusting whore. What's he paying you for? You don't need money! You're almost dead!"

The silent treatment, that potent little bullet, would have been more merciful than this tantrum you helped me create, Dr. C. I was egging him on with my raggedy tales of sex with Cole's imagined enemy. Cole had no leverage. I was soon to die, and there would be no memory of this to haunt me.

I had played the father card. Our wounds lead back to these old men.

"Besides," I said the line you instructed: "It's for the best. You're a terrible father." I took a breath. "A deadbeat father. What did you to do Bryn that made her disown you?"

He turned away. But then he turned back.

And here, set in motion, was what you guessed would happen if I were to return his cruelty. First came his anger in the form of a low, gruff bellow, and then his eight arthritic fingers wrapped around my neck. Even as he called me every horrible name in the book, I didn't take in his words. I soldiered on for Sig. Let him kill me so that she may live in love. Let me, on my single day of being someone's mother, be her protector. The little bones in my neck bent, and the fury in his red demon face burned so bright that I thought that I had crossed over.

What if I told you I still loved him, Dr. C.?

He pulled his hands away and I struggled to catch my breath.

What if I told you I loved her more?

Always the one to get the last word, he said, "I never loved you. No one ever did."

The door opened. "Cole! What are you doing here?"

"Sylvia!" he said, standing up straight, as if he weren't trying to choke the life out of me. He was drenched in sweat, his one eye bugged.

"Came here to see the love of your life?" she asked.

"Do you work here, Notley?" he asked. "Why are you in scrubs?"

She placed her hand on my head. "I'm here to see my friend."

He gave me another dirty look. "Nina is going around saying that Steve Elwood is the father."

Syl laughed. "It's true. Elwood was giving it to her real good while you were off with his daughter. You're mad, though. Cool, cool. Hey, I don't know if you noticed the cameras there and there," Sylvia pointed to the corners of the room. "Or the microphones. Probably not. The police are on their way. I'm going to stand here and keep an eye on Nina, so you don't strangle her again."

Cole laughed his contemptuous laugh. He glanced up at the cameras "You think you're so smart, don't you?" He had my morphine IV needle in his hand. He smiled down at me and stuck it into a vein on the top of his hand. "You don't even like your little A12 charity friend, Notley." He sang with Eddie's lilt, "She's my Nina, sweet as pie. The perfect girl for a special guy...."

"Don't sing Eddie Blaine songs at my friend," Sylvia shouted.

Cole caught himself. "It's my baby, Nina," he pleaded. "Someone to love *me*."

I remembered what you'd said: Cole's behavior wasn't about me. We were two damaged people with sixteen fingers between us, trying so hard to be loved and not quite getting there.

"You used to like me," I whispered. Such a fond memory, I am sickened to admit. My voice was hoarse. "You called me the prize in your junky cereal box."

Cole looked away from me like I had crapped my pants, which, I could have, as I couldn't feel below my waist.

I reached my left hand out from under the blanket, to the morphine pump that sat beside my bed. I pressed the up-arrow button. Up. Up. Up.

Cole contemplated the needle he'd stuck in his hand. He managed to get it into the fat vein on top on the first shot, staring at it for a moment or two to admire his handiwork. "Wow, this stuff is great. Nothing left to do with my short A12 life than become a morphine addict, right?" He laughed, druggy and drunk and someone else entirely. My love—he was gone.

Cole hovered over me, his hands shaking, his torso blocking the light from the window. "You shouldn't have done this, Nina. Nina? You're dead now. You're dead. Just like my mommy," Cole slurred. "Did I ever tell you about my mommy telling everyone she never wanted me? Laura too. She said it all the time. But not you. That's the whole point of you."

He had to have known what I was doing. That I had control of the morphine dosage. That I was trying to bring about his end as he was trying to bring about mine. This could have been sexy, I guess, but he was scratching his face and I kind of felt sorry for him. I hit those up buttons again. Palliative care, baby. I needed that morphine. The pain of my Caesarean incision crept back, like biting angry spiders.

He ran a finger across my cheek. "You wanted me. Badly."

"You didn't want me," I whispered, holding his A12 hand with mine.

"No. Eddie Blaine wanted you, though."

His voice became singsong, like a small boy. Time was moving backward for him. A child again, almost.

"Nina," he said, with tears running down his bright red face as he dug under his eye with his fingernails. He bent himself over my bed rail and laid his head next to mine, on my pillow, digging into his eye socket right next to my face, as if he were about to gouge his eye out. "My face is really itchy right now."

I looked up at Syl. She was taking my emotional temperature. *Focus,* she seemed to be saying with her eyes. *For the baby.*

"Cole," she started. "You don't need to do any of this."

Cole grabbed a handful of my hair. He pulled on it enough for it to hurt as he hoisted his face right above mine. "Hannah?" he said, trying to kiss me again, nicking the tip of my nose with his lips. "Hannah, I can't stand your father's music."

Cole smiled his last smile at me, his eye wet and red. He slid off the bed rail to his knees onto the floor.

Sylvia grabbed the bars on the back of my bed and kicked up the locks on the wheels. "Let's get you out of here. Now," she said, pushing me out of the door as the police came running down the hall.

***

When you and I talked to Steve Elwood about naming him the father, I cried so hard through that meeting, you were saying things that I couldn't really understand. We were sitting on the couch in your office and you Zoomed Sylvia into the meeting. "Eddie said he wished he'd taken you back to New Jersey, so you'd have a nice family," Sylvia said that day, looking so graceful as the wind blew across her face while she stood among her grapevines. "In the video? Think of this as us representing your daddy on how to handle Cole."

I was mad at her for saying that. What did Little Miss Harris Notley, aunts and uncles in every American city loving her and celebrating her and thinking nothing of that hand of hers, know about me and "real family?" My father was full of beans the day he said that stuff about taking me to New Jersey for Addie and her camera, anyway. He hadn't spoken to his family in decades.

Love is an action, not a word.

The day of that meeting, Sylvia said, "If what Paul said was right—that no good woman gets through life without becoming a mother—well, here's your opportunity for sainthood, Blainey. Blessed Saint Nina Ruth, who overcame every horseshit thing in her life to give her child a good family. I will name a wine Saint Nina Ruth if you go through with this."

I asked Syl to make the labels purple, my favorite color.

When Sylvia and I got to the NICU, where the baby was being guarded by you and a team of nurses, I began to hear my father's voice, distant, like it was coming through old speakers. Syl walked alongside my gurney, holding my poor, bruised hand. That side of me had already gone numb.

Sylvia squeezed my hand and began to sing to me:

> *O, sing thee daughters of Bondurant*
> *Our futures bright and true*
> *With loyal hearts and brilliant minds*
> *'Til death, we are Bondurant bluuuuuuuue!*

"I'm sorry," she whispered into my ear. "I've sang that song so many times I never really thought about that last line. I'm here because I wanted to see you and see the baby before— Tabitha will let me come over and see her, right?"

Auntie Syl.

Syl gets to see her. She'll have Auntie Syl to teach her the Bondurant song.

Oh, Tabitha. Siggy gets to have a wonderful life. Make sure my wish comes true.

I chose Siggy over Cole. I picked my daughter over a man, the way I always wished my mother had.

And the truth was, I loved Cole. I saw enough of myself in him for that to be true. He was, to me, the sun and the moon and the stars.

But Siggy deserved to be chosen.

That was the truth, Dr. Chen. Saint Nina Ruth. I made my sacrifice.

Call the Vatican and make it happen for real.

***

I'm going to hand this document off to Sylvia to give to you. Maybe she'll do some light editing, so it reads more like a novel and less like eleventh-hour brain dump.

I held onto life itself until I could see her little face.

I was half conscious. I recognized a few things: A nurse put me in a pair of sweatpants that rubbed up against my incision. Bryn, still in black scrubs, was holding the baby. Did she know about what happened to her father?

I didn't know Bryn, but I loved her. I loved her resolve and her anger. I loved that she held her half-sister in her arms like she would protect her. Bryn was lovable and I loved that Bryn knew she was lovable.

And there you were, Dr. Chen, sweaty and exhausted, but I could still see your joy. You kissed my forehead and thanked me for your daughter.

"She's beautiful," said Tracy, sitting next to my bed in a white vinyl recliner. Someone had given her scrubs to wear, too.

Death was near, and Tracy had called my baby beautiful. It was far too late to be petty. (Sylvia says, I will be petty next time I see Grandma Tracy.)

She said the same thing about you when you were born, too, kiddo, I heard Eddie Blaine say. *She said it over and over, that you were beautiful. You should've seen her when you were a baby. She looked at you like you were made of candy and diamonds. She was bananas about you.*

Bryn placed Siggy carefully in my arms and then braced her arms around my shoulders so I could bear the weight of my child. I sucked at bearing weight, and this time it really mattered. Your daughter looked like me, a little bit? And maybe like Rosie Sullivan, with a bit of Tracy thrown in.

Not yet, baby doll, I heard Eddie's voice, loudly. *Nah, as much as I miss you, baby, I think you should stay there a little while longer. As long as you can. You don't want to leave her any more than I wanted to leave you.*

Dr. Chen, Cole really did the most horrible thing to me. He made it so that I didn't want to die in the end. He made it so that I wanted to stay. Not to be with him—there was no him. But in his way, he gave me a reason to live, against every story I had told myself since that day in your office when I was eleven.

Bryn stood up and you sat beside me in my hospital bed, and we held her together.

You were the one crying, Dr. Chen. Not me. You were all in for this poignant moment. But I just sat there staring dumbly at her little face, thinking about how lucky she was to have you for a mother.

Bryn held her phone out, recording us. "Nina, say something to her. I promise to show her the video when she's older."

"No," I whispered, thinking of Eddie in those videos. "Please don't."

I saw that I disappointed Bryn, who was still filming us. Maybe that was the taste of motherhood I needed. But I wasn't the mother. You were the mother, Tabitha. I was just passing through.

A nurse put an oxygen mask on me, and gave me back my morphine, like I was going to be sticking around a while longer.

Maybe they'd bring me a drink, too? I thought. Hot chocolate? Maybe a shrimp cocktail?

Make an afternoon of it, baby, I heard my father's voice say. *Stare at that face! Don't take your eyes off that little punim. Listen to me when I say nothing else matters, Nina bella. You want to talk moon and stars, little lady, well, just look down at what you've got in your arms.*

I didn't want to miss anything, so I said all there was left to say:

I love you, Emily Lucille Chen.

Be good to your mama.

Acknowledgments

....

Thank you to my early readers, helpers, advice givers, mistake finders, good friends, and the angels who were there for me in the horrible year of 2020. Everyone listed here can guess which category they belong to: Tracy Manaster, Jorie Jenkins, Linda Abbott, Dave Gibbons, Kelly Sundberg, Courtney Sender, Dyna Moe, De Sellers, Cari Luna, Laura Stanfill, Epiphany Jordan, Karen Corday, Julie Gillis, Ritah Parrish, Amy Gentry, Marissa Korbel, Shawn Levy, Chrissy Tolley, Stephen O'Donnell, Jenni Ferrari-Adler, Renée Nicholson, Marguerite Avery, Kristen Bettcher, and the good folks at WVU Press.

Extra-specific thanks to Eileen Pollack, from whom I learned everything about Catskills hotels, to Dr. Melisa Ruiz Gutierrez, who explained how long it would take to die of a morphine overdose while we stood in line for Herrell's ice cream at our last Smith College reunion, and a shout to Sheerah Tan Cole, my Michigan MFA classmate who wrote the boldest, bloodiest stories, whose unique voice I remembered as I fleshed out Cole, who was named in her honor.

I'm grateful for the erudition and collegial spirit of my fellow booksellers at Annie Bloom's: Mal, Ruby, Daniel, Sharon, Rosanne, Will, Joanna, Cooper, Lela, Bianca, Greta,

Matt, Karen, Curt, Katie, Sandy, Michael, Laura, Caroline, Riley, and the ghost of our store cat, Molly. Support your local independent bookstore!

The biggest thanks go to my husband, Tim, the menschiest of mensches, who loved and supported me through the writing of this novel. The day Margy made her offer, Tim gifted me a Canter's Deli enamel pin, because Canter's is Eddie Blaine's favorite restaurant. He's very attentive, and he knows I love Canter's, too. Tim, you are the sun and the moon and the stars.